LOVING LIZ

Visit us at www.boldstrokesbooks.com

What Reviewers Say About Bobbi Marolt:

"[*Between the Lines*] is a journey to sexual fulfillment bristling with smart, intense dialogue between two characters who are definitely more than women-loving-women romance novel stereotypes." —Richard Labonte, *Book Marks*

"*Between The Lines* is an excellent read for that lazy sensual weekend where you need a little romance in your heart, a little laughter in your soul, and a good read for that moment of escape. The characters in this book are eccentric and comedic. …There're fun, sexy, romantic, and heartfelt moments embedded into the pages as the story unfolds."—*Kissed by Venus*

By the Author

Between the Lines

Loving Liz

LOVING LIZ

by

Bobbi Marolt

2011

ISBN 10: 1-60282-210-7
ISBN 13: 978-1-60282-210-8

THIS TRADE PAPERBACK ORIGINAL IS PUBLISHED BY
BOLD STROKES BOOKS, INC.
P.O. BOX 249
VALLEY FALLS, NY 12185

FIRST EDITION: MARCH 2011

CREDITS
EDITOR: CINDY CRESAP
PRODUCTION DESIGN: SUSAN RAMUNDO
COVER DESIGN BY SHERI (GRAPHICARTIST2020@HOTMAIL.COM)

Acknowledgments

Many thanks to:

Cathy "Ma Barker" Rowlands: For your input and endless support.

Cheryl Craig: For reading and for the terrific vibes you and JLee sent to Connecticut.

Cindy Cresap: I owe you—big time—for helping me dodge a bullet.

Lynn Richardson: Your kumbaya moment made my day and gave Marty the perfect reaction.

Nikki Grimes: Thank you for your support, and for cleaning up my "acts."

Melissa McGuire: For reading, for terrific support, and for your friendship.

Radclyffe: I owe you bigger.

Sheri: A perfect cover from the perfect "cover girl."

And, of course, Carsen Taite, for being a good sport.

Dedication

For Jo, who lovingly rearranged her schedule and drove
through the night when I needed her most.

And for Shohreh Shahabi, MD, gynecologic oncologist,
who caringly rearranged her schedule to preserve my life.

CHAPTER ONE

I'm on Forty-third and Broadway," Marty Jamison said over the phone to her assistant Nina. She slammed the door of the disabled taxi. "Traffic is backed up and my cab just died. Tell Bert I'll be there in five."

She made a mad dash across the street and didn't dare look at her watch with hope that time might have stood still for the last thirty minutes. The St. James Theater was a street away and she could double time, with added hope that she'd make the opening curtain for the matinee show.

With skillful maneuvering and a sudden left turn at 44th Street, she avoided brutally trampling tourists. As she reached the doors of the St. James Theater, she yelled to the door attendant, "What time is it?"

He opened the door. "One fifty-two. Bert's gunning for you," he said when she flung herself into the building and rushed to her dressing room.

Bert was stage manager and never tolerated tardiness. Normally, final call meant the performers were in the theater thirty minutes before show time. For Bert's final call, you were in costume and hanging out in the dressing rooms forty-five minutes before the orchestra began the overture. Bert was a strict bastard. His shows never ran late, and he was the best stage manager in town.

Marty dodged props, people, and fire extinguishers that littered the brief maze of hallways. "You're late," a blurred man said as she ran past him. When the bold and thunderous crack of timpani rang throughout the theater and began the overture, she knew her curtain was doomed.

"No kidding," she said and pushed open the door to her dressing room. Bert sat in her chair at the makeup vanity. His reflected eyes stopped her in her tracks and he swiveled to face her.

"I'll be ready in five minutes," she said and tossed her handbag to him. She looked around the room. "Where's Nina? I need to get dressed. I can beat the overture."

Bert pointed toward the door. "Nina left and everyone else dressed Allison. You should be on the wing, Jamison. Allison's there instead, and she's been announced to the house. I could do a no-no and hold the show for five minutes, but you don't want to be the one who tarnished my record, do you? Give Allison the show."

Marty's heart hammered against her chest. Yes, she did want to be the culprit, but she dropped onto a soft chair and let out a final labored breath. The show would close in three nights, and her understudy had gone on only three times during their eighteen-month run. Allison wasn't a threat. Marty Jamison was a professional who insisted on performing unless hampered by outside forces: a funeral, laryngitis, or a terrorist attack to name a few. In today's case—traffic and a flat tire. She looked at her Tony Award on the vanity. The recent acknowledgement for her performance told her it was okay to take a break, although her public would be disappointed, if not totally pissed off.

Marty looked around the room as though she could see each note of the score dancing through the air. "I guess it's hers."

"You're the best, Jamison."

Marty pushed herself from her chair and followed Bert to the wing. She hummed along while the medley of show tunes grew louder. Around the final corner to the stage, Allison stood with her eyes transfixed on the catwalk that spanned above the stage. Marty looked up and saw Allison's fiancé say, "I love you." She smiled and approached her understudy.

"I think he means it," she said and quickly noted the disappointment in Allison's eyes. "It's your show, honey. Break a leg."

"Thanks." Allison moved to her position at center stage. The conductor ended the overture and the curtain rose for the silent house. Applause was plentiful.

Marty watched the first ten minutes of the opening act and then headed outside. A few feet from the theater, the heavy scent of fresh bagels captured her attention, and she glanced into Times Square Bagels. Tempted to stop for a snack slathered with cream cheese, she redirected her attention to two women who shared a table near the window. One looked familiar, but she couldn't quite place her. When Marty smiled at her, the woman smiled back. Her flattering, soft yellow summer dress appeared a comfortable half size too large. Dark hair grazed her shoulders, and she wore blue reading glasses that complimented her outfit. The woman leafed through a thick stack of papers. Occasionally, she looked up and spoke to her companion.

"Liz Chandler," she said to herself. "If there was ever a perfect time to lose an opening curtain, this is it." She pulled open the door, approached the two women, and smiled. The woman on the left had just taken a large bite of quiche.

"Hi. I'm Marty Jamison. I'm sorry for intruding, but"—she looked toward the woman to her right—"you're Liz Chandler, and I'm thrilled to meet you. I love your books."

"Yes, I'm Liz. It's a pleasure to meet you, Ms. Jamison." She removed her reading glasses and nodded to her companion. "This is my editor, Trish the hungry."

Trish turned an interesting shade of red and could only offer a handshake and a vigorous nod.

"Hello, Trish. That's great quiche, huh?" Marty turned back to Liz. "I've read all of your books. They're fun and hot. Nice work." Feeling awkward but giddy for having met the best lesbian novelist in the business, she set her handbag onto the table and riffled through a myriad of cosmetics, cell phone, wallet, keys, and sunglasses. Finally, she pulled out two theater tickets and handed them to Liz.

"Your books have entertained me for years, and now I want to return the favor. Those tickets are for tonight's performance of my show, if you'd like to attend. I've signed the back, and that will get you backstage afterward. I'd enjoy seeing you again." Marty flashed a large smile and winked at Trish who simultaneously nodded and chewed.

Liz studied the tickets and looked up at Marty. "Thank you, Ms. Jamison."

"Just Marty. Well, I think I've barged into your business meeting, so I'll be on my way. Good-bye," she said and left the café.

The sound of steel drums resonated and she followed their echo to the bleacher area of Times Square. Two men played compositions of tropical beaches and liquored fruit beverages while visitors, and probably some locals, sat and listened to the harmony of the musicians' current island song. Fond of the steel drum sound, she strolled over to listen. The afternoon was warm, and she had to admit it was wonderful having a sunny Wednesday afternoon off work.

A couple of seats were vacant on the bottom row and Marty wound her way through a smattering of tourists and snagged a space. She contemplated stopping in Sephora to sample new perfume scents, but the lazy sound of island music kept her in place. For fifteen minutes, she listened to the calypso tunes and watched pigeons and pedestrians as they came and went. Warm winds blew through the square.

What were the chances of her having just met Liz Chandler? She wished their meeting had had greater length. The author was more attractive in real life than on her book covers. That was the first thing she'd noticed about Liz. The second thing was Liz's calm demeanor at having met Marty. Most people gushed, but Liz was full of reserve.

"Slide over," a woman said.

After a quick scoot to her left, Marty was about to ask the woman if she could be any more rude. When she turned to offer a piece of her mind, Liz dangled a bottle of chilled spring water from her fingertips. It dripped onto Marty's lap and she smiled.

"Perfect," she said.

Liz took the vacated space. She twisted the bottle open and handed it to Marty. "You looked parched."

"I am. Thank you." She took a swig and capped it again.

"No matinee today?"

"Fate threw me a curve, and my understudy booted me for the afternoon."

"I've read that the show closes this weekend. Do you have something new lined up?"

Marty nodded. "I have a half-baked drama that has yet to thrill me. My manager read the script, told me of the possibilities, and I signed on the dotted line after a quick read through. I don't know why I assumed music would be involved."

"You prefer dancing and singing?"

"Yes, and I don't get enough of those roles. I've received two Tonys for dramatic work, but it's music and dancing that gets my blood flowing. Such is life on the boards. We'll work it out." She listened to the drums for a moment. "How about you? Do you have any new books coming out?"

"*Taylor Rock* was released two weeks ago. I gave Trish my final manuscript today. She was disappointed that I'm taking a sabbatical. I think she's my biggest fan."

"A break? That's too bad for your fan base. For me. I've enjoyed your novels. Not too heavy, just enough romance, some nice sex. They're great reads when I have a little time. Maybe you'll sign them for me one day? I have all of them, except *Taylor Rock*." Marty liked watching Liz's hair whip against her cheek. She also liked the prospect of having her novels signed. It would allow her to see Liz again, and the thought brought a smile to her lips. She glanced at the entrance to Sephora and thought a new bottle of perfume might have a role in this evening's performance after all.

"I would do that. Twenty-two novels." She squinted into the sky and looked back at Marty. "That's a lot of signatures. It sounds like you'll have to invite me over for that feat."

"No way will I lug them anywhere, that's for sure. Will you make it to the show tonight?"

"I'll try. There's this thing I have to attend, and it may not go so well. I appreciate the tickets. Thanks." She looked at her watch and stood. "I have to get to my attorney's office."

"Ouch. I hope that's not serious." When she stood, Liz took a gentle hold of her hand. Marty returned the squeeze. "Maybe I'll see you later, then. It's been nice talking with you."

"I'm glad we met today," Liz said and her thoughts were obviously elsewhere. "Good-bye."

"Good-bye," she said and watched her cross Broadway and disappear among the crowd. "You are one cute woman, Ms. Chandler." Marty let out a joyful whoop. "Damn."

New perfume, a haircut, a manicure, and seven new CDs later, she made her way back to the theater instead of going home before her evening performance. She'd order a salad, have a nap in her dressing room, and Bert wouldn't have to pace the hall waiting for her.

❖

Before the start of the evening show, Marty finished getting into costume with Nina's assistance.

"Nice trim," Nina said. "I would have cut your hair for you." She completed the back lacing of the blouse with a final tug on the laces and then tied a bow.

"I know. I got caught up in some weird thoughts and decided an immediate haircut went along with them."

"What weird thoughts prompted a haircut? I smell new perfume, too. I'm guessing Dolce and Gabbana. Subtle, not over-priced." Nina spun Marty around to face her. "You screwed up your eyeliner. Sit. I'll get you cleaned up." She pushed her into the chair.

"You've been my assistant for nineteen years."

"Nineteen long and arduous years." Nina rolled her eyes. "Yes. Why?"

"Have you ever known me to act silly about a woman I'd just met?"

"No." Nina dabbed some cold cream onto the smudge and wiped it off with her thumb. "Did you?"

"Did I meet someone? Yes. Did I act silly?" She thought. "I think I did. I let out one hell of a hoot in the middle of Times Square and scared a flock of pigeons. Probably a few people, too. Then

I proceeded to buy several items that I thought I needed, haircut included. Not that I don't need those things. I can always use them, but—"

"You're babbling. Simmer down and tell me about the woman."

"She's Liz Chandler. She writes lesbian fiction."

"Okay." Nina applied the missing eyeliner. "I don't read that stuff. I don't know her."

"Five minutes, if you're here, Jamison," Bert yelled through the door.

"Long story short, she's damn cute and made me tingly inside. Women just don't do that to me. They grow on me." She shook her head in disbelief of her attraction. "I think she's about my age."

"Old geezer," Nina said. She wiped a smudge of lipstick from the corner of Marty's lips and then pulled her up from the seat. "You look great, sugar."

"I gave her tickets to the show. Third row, right orchestra, aisle. She's a brunette." Marty remembered Liz's hair blowing wildly in the wind. She was a sharp dresser, but her hair didn't top her list of worries.

"Aw," Nina said with a nudge. "You have a crush. You're bubbling. So after the show you ask her out for a little chitchat."

"Crush?" She grinned. "Yes, I do. I hope she's in the audience."

"Who could resist?" Nina answered in a bored manner and pointed toward the door. "Go on. Get out of here."

Marty yanked the top of her blouse down, enough to show a fuller bosom. "Too much?"

"You look like a tramp." Nina poked Marty's breasts back into the blouse. "Just go out there and knock 'em dead. You don't need more tits for that."

"Where's my gun?" With the prop, she would shoot a man at the end of the first act, but first she'd sing her show-stopping number that had nailed the Tony for her. During fourteen separate performances, the audiences taunted her until she performed the song again.

Nina tucked the pistol into the back of the skirt. "Go shoot the bastard, will ya? I need a nap."

Marty grabbed Nina and planted a fat kiss on her cheek. "Love your support." She whisked herself out the door and followed the twists of short hallways. Inching behind the orchestra, she made her way to stage left.

"Glad to see you could join us this evening," Bert said. "Got your gun?"

"I'm a pistol packin' mama." She stepped toward the curtain and Bert yanked her back by her arm.

"Where do you think you're going?"

"I just need a peek at the third row." Bert released her arm and she pulled back the curtain enough to see Liz's seats were empty. "Damn," she muttered in disappointment, but read the other patrons as a friendly house. House lights, at Marty's request, were always bright enough that she could see and play to the entire audience, not just the first few rows. She let go of the curtain and stepped back to the wing.

"Felice is in the audience," Bert said.

She cringed. Felice Tate was the one person she didn't care for. Felice was hot to dethrone Marty's rule as the First Lady of Broadway, and the diva wannabe said so in as many words. Marty wasn't afraid of Felice, because she'd seen her type go down quicker than the final curtain that closed a bad show. No, Marty wasn't afraid. She simply disliked Felice's arrogance.

"Do you know where she's seated?"

"Right orchestra, third row, third seat."

"Really?" Two seats from those reserved for Liz, and she hadn't noticed Felice. "I don't want her in my face tonight. I'll give you ten bucks to pull the fire alarm."

"Right. Ten bucks to scare the hell out of fifteen hundred people and have them stampede the theater. That's great, Jamison." The overture came to the final measures. "You're on."

Marty found her mark at center stage and faced the curtain. Her flesh turned into goose bumps. Tight, prickly skin told her she was home. She'd always felt the electricity of an opening curtain, no matter how many times it went up. Good shows, bad shows, she felt respectful of that drape in whatever theater, for whatever audience, to whatever end. With confidence, she would dazzle her audience tonight, with or without Liz Chandler's presence.

The maestro ended the final note. Marty watched the red velvet wave of the curtain rise slowly in front of her. Charged with anticipation, she wanted to smile, but that wouldn't have been in keeping with her character. Applause began before the curtain had reached knee level. As the drape reached her waist, she was ready to burst. When the audience was full in her vision, their standing ovation forced her to wait several minutes before she could begin her monologue.

It was a great night at the St. James Theater.

While act one progressed, she managed an occasional glance toward Liz's seats. They remained vacant after forty-five minutes, and she accepted the fact that the seats would stay vacant. However, Felice's look of bored indifference caught her attention and it irritated her, to her surprise.

At the close of act one, Marty completed her ballad, reached behind her, and pulled the gun on her nemesis. In a defensive maneuver, the actor raised his hands to his face. She tightened her finger on the trigger. Click. She pulled the lever again. Click. No shot rang out. No smoke rose from the barrel. The click wasn't even loud enough to echo through the house. *Shit,* she thought and heard a snicker from the audience. No one had to tell her it was Felice's snicker.

The recipient of the missing bullet covered the faux pas, giving her time to react appropriately. He bellowed in a sinister voice, "Ha ha ha! You thought I'd fall flat on my face. You haven't seen—"

Marty stifled a laugh at her cast member's demonic ha-has. Quickly, she threw the gun at him, rushed him, knocked him to the floor, and then proceeded to choke the life from his character.

"Good recovery," he barely said as the curtain came down. "Ease up on the throat."

Marty released her hold and a severe case of the giggles overcame her just before the curtain reached the floor. She rolled off her cast mate and continued laughing until Bert stood over her. His smile, his look of satisfaction, gave him away without words.

"You smartass," she said through her laughter. She reached up and he helped her to her feet. "Did I deserve that?"

"It pays to come to work on time," he answered. "You did well, Jamison. Now, clear the stage and get ready for the second act."

❖

The remainder of the performance ran smoothly, and the final curtain fell just past ten o'clock. Marty's excitement didn't end when the curtain came down. She hugged and thanked all her fellow actors, for yet another night well done.

"Excellent work," she said to the last member and entered her dressing room. "What a great time we had."

Nina helped remove her costume. "Do you think Wonder Woman will come backstage?"

"If you mean Liz, I didn't see her in the audience. So much for my carrying on, I guess." Marty yanked her blouse over her head and waved it as a fan against the top half of her torso. "I need a shower before I greet my guests." She kicked off her boots and slipped out of her skirt.

"Maybe you'll run into her another time." Nina reached into her pocket and pulled out some cash. She counted out fifty dollars and handed it to Marty. "Here. That's half of what Bert paid me to take the bullet out of your gun."

She smacked Nina's arm. "What the hell did you do that for?"

"I knew you'd recover and both of us made a buck. Drinks are on Bert tonight."

"You're killing me, Nina." She tossed the money onto her vanity. Stripped bare, her body absorbed the chill as perspiration dissipated and Marty headed to the shower. "You can let people in. I'll be quick."

"Your ass is falling," Nina said.

"I'm forty-two," she said over her shoulder. "Asses fall." She closed the bathroom door.

Cool water soaked her hair and she lathered her body quickly. Marty briskly scrubbed away at her makeup and sweaty flesh. Not ten minutes into the shower, she heard a knock at the door.

"Sugar?" Nina entered the bathroom.

"Is something wrong, Nina?"

"How do you feel about greeting Felice?"

Marty turned off the water and stepped out of the shower. Nina handed her a towel. "Tater tot wants to see me? This could be fun. Sure, invite Felice in."

Wrapped in a silky peach robe, Marty walked into the room. A towel draped her wet hair. Nina had allowed at least fifteen people into the dressing room and Marty happily greeted them all. Felice was last.

Felice lifted her forearm to a handgun position and pulled the trigger. "Bang," she said, adding a triumphant smile.

Marty smiled. "Hello, Felice. Were you awake long enough to see the end of act one?"

"My escort nudged me once or twice."

However appropriate "escort" was for the Times Square area, she let the thought go. It was humorous enough seeing that pixie of a woman standing before her.

"At least you got a good nap. Comp tickets? Surely you wouldn't pay to see me perform."

"Oh, I paid full price. I was curious. Didn't anyone tell you I was offered the role and turned it down? I'm guessing they thought you might be too old for the part."

The statement was Felice's psychological game. Marty wasn't too old. Elaine Stritch still played the theater, Bebe Neuwirth wasn't getting any younger, and they were just for starters. For most lead theater roles, age wasn't much of a factor. Felice was sniping.

With all the belittling comments Felice made to gossip columnists, never once did Marty return the verbal volley. Tonight was different. Maybe because she was disappointed that Liz hadn't shown up, or maybe because Felice wasn't important to her, she took the bait.

"Thank you, then." She grabbed her Tony from the vanity. "And thanks for this. How many of these do you have? Three? Four?" In fact, Felice had never had as much as a nomination. All of Felice's shows had been Off Broadway.

"Broadway isn't about awards. It's about craft."

"Then I suggest you go on out there and be crafty."

Felice scowled at the comment and then perked up when she looked over Marty's shoulder. "Who's this lovely vixen that's making her way toward the great Jamison? A new girlfriend?"

Marty turned around. Surprised, relieved, and elated that Liz stood directly behind her, she felt a stupid Cupid pang in her chest and never had time to smile. Liz elegantly wrapped her arms around her and kissed her as though they'd been together forever.

Shocked with the kiss, their union blew such delight through her that even Cupid would have opened his eyes in surprise. Oh yeah. Marty knew a good kisser when kissed by one, but she also knew a good act when she saw one. Advantage hers, she savored the delicate warmth of their intimacy until Liz broke the kiss just when Marty's legs were about to fall out from under her.

"I heard Felice's comment and you looked stressed," Liz said for Marty's ears only then moved slowly away. "Your show was wonderful, kitten. Ready to go home?"

"Well," Felice huffed and walked away.

Grinning, and still clutching the Tony Award, Marty presented the statue to Liz. "Best performance by a featured female actor in a play," she said. "Thanks. That's twice you've rescued me today, and I liked that one best." Feeling awkward wearing nothing but a silk bathrobe, she tucked the lapels closer together.

"Thank you." Liz took a bow. "I enjoyed your show."

"You did? Your seat was vacant all night."

"I was there. You sang, you didn't shoot the man, all was well at the end, and I'm about to drink free champagne." Nina handed each of them a full glass. They tipped their glasses together for a ringing, wordless toast.

Marty scrunched up her nose. "Stage right?"

"Right orchestra." She held up the Tony. "You're a little confused on direction, Ms. Jamison. Should I return this to the academy?"

"No, that's the gold guy. We're the American Theater Wing."
Marty glanced over Liz's face. "I'm glad you attended the show."
She looked around the room of friends and guests. "Did someone
come with you?"

"All alone," Liz answered with a captivating smile.

"Would you care to join me for some late night chatter at
Sardi's?"

"I'd prefer Rosie O'Grady's. It's quieter."

"Great." She looked down at her robe. "I suppose clothes
would be a good idea."

While Liz mingled with other guests, Marty slipped into
the bathroom and dressed quickly. She rummaged through the
Sephora bag and sprayed her neck with perfume. Nina dried,
waved, and styled Marty's hair, and twenty minutes later, she was
ready to go.

"You need a dye job," Nina said. "You have a salt and pepper
thing happening. Go get 'er, tigress." She pushed Marty away from
the chair. "Call me. I want the dirt."

❖

Their walk to O'Grady's was quick. A few cast members were
present and waved for Marty and Liz to join them at the bar, but
they declined. Seated in a side booth with low lighting and candles,
the ambience of the back room was warm and cozy. They ordered a
round of Irish coffee and received them quickly.

"This is the best Irish coffee in town."

Liz lightly stirred the cream that floated on top of her coffee.
"It's a dark roast. Like your hair." She pulled her spoon from the cup
and took a sip. "Thank you for inviting me tonight. I'm usually good
with seeing the big shows, but yours slipped by me."

"I'm glad I could accommodate. Tell me about your final book.
Why the sabbatical?"

"It's simple. I've kissed, ran away from, seduced, charmed,
fought, and slept my way through so many characters that it's
become too repetitive. I'm bored."

Marty nodded. "I can see that it would get monotonous, but I've enjoyed relaxing with your novels. I imagine you have quite a following of readers and they'll be disappointed, too."

"I sell well, if that's what you mean. And look"—she fished around in her handbag, pulled out the Tony Award, and set it on the table—"I've received my first Broadway recognition."

Marty snorted her laugh. "Oh my God. You kept it? That's too funny." She appreciated the surprise, and stashing the statue took guts, but Marty quickly pulled the Tony to her side of the table. "What are your plans? Will you try mainstream publishers? Maybe you'll become the next Nora Roberts? Or will you go more daring like Jackie Collins?"

"Do people still read Collins?" Liz fell silent for a moment. "I'm not sure what I'll do. A screenplay would be challenging. Thanks to a demanding publisher, I belong to just about every writer's guild in the country. I can write for Broadway, if I choose."

"Really? We need new writers and fresh material." Her enthusiasm grew into bubbling. "We could brainstorm ideas, if you want. I have plenty of them, but I'm far from a writer."

"I'll think about it. That sounds like fun."

Loud voices filled the front of the restaurant, and soon Felice sat at a nearby table with her following of older men. Marty smiled politely and nodded to the boisterous crew.

"Hello again," Felice said. "No late night snuggle after all?"

"The night is young, Felice." Liz smiled and reached for Marty's hand. "Is she always so obnoxious?"

Marty enjoyed the slow, soft touch of Liz's fingers caressing her hand. She wanted to lace their fingers together, for a feeling of permanence, but thought better. It didn't matter how real and needful the touch felt. She chalked up the touch to another performance.

"Yes, and it gets worse sometimes. The sad thing about Felice is she has potential and could probably make it on Broadway, but do you see that group of cronies with her? They buy properties for her to perform. They're not horrible shows. Her reviews are often mediocre, but she's received at least one Obie nomination. The only people making money are those fat men who keep telling her she's the greatest thing since, well, me." She shrugged. "Felice loves the attention and she loves throwing her barbs at me." Laughter sprang from Felice's group, and Liz looked over at them.

"I can see that. Speaking of barbs, I owe you an apology for the one I threw at Felice." She gave Marty's hand a final squeeze and then let go.

"What do you mean?"

"I don't habitually kiss strangers, but I didn't like the way she spoke to you in your dressing room."

"Well, it didn't hurt. The kiss, I mean. It was my pleasure." Disappointed that Liz responded with only a nod, she changed the subject. "Are you a writer by profession?"

"Yes, but I write technical manuals for various companies. I wrote novels out of boredom." She looked at her watch. "I'm sorry. I know this might seem awfully quick, but I'm afraid I have to end the evening. I feel as though I've been up forever and today wasn't that great of a day. Your show was great, though. I see why you won the Tony."

"Will I see you again? I recall some books that are in need of your signature."

"I'm moving in the next three days. If you give me your number, I'll call you once I've gotten some things unpacked."

The brush off. That was the last she would see of Ms. Chandler. She supposed there was another woman at home, but she dug through her handbag until she found a paper and pen and then wrote her phone number down. At the least, she could get her books signed and maybe develop a friendship with Liz.

Marty handed her the paper, but Liz looked distant. "Are you okay?"

Liz snapped quickly back to attention and straightened her shoulders. She smiled when she looked at the phone number. "Yes, I'm just tired. Give me a few days and I'll give you a jingle."

"You jingled me when you kissed me."

"I liked it, too." She glanced at Marty's lips, but yawned. "Sorry. It's not your company. I've had a hectic, long day, and I need to get some rest. Walk me to a cab?"

At the curb, a car was immediately available. When she opened the door, Liz turned back to Marty. "I had fun tonight. Good night."

"Me, too. Good night." When the taxi pulled away, Marty hailed another one. "I could have easily sat through a few hours of conversation with her. This night ended much too soon."

CHAPTER TWO

Marty's show closed, and she immediately read and reread the new script, aka the half-baked show. She tried to figure out how to change bland into something delicious, but nothing clicked. Creating a project wasn't within her comfort zone, but she flourished with performance. Therein lay the problem. Her new play was a one-woman show, and Marty wasn't confident that she could carry an entire night. She'd always worked with an ensemble of performers.

"I wanted something different," she said to the pages on her lap. "Now I'm wondering if I made the wrong decision."

Another problem was a low budget that had her working the boards for less than half her usual rate. One redeeming quality to the show was the venue. At least someone saw fit to stage it Off Broadway. She would get through her six-month contract then turn it over to another actor, or the show would close and then she'd be back in town. Another good point, the schedule called for only five performances a week. That was a walk in the park when compared to her usual eight shows.

The story itself was common to theater and screen: A Broadway star takes fame to heart and ends up alienating her friends, colleagues, and lovers. She turns bitter and places the blame onto those around and no longer around her. With the heavy-heartedness of *Sunset Boulevard* and *A Star is Born,* each having ended in tragedy, Marty's character plans to turn the gun on herself.

"The dialogue isn't even interesting." She leafed through the pages and mocked the words. "'*I don't need another bullet. You're killing me.*' I think we should insert a song there." She laughed at herself. "Could do with some rewriting."

Writers. Marty sighed. Two weeks had gone by since she met Liz, and she still hadn't called. Disappointed, but finding no logic in losing her agility by sitting on the sofa, she turned on a CD of fast tunes, secured ten-pound weights around each ankle, and began a rigorous workout. "Gotta do it to dance" was her motto.

Thirty-five minutes into her exercise routine, the phone rang. She pressed TALK without looking at caller identification. "Hello," she answered more cheerfully than usual.

"Well?" The gravelly, over-smoked voice told her the caller was Nina.

"What's up? Are you bored without me to fuss over?" She stretched onto her back and executed leg lifts.

"Never. People like you are a dime a dozen on these streets. Is there a story on you and Wonder Woman? Did you ever go out? Did you get laid?"

"I haven't talked to her in two weeks. She said she's in the process of moving."

"Do you think she gave you the slip? Ditched you? Traded you in for a younger model?"

"That could be. You did say my ass was falling." Marty pushed up from the floor, turned on her stepper, and worked her glutes with a high resistance. "I guess my charm was lost on her."

"Nah," Nina said. "She'll call. The way she lip-locked you, she'll get unpacked and then stroll back into your life."

"Maybe. Hey, I need you for the next show. Are you available?"

"I'm always here for you, sugar. Call me when you're ready."

Marty's phone signaled another caller. The display flashed Liz's name and number. "I gotta go. She's trying to get through now. I'll call you." Without saying good-bye, she clicked into the next call. Caught off guard when Cupid slung arrows of outrageous giddiness toward her, Marty giggled. "Hello," she said, embarrassed at herself that a near stranger could make her feel so smitten.

"Hi. It's Liz Chandler. Are you busy? I'm standing at your front door."

"What? Really?" She leaned forward and peered through her second-floor window. On the stoop below, Liz leaned against the concrete banister. What a lovely vision. "You sure are. How did you know where I lived?" She tapped on the glass.

"You're in the book." She looked toward the window and held up two candied apples. "Come on out. I have something sweet for us."

"I'll be right down." She closed her phone, tore off her ankle weights, ran barefoot down the flight of steps, and out the front door. When the heat of New York in mid-August whacked her, she still marveled at the clarity of the sky. "It's gorgeous out here." Had Marty run into sleet up to her hips, the day would still be perfect with Liz standing there looking wide-eyed at the candy apples. "For me?"

She handed one over. "For you."

"Thanks." She watched while Liz unwrapped her treat. If Liz's smile were any sweeter, Marty'd trash the apple and nibble her instead. *Slow down,* she thought. *Settle down. Don't make a fool of yourself. You've just met this woman.* But that woman gave her the shivers all the way to her knee bone. Good shivers. Marty sat on the concrete barrier and tore off the cellophane wrapper from her apple. Liz sat on the opposite wall. "How've you been?"

"Good. I'm sorry I didn't call sooner, but everything's moved and stacked neatly. I'm lazy enough that I'll live out of boxes for a while."

"This makes up for not calling." She bit into the apple.

"I've been thinking about your offer of brainstorming script ideas. If that was a valid proposal, let's do it."

Marty's face turned red. Yes, her suggestion was real, and she wanted to tell her as much, and she would tell her, if she could get her teeth out of the apple. Instead, she nodded.

"There's no rush since you have something else going."

Surely, the heat from her face would soon melt the cement-like sugar. She nodded again and tugged at the apple.

"You're stuck, aren't you? Let me help."

Marty felt like a pig ready for roasting, but waited patiently while Liz slowly worked the apple back and forth. Their eyes held a gaze, and Liz's long eyelashes made embarrassment bearable.

Saliva built up in her mouth, and when she swallowed, a small trickle dripped from the corner of her lips. Liz snickered when Marty wiped it away. After a final pull, the apple came free and she checked to make sure her incisors were intact.

"Thanks," she said. "You know, a moment ago, I had an internal conversation to not make a fool of myself. It didn't take."

"That wasn't foolish. It happens."

Unlike their first evening together when Liz's thoughts dragged her attention away, this felt casual and relaxed. Liz handed the apple back and stood beside her. Marty liked today's Liz better.

"Where's your new place?"

"Just around the corner. We're neighbors."

Could life get any sweeter? "I'd be happy to help you organize, and I especially enjoy painting. It helps keep me fit."

"No painting is necessary, and you do well at keeping fit." Her eyes scanned Marty's body.

"Job security demands it. I think you'll like this neighborhood."

"Good. I've made some recent changes to my life, and I need to find a new circle of friends."

"That sounds like big changes. Did you end a relationship?" Baggage, the last thing she wanted.

"Yes. I ended twenty-four years' worth of relationship."

Liz bit into her apple. Hers was a small bite, a delicate bite that wouldn't repeat Marty's stick and drool ways. She chewed slowly, leaving enough time to have the information digested.

Great. Twenty-four years wasn't just baggage. That was a warehouse of Samsonite. Liz might be ready for a date in two years.

"Twenty-four years. Ouch. That's a long time. Wow. That'll take some time to get over. New friends sound like a good idea, and they'll help smooth the rough edges." She half-expected Nina to walk around the corner and tell her to stop babbling.

Liz smiled with her candy-apple red lips. "The breakup wasn't that devastating for either one of us."

"It was amicable?" She perked up. "That's rare, but always good. What happened?" They sat together on the concrete step.

"I was eighteen when we got married. After college, he continued through med school and we became better friends than we were lovers. While I took on more clients, I put him through school, and that was the end of us, pretty much. We've been coasting for decades."

"Him?"

"My husband."

"You married a man?" Marty asked. "Of course you married a man. You mean to tell me the biggest deal in lesbian fiction is straight?"

"Yes. I don't want to mislead you."

"Oh, no. You didn't mislead me." Marty set her apple on the concrete at her feet. She crumpled the cellophane in her hand as she spoke. "Okay. I thought you were gay. Your books naturally push a woman's mind in that direction. Not to mention your kiss." She crinkled the plastic anxiously. "Oh, yeah. That was convincing. So was the way you looked into my eyes when you worked the apple from my teeth. Do you remember that part? That was convincing."

Marty wasn't angry, and her words weren't harsh. In fact, she felt foolish because the notion that a celebrated author of girl-on-girl novels was straight had never entered her mind. Marty had been single for two years, and she was ready to find Ms. Right again. Liz was the first woman that grabbed her attention. She had even given thought to checking out Liz's love scenes on a more intimate basis. She hadn't planned on doing it today, not tomorrow, but hopefully in a few weeks, or maybe as long as a month from today. A month would have been perfect. She laughed to herself. Nah. Straight? That announcement couldn't possibly be true. There was always room for hope. A final squeeze of the plastic accented a final question.

"You're kidding. Right?"

Liz pried open Marty's fingers and removed the cellophane. "I think this is dead now. I'm not kidding. I'm straight." She shrugged.

"Dynamics are everything, aren't they?" She shook her head, an attempt to understand the statement. "What happened? Twenty-four years is a long time to shrug off."

"Our marriage should have never taken place, and we knew it soon after we tied the knot. We were young, dumb, and we stayed together because we got comfortable. When he finished med school, we talked about divorce but never followed through. Dr. and Mrs. Chandler became those dreadful people who have open relationships, although we weren't sleeping together."

"He cheated on you?"

"It worked both ways. No secrets. I had a few liaisons, but nothing serious. Casual sex."

Marty reflected back to Liz's state of mind on their first meeting. "The day we met, you had an appointment with your attorney. Was that the day you signed the divorce?"

"Yes."

She looked seriously at Liz. "Are you really okay? That's a lot of emotion to sort through. Even if you were no longer in love, you've been glued to Dr. Chandler's hip."

"The day we signed the papers, and until yesterday, I wasn't okay. I wasn't sure how to handle...freedom." She smiled at Marty. "Anyway, I sound like I'm dumping on you, but I'm not. I wanted you to know because I...well, forgive me for being direct, but I have the impression that you're attracted to me, and I didn't want that to come between a new friendship."

"I appreciate your candor. Some people would see you as narcissistic."

"How do you see me?"

"Honestly?"

"Yes."

"The answer is as clear as the plastic in your hand." Marty looked long into Liz's eyes. "Okay, I'll be candid. You wrote a lesbian novel for every year of your passionless marriage, you contained yourself within that comfortable lifestyle for whatever reason, and you lip-locked me to the point that my flesh performed a happy dance all over my body. There's no way you can tell me you didn't enjoy kissing me." She laughed. "To me, it's perfectly obvious that you had some huge closets on Fifth Avenue."

"Actually, we lived on Thirty-sixth and Madison." She never batted an eyelash.

Marty held up her hands. "My bad." Her smile couldn't stretch wide enough. "No further comment on your closet space?"

"No. Was I wrong? Are you attracted to me?"

"Like lightning to the Empire State Building. It doesn't matter, though. Not if you're straight."

"I suppose you're right. Good. That's settled." She cleared her throat, maybe an apologetic act, and promptly changed the subject. "Are you busy?"

As far as Marty was concerned, Liz's announcement wasn't settled. Too much coincidence existed when Marty considered all those novels. Not to mention her kiss and her searing brown eyes. Yes, Marty knew a good act when she saw one, but she also knew a bad act. One sat directly beside her.

"No, I'm not busy," she said. "I was exercising and trying to figure out a fix for my new show."

"How about coming over to my place? I'll put you to work sorting through boxes with me and then we'll have a look at the script. Maybe we can come up with some ideas for the show."

Intrigued with Liz's inner-workings, Marty was curious to look inside the boxes. She slapped her thighs and stood. "You know what? I'd like nothing more than helping you sort through your clutter and then hand the script over to you." She ran upstairs for the play and a pair of shoes. "I'm yours," she said when she returned to the sidewalk. "You lead the way."

She wondered if Liz appreciated the double entendres.

❖

Liz's loft was a roomy, renovated warehouse, and the scent of fresh paint lingered in the air. A row of windows completely lined one side of the apartment. Stacked neatly and tightly against another wall were twenty-four years of boxes.

"I've set up my bedroom and workplace, but that's as far as I've gotten. Are you sure you want to do this?"

"That's what I'm here for." Marty looked around the vast room, danced a playful shuffle, and nodded. "You have a nice place. I could use some of this space." She scanned the boxes. "You didn't label them? This'll be fun. Where do we start?"

Liz pulled a box from the top and set it on the floor. "Right here."

They plowed through box after box for three hours. Marty filled empty containers with discarded items while Liz placed towels, dishes, and various forms of whatnot on, in, or near their probable niches. Together, they hung clothes, hung art, set up electronic devices, and then took a break before they emptied the final boxes.

Liz took a long look around the large living area. "We did good. The furniture works better in these positions."

"You could use some track lighting. Soft spot lighting would work for your art pieces." She stood in front of the two Roy Lichtenstein art pieces they had hung. In one, a woman in the picture talked on the phone. The text bubble read "OHHH...ALRIGHT." In the second piece, a dark-haired woman smiled from a bubble bath. "Why do you like his work?"

"I like the simplicity and his colors." She pressed her fingertip against the bathing woman's hair. "Did you notice? Her hair is salt and pepper like yours, and she has it pinned up in the same way. That could be you in the bath."

Marty felt nude when scrutinized by Liz. Her eyes moved slowly around Marty's face, down her neck, and across the opening of her v-neck top. The look in her eyes told of twenty-four years of desire, no longer written on page fifteen or somewhere within chapter nine. The truth now escaped her. It poured from her eyes, from the single twitch of her lips, from her slow and deep breath, and from the rise of her chest. That look was one found in the bathroom of a sleazy bar, or in the shadows of a darkened alley, where Marty would find herself backed against a wall, or a cold chain-link fence. If she moved one muscle, she'd envision her clothes being torn away.

Marty was too playful and curious to let that serious gaze go unnoticed. Liz wanted her, and she couldn't feel any differently about the fact.

"Who was she?"

Liz snapped her eyes upward. "Who do you mean?" There was no look of embarrassment, but a friendly smile.

"I get the feeling a young woman had your hormones caught in a raging cyclone, but dropped them and you onto a field of debris. That would explain your books."

She shook her head. "Nothing like that ever happened. I've never slept with another woman."

"That could explain your books, too. Frustration and desire, even fear, can loom heavily and find themselves in paperback."

"That's a typical lesbian response."

"A what?" She laughed and sat on the sofa. "What the hell does that mean?"

Liz straightened the Lichtenstein and turned toward the sofa. "You like thinking all women are dykes. Well, we aren't."

"I don't think that way at all. You looked as though you were about to rip my clothes off and dive inside me without as much as an 'excuse me, but.' How do you explain that?"

"I wrote a character that looked much like you. Seeing you is like having her next to me. It's an odd feeling."

"I know the book you're talking about. The title was *No Business, Show Business*, and the character was Abby McNair. You wrote your best love scenes for Abby."

"You've personified Abby, and I feel comfortable with you because of her character. That's why I easily kissed you in your dressing room."

"I'm not Abby, and I'm certainly not fiction."

"Of course you aren't fiction. I was reflecting on the character. Comparing the two of you, I guess. I know the difference between you and fantasy. I hope I haven't made you uncomfortable."

"I'd be out the door if I felt discomfort, but there's no sense in us butting heads over Abby. Do you still want to look at the script with me?"

She smiled. "Lighten the mood, huh? Yeah. Shoot me a synopsis first."

"A synopsis? Let me think." Marty grabbed the play from the kitchen counter and returned to her seat. Liz relaxed at the other end of the sofa. "Basically, the play is a monologue. The character is an insomniac and has a night-long conversation with her subconscious. Herself."

"What does she talk about?" She reached for the play.

"Infidelity, relationships gone wrong, stardom, and obnoxious friends. Most of the dialogue is bland." She watched Liz flip through the pages and occasionally stop to read a line or two.

"Some of this is funny. Maybe your delivery is stale. Why is that?"

"Probably because I don't have a single song or dance number."

"You've pigeon-holed yourself. Shame on you."

"Yeah. I should have given more thought to the show before I signed. I've come to realize there are two distinct voices, and I think they need distinct sounds. I'll wreak havoc on my vocal chords by changing character."

Liz pointed to a section on the paper. "In this segment, you're brushing your hair in a mirror and speaking to your reflection."

"And it's one of the dumbest scenes. I feel like Felice Tate's managers have dumped a pile of manure onto my lap. The audience will laugh me out of town, or at least well off Off Broadway."

"I think that's an overstatement. My thought is the play needs two women to feed off each other. Have you talked to your producers?"

"No. I'll wait until production begins. We'll have a sit down and go through the script. Producers included."

"What do you like about this play?"

"The character's anguish for the way she mishandled her life. She contemplates suicide, and she contemplates murder, but in the end she blames no one but herself."

"Who does she want to kill and why kill them?"

"She's bitter about her life and angry with her friends. She's turned Diva and wreaked havoc on her career." Marty reached for the script and scanned the pages. "Here it is. She's tired of having to explain her actions and desires to friends and cast members. She simply wants to be herself, and to receive what she demands. The character has no real desire to kill anyone. Her thoughts of murder are hypothetical."

"I don't understand that state of mind, about not wanting to be asked why."

Marty dropped the pages to her lap. "Are you kidding me? I think you understand her emotional state quite well. Random questions: What color are my eyes?"

"Sapphire. Pretty blue. Sparkling blue."

She stopped a smile. "Thank you. Will the Yankees win the series this year?"

"Maybe. I hope not, but maybe they will."

"Do you hear those Mexican laborers speaking Spanish in the loft next door?"

She turned her ear toward the window. "I hear them."

"Do you want to go to bed with me?" Liz fell mum. Her color changed instantly from Caucasian to sunburn. Her lips moved to speak, but nothing followed. Her thought processes raced in her eye movement. They moved from Marty's eyes, to the floor, and up to the bathing Lichtenstein. Perhaps her eyes searched for spontaneity or a witty response, but still no words followed. Liz's inner workings were jammed like the keys of an old typewriter. "There. That's how the character feels. She can't breathe."

"Is it so important to you?"

"No, but women together is important to you. In all my years, no one has ever asked me if I was attracted to them. Not even if they were drunk on their asses. I don't think you can deny your desire for women, possibly even for me. Why do you find women so frightening?"

"I wouldn't write about women loving women if I found us frightening. I write from…from…hell, I don't know. Maybe my books are from personal experience. No, not experience, but they're easy to write. As a woman, I'm qualified to know what a woman would feel, and would like to feel, physically and emotionally. It doesn't matter that I'm straight."

"Of course you know women, but you married a man. Have you thought about writing mainstream romance? You'd get better bucks from a large publisher, and I think your work would do well if you throw in a guy and change some personal pronouns and body parts."

"My writing isn't about making money."

She nodded. "I know. For what my opinion is worth, your work is about entrapment."

"And by that you mean my entrapment?"

"That's exactly what I mean." Feeling that she had overextended her welcome, Marty apologized. "I'm sorry. You have permission to slap me."

"I'm resilient, but I understand your curiosity." She closed the script. "Maybe you have part of me right. My life is changing and anything could happen. I've met and kissed you, and that was all in the same day. Some people would call that an interesting beginning."

"What do you call it?"

Liz kept eye contact with her. "Fate," she said. "Maybe my subconscious is testing probability and outcome."

Marty wanted to dive across the sofa and show Liz exactly how likely her attraction was, but she would never force herself on anyone.

"Is that an admission of guilt?"

"Call it what you like," she said and opened the play to the last page. She cleared her throat and gave a quick summation of the story. "Your character goes to sleep and the curtain goes down. No suicide or murder has taken place. We have, simply, a sleepy woman preparing for tomorrow." Lifting her eyes to Marty's, she quoted the last line. "*It won't be curtains for them, or for me. I'm not that lost of a soul. Tomorrow is curtain up.*" She closed the script.

"At least I like the ending. She's not so tragic after all."

"Your dialogue throughout says that much. I don't think you're visualizing this in the comedic sense it was written."

"I'm fighting it, I agree. Alone, the whole show, I'm kicking myself."

Liz pushed up from the sofa. "I'm going to copy this, if you don't mind. Maybe I can come up with some ideas for you to mention at your meeting. Make us some coffee?"

Marty puttered in the kitchen. While Liz copied and bound the script, she hummed a song from the musical *Breakable Goods*. Marty softly sang along and wondered if Liz had chosen the song at random or had the song's sexual overtones been a conscious choice. Either way, the tune fed into her ego. It made her feel special because it was her favorite song. From the kitchen, she watched Liz finalize the copied script.

"Coffee ready?" She entered the kitchen and placed the copy on the table.

"Yup. Cream and sugar?"

"A bit of both, please. This should happen the other way around, but I'm enjoying your attention."

"I'll bet you are," Marty answered and sat across from her. "Shit. I'm doing it again. Sorry." She glanced toward the nearly boxless wall. "Do we finish today?"

Liz looked over at the remaining items. "Sure, if you—" She stopped abruptly. "Maybe I should do those alone."

Marty's eyes grew large with excitement. "What? Aw, come on. With that look on your face? What's in those boxes? Your girlie magazines? Toys?" She made a mad dash toward the windows. Liz flew ahead of her and blocked the boxes with her body and arms.

"Stuff. Props, mostly." She warded off Marty's left and right grabs for a box.

"Props? Now we're talking my game. How do you use them as a writer?"

"With each novel, I have certain physical items that represent a portion of the story. You use props, and I sample them or carry them with me. Like this one, from my book *Advance Copy*." She handed her a small, faux diamond chip ring. "I built the entire story around this cheap ring I found on the street."

"Really?" She turned the ring around in her hand for her inspection. "I remember reading about this ring." She handed it back. "Motivational material. Interesting. Do you have"—she scanned her memory for book titles—"the blue pashmina scarf from *Residence Inn?*"

"Let's see what's inside my box o' tricks."

She opened the container and Marty peered over her shoulder. She reached between Liz's body and arm but playfully had her hands slapped away more than once. Liz picked up an item and then shoved it back into the box.

"Hold on now. That was an interesting look on your face. Show me the prop you just scuttled away. Was it the pack of flavored Trojans from *Newport Reviewed?*"

"Yuck. I never wrote about condoms."

"You did, too, and more than once." She tried another reach into the box of goodies. Again, she felt a slightly stinging slap. "In *Newport Reviewed* and *Suddenly Yours* your characters—Oh, wait a minute. How did you sample those? They were strawberry in one book."

Liz blushed her own shade of strawberry. "Never mind, pest." She reached into the box. "Here's the scarf. Pretty, huh?" She wrapped the cozy wool around Marty's neck. "Keep it. I want you to wear that for me in the dead of winter."

"No sooner? How about now?" She moved closer. "I can pretend it's cold. Playing make-believe is my job." She tickled Liz's nose with the corner of the scarf.

"Nope." She scratched her nose. "I'll take it back and return it to you on Groundhog Day."

Playfully pouting, she removed the scarf and peered around Liz's shoulder again. "I'll wear it in February. Do you have the silver cigarette lighter from *Grand Rapids?*"

"Yes." She reached inside the container. "This was actually a gift from my husband, when I smoked."

"It's pretty. Anything in there that takes batteries?"

"I'll keep you guessing."

"Come on! Do you have the big purple dil—"

Liz immediately covered her ears and scrunched up her nose. "No. Don't say it."

"Don't say what? Dildo?"

"I hate that damn word."

"That's funny. You use it. A lot. Your characters, I mean. Well, maybe you do too, but in your books someone's always strapping one on or performing a personal act." Again, Marty's eyes widened. "How did you test toys?"

"That's another question I won't answer, but yes, I have written about them. I never realized how much." Liz took the lighter and placed it in the box. She turned back to face Marty.

"I'll let you off the hook." Marty reached around with both hands and closed the box. "I guess you've had enough of me for today."

"Honestly? You've made me smile more in these few hours than I have in years."

"Great. That still leaves several years' worth of smiles I can replenish." She wasn't about to give up.

Liz jerked her head toward a door. "I have a small balcony slash fire escape. Care to risk the heights with me and have our coffee out there?"

❖

The early evening had grown hot and humid. When they settled with their coffee, they watched two men passing a football to each other.

"Frankly," Liz said, "I've never met anyone quite as invasive as you. I hadn't anticipated this side of you."

"I've been rude, I know. I can't help it, though. You've so much stuff to play with, many questions, and something still tells me I'm not off my rocker." She sipped her coffee and looked to the street below. She pointed to the football enthusiasts. "We're like them, I guess. Back and forth. I wonder which of us will drop the ball. I'm great with recovery." She looked over at Liz. "Invasive? Is that how you see me?"

"You're like a stage mother. Like Rose, from *Gypsy*. You seem to know what's good for me."

"Playing Rose is a role I've always wanted."

"Would be fun watching you play Rose with Felice playing her daughter Louise."

Marty laughed. "Oh, God, I'm not sure I'd want to go that far, but Louise is the perfect role for Felice."

"Do you think you're special? Above her? Maybe you're afraid you'll lose your audience to someone younger?"

She hesitated. "No. What the girl needs is a good spanking and then a good script. Sometimes I feel badly for her until she makes a public remark that a gossip columnist shoves down my throat the next day."

"This thing between you and Felice, is it a war?"

"It's Felice's war. I just laugh at her a lot." Both sipped their coffee and sat silent. Marty was comfortable, enjoying Liz's company and relaxing. She wondered about the contents of the prop box. She liked the playful mystery within, and the greater mystery of Liz. "Are we at war?"

"What do you mean?"

"We've known each other a short time, and I'm bothering you about your...what shall I call it? Your denial, I guess, but I don't feel you're annoyed with me."

"If you annoy me I'll tell you. As for the short time, what's wrong with that? When I write, I have to throw people together in a few short pages to show their intent with each other. Why can't that happen in real life, too? I'm sure it does, sometimes. Wham. The attraction is there. Form an opinion, a plan, and then see it through."

"Is that what you're doing? Throwing us together? Oh, darlin', this will be an interesting relationship."

Liz released a gentle sigh. "Welcome to my world. You've told me your attraction to me is like lightning to the Empire State Building."

"What do you plan to do about it?"

"I'm not sure, but, if nothing else, I'll be a friend."

"Let's go the distance here. Are you attracted to me?"

She was quick to answer. "I think you're attractive and I think you're fun. You make a nice cup of coffee, too."

Marty set her coffee cup on the iron grate. She stood and pulled Liz to her feet. Almost breast to breast, she kept that distance between them. She didn't hug Liz; she didn't kiss her cheek. When Liz leaned closer, Marty winked at her.

"I've had an enjoyable afternoon with you, but I have a meeting to attend." She picked up their cups and Liz followed her into the kitchen.

"Call me?"

"You can count on it." She closed the door behind her and descended the front steps. Outside, she reached into her pocket for her cell phone and called Nina.

"Why didn't you return my call?" Nina asked.

"I haven't checked my voice mail. Something wrong?"

"The meeting was cancelled."

"I didn't know you were invited."

"I'm special," Nina said. "Of course I was invited. Do you think I work just for the peanuts you pay me? I like the perks."

"Are you busy tonight?"

"No. Come on over. We'll get drunk and talk about people."

Liz flashed through Marty's mind. "Yes…people."

CHAPTER THREE

S he walked lazily to Nina's. The cancelled meeting was a pre-production dinner. Other than a free meal and a few laughs, she thought the idea a waste of time. She was happy with the cancellation, but wished she had known sooner. A few more minutes getting to know Liz wouldn't have been painful.

Marty smiled with the thought of her. Liz wasn't exactly enigmatic, but she was a challenge that Marty rarely faced. Not one to bother with straight women, or at least professed straight women, she still couldn't deny the tingles she felt in her presence, especially when Liz seemingly made a mental note on the layout of Marty's breasts. Liz had mapped her and might be interested in following that map to unknown treasures.

"Good Lord, Jamison," she said. "You're giving yourself too much credit."

She picked up a bottle of red wine and, thirty yards later, she rang the front buzzer to Nina's apartment.

"Yeah, you're in," Nina said after she buzzed back.

They settled at the breakfast nook and Nina poured two glasses of wine.

"So," Nina said, "how was your afternoon?"

"Nice. Enlightening, too. I think she's thrown me a bone, but I'm not so sure I want to get involved."

"Don't be so practical. She's hot, you want her, seal the deal."

"Seal the deal? That's funny."

"Sugar, you've been looking around for a few months now. You aren't the type to stay single much longer. Feel her out. No pun intended. Better yet, intended."

"I like her company and she has a lot going for her."

"She looks like a great kisser, too, from that little peck she gave you in the dressing room. I won't even begin to wonder what that was about." Nina tipped her wine glass against Marty's. "So you've had a little taste."

"Excellent kisser. Oh, for sure." She shrugged. "I don't know. Maybe I'll dig a little deeper. She and her husband recently divorced and that could make me a rebound for her."

Nina's jaw dropped. "She's straight? Holy Toledo. I'd have never thought that."

"Yeah, well, if you saw the way she looked at me earlier today, you'd never assume she'd been married for twenty-four years. If the woman had come two inches closer to me, she'd still have me wriggling about in her arms." She took a long swallow of wine and refilled their glasses.

"I can't imagine what she's thinking. Why do you suppose she writes for lesbians?"

"What do you think?"

"I guess she's closeted. I see your predicament now."

Marty nodded. "She read some of my new play and she thinks it's a two woman show."

"I had your manager e-mail a copy. The script is hilarious."

She groaned. "Liz thinks that, too."

"Great minds. Maybe you could give Allison a call. Or Felice." She smiled.

"You're killing me, Nina."

"Now, wait a second. Hear me out. Felice has the misguided notion that she can act you off the stage. This play could be her chance to put her money where her mouth is, and you'll have the chance to embarrass her."

"That's silly. I wouldn't want to jeopardize any show, and you know I don't have a vendetta against Felice. She's just a little virus that I can't shake. Besides, the show is still one woman. Listening to you suggest Felice, I'm beginning to count my blessings that I'm the entire cast."

She shifted uneasily in her chair. She did have a certain amount of fear regarding Felice, but wouldn't say it out loud. The realization was more than enough. Twenty-two years ago, Marty's youthfulness and determination, coupled with the guidance of mentor Joyce Manning, triggered her rise to the top of the Broadway food chain. On the other hand, perhaps the trigger was two years later for her show *Breakable Goods* when she appeared in a sequined dress with a V front cut to below her bellybutton. The dress barely covered her nipples. Maybe Felice would one day have a similar costume that catapulted her to the top. No. She reminded herself that there was more to her success than the perfect fabric.

Nina pulled a cigarette from her pack. "Want one?"

"One drag." She took a long drag and exhaled slowly. "I was smokeless for three weeks, until now. I'm gonna miss cigarettes. I know I will."

"My prediction is you'll be smoking again soon, especially with the new show you have going and then adding this Liz thing to the heap." Marty didn't doubt Nina. "What's going on inside of you?"

Discarding her thoughts of Felice, Marty focused on Liz. "I like her. I wish I didn't, but I do."

"I'm on your side, sugar. Enjoy yourself, but if it looks like it's going to hurt, stop. Rachel wrecked you and I mopped up after your tears for months."

"I'd given so much to her. I introduced her to world leaders and to powerful people in show business. We traveled the world and her entire ride with me was first class. To this day, I can't believe I found her in our bed with another woman."

"Did you ever wonder if she felt something was missing?"

She narrowed her eyes and finished her wine in a large gulp. "Yes. I should have bought her a chastity belt. Live and learn."

"As long as you've learned. Well, I don't mean to open old wounds. That said, for your new show, your only costume is some type of nightwear. Do you want me to suggest a color to the wardrobe department?"

"Sure."

"I'll try for a canary yellow teddy. If the show is panned, they'll still come to see your fabulous legs."

"Ever confident in me. That's what I like about you, Nina. You're consistent."

"That's what I'm here for." Nina emptied the bottle into their glasses. "You have great legs, sugar. If I were a lesbian, I'd go out with you."

"Thanks."

"I'll bet Liz thinks the same." She grabbed another bottle of wine from the rack. "I like the new show: the nobody from Queens makes good on Broadway. It's you, and it's funny. I think this change will be good for you."

"Or maybe it's another mistake. I should have thought about the show before I signed the contract."

While Nina poured the second bottle of wine, Marty's cell phone rang. "Another bet is that's Wonder Woman calling."

She opened her phone and checked caller ID. "Hello, Liz," she said and stuck her tongue out at Nina.

"Hi. I thought your meeting might be over. I wanted to remind you that you left the scarf here."

"I think you should hold it for Groundhog Day."

"I won't have scared you off by then?"

"Maybe I'll scare you first. I'm the one who is attracted like lightning."

"Maybe that works both ways. So how daring are you, Marty?"

"Quite. Why?"

"Come back to my place for a bit."

"I can't. I drank too much wine. I'll probably take a wrong turn and end up face down in the Hudson."

"That won't be fun. Maybe take a cab? I'll buy."

"You're teasing me now."

Marty was tempted to return, which would have been especially easy with all the wine she'd consumed. She wasn't fall over drunk, but a good buzz had taken hold of her. Her legs were rubbery and she hadn't even stood yet. Not only the lack of control to her legs, but also a lack of emotional control and physical need kept her from returning. She was thankful for retaining enough brain function to understand Liz's charm would be irresistible, and she wasn't ready to seal the deal.

She thought back to the day in Times Square when Liz's hair had blown across her face. Marty had wanted to push the loose strands behind her ear to satisfy the desire to touch her. She laughed to herself. She hadn't had the nerve to push a few hairs away, yet Liz had enough confidence to kiss her. Ah, yeah. That kiss was warm and welcoming. She perked up when she remembered Liz had nibbled her lip. Her body warmed with the sudden memory, but maybe the wine caused her rapid temperature change. Liz wasn't acting. She'd given Marty free rein with her kiss. An invitation. She could have had her that night, if she'd wanted to pursue her. Marty's physical glow heightened and she decided it wasn't from the wine.

"Marty? Are you there?"

"Yes. It's not a good idea for me to come over tonight. I'm at Nina's and I'll stay here." She looked at the floor. "There's no river in her living room, so I think I'll be safe. Thank you for the invitation, though."

"Okay. Sleep well. Good night."

"Good night." She closed her phone and tossed it on the table.

"No guts, no glory," Nina said. "I'll give you credit. You're stronger than I thought."

She looked at Nina. "What am I getting myself into?"

Nina shrugged. "I don't know, but I want to hear all about it. Come on. It's late and I want to go to sleep." Marty followed Nina to the guest room. At the door, Nina hugged her.

"Don't awaken me before nine, please."

"Lazy ass." Nina closed her bedroom door.

❖

Marty turned off the table lamp and lay back. She stared at the ceiling, and then at the window, and then at the digital clock with blue numbers. Blue. Liz had called her eyes "pretty blue" and "sparkling blue," and Marty had wanted her to say it again, softer, closer.

"What's wrong with me? We met only two weeks ago," she said to the blue numbers twelve, eighteen, and their connective colon. "What's wrong with her? Hell, neither one of us makes sense."

She grabbed her cell phone from the nightstand. When she opened it, she scrolled the calls received list until she came across Liz's name. More blue numbers. She looked at the clock and it read twelve twenty.

"If she's sleeping, she'll think I'm three sheets to the wind." She pressed the call button and waited. "I must be, to make this call. Shit. I shouldn't—" Her finger had just touched the end call button when Liz answered.

"I'm impressed," Liz said.

Good God. Her voice sounded sexy, close, warm, and cuddly. Sensual. She breathed sensuality. Marty felt so near to her that if she rolled to her side, Liz might be there.

"What impresses you?"

"Many things, but tonight you left me with the feeling that I'd be lucky to ever see you again."

"Good," Marty said.

"Good?"

"People need to want for something. Desire motivates us."

"That sounds like something I'd write. Do you want me to want you, Marty?"

"I want you to tell me what you're all about. I'm offering you a blank sheet of paper."

"*Tabula rasa.*"

"Pardon me?"

"A blank slate," Liz said.

"Latin lesson over? Now tell me what's happening."

"Do you want to hear the 'two ships in the night tale,' or would you prefer the 'I don't know what the hell it's about, but it's been a joy so far' tale?"

"Your last scenario sounds more legitimate. If you don't tell me your intentions, I can't see you anymore. Even as a friend."

"That's extreme."

"Yes, but necessary. I'm interested in knowing you beyond friendship. That's my want. If you have no intention of offering me even a morsel of follow-through, I need to know right now." There was no response, but she still heard soft breaths. She closed her eyes and imagined cuddling with Liz while they talked their night away. "Two weeks. All totaled, I've spent only a few hours with you, but I've never been so interested in knowing someone. That's not like me. You've obviously touched something tender inside me, and I can't let it go until you tell me otherwise."

"I think the woman means business. I've never been told to take a hike."

"I'm sorry." She rolled to her side and hugged the extra pillow close to her. "Wine makes me bold."

"Oh, Marty, don't take away from the truth of your words. I've made a few gestures that you've picked up on, and I don't blame you for the attitude."

She released her pillow. "Attitude?"

"Listen. I'm wide-awake now. If you want to talk to me, I'll be at the bleachers at Times Square." She hung up.

"Attitude? No no no." Marty closed her phone, pushed out of bed, and dressed. "Attitude is Felice. Attitude is the Yankees. Attitude is not what I gave Liz." She marched to Nina's door and knocked twice. "Nina?"

"Yeah?"

"I'm leaving. I'll talk to you tomorrow."

"You okay?"

"Yup."

"Lock the door."

Marty stormed through the hallway and entered the elevator. Impatiently, she tapped her toe while the elevator slid to the lobby. Attitude. She tapped her toe faster. She'd show Liz attitude.

Chapter Four

Marty paid the driver and stepped into the hot, humid, and windless night air. Perspiration clung to her flesh. She could almost feel her hair frizzing.

Times Square was lively at that hour. Light jazz sounded from a three-piece ensemble of woodwind instruments, although she'd have preferred more steel drums. A troupe of mimes moved in rhythm to flashes of neon and worked the crowd. She scanned the bleachers, but a tap on her shoulder turned her attention behind her. She swung around. Liz stood waiting and no wind blew her hair into disarray. She held a large bottle of water. Without a word, and without losing eye contact, Marty took the bottle, sucked a long drink, and handed it back.

Liz sipped from the container and brushed her tongue across the wet rim. "I taste nicotine. You've been smoking."

"It comes with the territory. Cigarettes are a hard habit to break."

"I know. I've managed to quit." She looked at Marty's lips and stepped closer. "But I still like the peppery bite, especially on someone's lips. Why did you come?"

"Intrigue. You're similar to the mimes behind me. You make verbal gestures, but you don't say what you mean." She motioned to the dazzling display of neon that enveloped them. "I find something gratifying within the colorful flicker and throb of these lights. I love the sight and feel of them surrounding me. You have that allure."

Liz's lips curled slightly at the edges. "That's romantic. I'm touched."

"Don't jump to conclusions. I'm also here because you pissed me off."

"Did I? At least your anger brought you here. You did give me some attitude, though."

"That was the wine talking and you were pissy, too. I'm not angry now, and I'm glad I'm sober enough to take you up on your challenge. Now it's time for a midnight confession."

Liz smiled fully. "I think I might like this."

She shook her head. "Maybe not. On the ride over, I'd decided I would seduce you, get you into a bed tonight, and then say *au revoir*."

"Really? You'd dump me like that? Now I think I'm angry."

"Don't be. It's not going to happen." She took Liz's hand and held tightly. "Come on, I have something to show you."

"Demanding, aren't you?"

"Actually, I'm more of a pussycat."

As they walked past the flashing neon of Times Square, Marty pulled her cell phone from her pocket. She pushed speed dial number nine and waited several rings.

"Hello, Marty. You're up late."

"Yeah, a bit. I'm right around the corner. Can you let me in for a while? I have a friend with me, too."

"Sure. I'll meet you out front."

She closed her phone and turned onto 44th street.

"Where will my abduction lead us?" Liz asked.

"Into a dark, cavernous room. I want you to meet someone."

The Stanwyck Theater was half a block off Times Square. The building dated back to vaudeville when acts by comedians, acrobats, strippers, and numerous other variety acts stuffed the theater's wings. It had a smaller seating capacity than most venues, seating only a thousand.

Housed in early nineteenth century neoclassic architecture, the Stanwyck was the only theater that bragged of four polished pillars at her entrance. She was a ghastly rogue, seemingly plucked from City Hall and randomly dropped into the theater district of Midtown Manhattan. The Stanwyck stood proud, never apologized for her appearance, and she pulsed through Marty's veins. When they arrived at the building, she placed a kiss onto a cool, marble pillar.

"Do you often kiss inanimate objects?"

"This one, yes. The Stanwyck is my home, and I want to show her to you." She knocked on the front entrance and a security guard opened the door.

"Good to see you, Marty. You two come right in." He held the door and allowed them to pass through first. "We've got a crew working on electricals tonight. If you go on stage, you might have some spotlights on you."

Marty led Liz into the house and seated them at the rear of the mezzanine. The theater auditorium was dark except for a solitary light that glowed dimly at center stage. The stage was empty.

"Who am I to meet?"

When Marty's eyes adjusted to the darkness, she looked around the fading mural walls and then at the hand-painted ceiling. Behind crystal chandeliers, the masks of comedy and tragedy needed some makeup. On the seat in front of her, she ran her hand over the red velvet cushion as though she caressed a fine work of art.

"I want you to officially meet Marty Jamison. The Stanwyck has been my favorite playground for as long as I can remember. My grandparents met on this same stage when this was a house of burlesque. He was a comedian and she was a stripper."

Liz laughed. "A stripper? All the way or like Gypsy Rose Lee?"

"Grandma let most of it hang out. She must have passed her gene to me."

"You don't strip, though."

"I've come terribly close. Sometimes I scare myself." She looked down to the stage. "My parents were actors and they worked this theater for years after vaudeville folded."

"You developed a relationship with theater at a young age. This is your blood."

She nodded. "My mother and father were consummate performers. They taught me how to act and dance. Singing came naturally, but I don't think I'm one of the better vocalists."

"I have to differ with you. I have all your soundtracks."

"Thanks. My childhood toys were props and costumes. One day I was a barmaid wearing feathered boas, and the next day I was a dusty cowboy hitting on the barmaid."

"You knew you liked girls when you were that young?"

"I sure did, and one of the things my parents taught me was love happens, and they told me not to question it."

"Sound advice," Liz said.

Marty rested her arms on the seat in front of her and inhaled deeply. "Can you smell the cinnamon? The same aroma was present when I was a child. Twice a year, the maintenance crew treats the wood with special oil that's spiked with cinnamon. It's a scent unique to the Stanwyck. I love the smell of this building."

"It's warm and inviting. The scent reminds me of Christmas," Liz said almost in reverence. "It's scary in here. I half expect a ghost to appear."

"Funny you should say that. That light at center stage is the ghost light. It's always on for safety, but there's a legend that the light remains on for spirits that haunt a theater. One spirit is the Lady in White."

"Who's the Lady in White? Like the Carol Burnett clean-up lady?"

Marty laughed. "No. Good guess, though. The spirit is a legendary ghost that inhabits all theaters. You hear all types of stories. For the Stanwyck, she sits onstage and hums. Some say they've seen her walking up the aisle. The legend goes that her husband hung himself during a performance."

"Have you ever seen her?"

"I think I did when I was a child, but I may have imagined her. She was a mist that took shape and I named her Martina, after me. Martina sat at the footlights and hummed a wistful song I didn't recognize. I hid behind the left drape so I wouldn't frighten her away, but I was more scared than she would have been. When she finished the tune, she stood, walked off the stage, and passed right by me. It's because of her lead that I always exit from the left. I thought she was telling me something."

"Your eyes are sparkling, even in this low light," Liz said. "They show a lot of love and respect for this room."

"A lot," Marty said. "Did you know of Joyce Manning?"

"She was the matriarch of Broadway some years ago. You resemble Manning."

"That's her. I had a bit part in *Cats,* and one night Joyce was in the audience. She came backstage to congratulate me. She said, 'Jamison, you're good and I want you to go places.' Joyce tucked me under her wing that night. My parents taught me to act, but Joyce taught me how to grab an audience and bring them to their knees. We became close friends."

"She was…what? In her sixties when she died?"

"Sixty-three, going on forty and with a big heart that suddenly gave out on her." She wiped a tear from her cheek. "I miss her every day."

Liz touched Marty's arm. "I'm sure she's smiling down on you."

She didn't want her evening with Liz burdened with emotion and retrospect. Suddenly, she stood. "Where do you usually sit for a show?"

"About seven rows from front orchestra."

"That's a good area. Have you ever seen the house from the stage?"

"No. Show me."

Marty grabbed Liz's hand and ran to the apron. At direct center, she placed her hand at the crescent edge of the stage. With her other hand she motioned around the hand-carved oak bow that separated the stage from the apron.

"This arch is called the proscenium arch. More simply, the proscenium."

"I know the word comes from the Greek word *proscaenium* and means an entrance."

"You're definitely a word person. I didn't know the word origin until now. This"—she patted where her hand rested—"this is the apron, and right behind these footlights is the exact spot where Martina sat." They walked to the side of the apron and she escorted Liz up the steps to stage right. Marty grabbed the framing curtain's edge. "This thick sheath of material"—she wrapped the heavy red velvet material around her body—"God I love the feel of it." She took a whiff of the fabric. "It's the same Grande Drape that was here when my parents worked this theater." She crossed to stage left and manually lowered a different curtain. "This is called the act curtain. I want you to see what an actor sees, once the curtain goes up." She guided Liz to the central area directly behind the curtain. "This area is down center stage." She yelled into the house, "Anyone near the electricals?"

"Here," an unseen presence said.

"Will you hit my friend with an overhead and a center spotlight, please?" Hot light covered Liz from above, and another hit the front of the curtain. "Here we go," Marty said while she raised the curtain. Liz immediately shielded her eyes when the spotlight hit her.

"Wow. That's intense." When her pupils corrected for the spotlight, she lowered her hand and looked into the house. "I see only the first few rows." She walked to the edge of the apron, followed by the spotlight. "A little more here, but the rest of the room could be vacant, for all I would know."

"Doesn't that suck? It's like playing to a small group, and I always hated performing to darkness. After I became well known, I received the privilege of having the lights adjusted for me." She yelled once more to the lighting man. "Turn the house lights to my level, please." The lights brightened until Marty saw to the final row of the mezzanine seating and the balcony seats.

"Much better," Liz said. "The lights aren't harsh enough to annoy the audience, but I can see the people."

"And, if the audience looks tired, I'll jack up the performance." Marty had the lights turned off and sat on the floor. Liz sat next to her and looked toward the house.

"Have you ever thought what you might be, if the theater never existed?"

"Never once. Why jinx a great gig?" Marty stretched her legs in front of her and crossed them at the ankles. Liz's eyes and head followed their length from the toes and up to Marty's eyes. "I wanted you to know this about me. There's more to me than the side that thinks you're wildly attractive."

Liz lowered her eyes to Marty's shoulders and breasts, maybe taking a second look to be certain not a centimeter had gone astray during their few hours of separation. Her eyes moved slowly along Marty's neck.

"Does that mean no seduction scene tonight? You're not about to steal my girl-on-girl virginity on this dusty floor?"

"That's exactly what I mean." She moved closer. "You'll have to try harder, if that's what you want."

Liz rested her forehead on Marty's shoulder. Marty wished the spotlight covered them so she could see the rich chestnut color that was lost under the dim ghost light. Marty sifted her fingers through soft waves of hair and allowed her lips to touch Liz's head.

"I guess it's my turn to confess." She looked back into the auditorium. "About twenty years ago—"

Marty stopped her with a hand to her back. "The house is empty. Play to me. I'm a captive audience."

Liz turned to her. When Marty saw an intense and sad look in her eyes, she wrapped her arms around her and loosely held her. Cheek to cheek, Liz breathed nervously and suddenly pulled away.

"Sometimes life isn't fair."

"I agree," Marty said. With the backs of her fingers, she brushed a tear from Liz's cheek. "My Protestant upbringing taught me that confession is between God and me. If you have something to tell me, tell me out of personal need. Don't tell me if you feel you owe me one."

Liz wiped another tear with the back of her hand and breathed a short laugh. "Are you ready for this? I'm about to tell you an incredible story, and I don't want you to bolt from the theater or from my life."

Marty raised her chin, took a deep breath, and exhaled. That statement fascinated her. There was uncertainty in Liz's eyes when she ran her fingers through her hair and rolled her shoulders.

"If you're uncomfortable, don't tell me, but I'm easy to talk to, and I promise I won't bolt."

"I have one confession, and I don't mind sharing it because I need to hear myself tell the story and you need to hear it. About twenty years ago, I attended *Breakable Goods*."

Marty straightened with that surprise. "That was my show. My favorite."

"It was my favorite, too, and your performance has remained embedded in my mind for twenty years."

"That's terrific. Our cast was the best in town, and we were lucky to have each other. Our reviews were good, but not as wonderful as yours." She smiled. "Go on."

"When you walked out on stage, you hit me with a flame thrower. There you were, dressed in a sparkly red dress, and your eyes were bright aquamarine gemstones shining down on me. I couldn't believe how brilliantly your eyes sparkled. Your fabulous hair was full and thick and bouncy against your shoulders." She motioned a wide V from her shoulders to below her waist. "Your dress was cut to here. I wanted to yank you from the stage and lick your lipstick from your mouth." She stopped and her face was brilliant red. "The night I kissed you in your dressing room, your lips felt so damn good. I could have died happy that night."

The proportion of her revelation was staggering. Liz had entombed her emotions within a loveless marriage while she craved the attention of a woman all those years. At least she'd craved Marty's attention. Never acting to satisfy that need, she knew all too well the meaning of want. Marty felt sad for her, and listened, captivated.

"Go on. By all means, tell me how lovely I am." She nudged Liz's knee. "We girls like that, you know?"

"Lovely? Yes, you were, and even more so now, but lovely wasn't the word I had in mind. You threw me into a tailspin and you didn't stop there. Later in the act, when you appeared wearing only a short towel, I said 'Holy shit.' My husband asked me what was wrong, and I told him I thought I'd left the curling iron on." Liz paused and swept her eyes over Marty. "I couldn't take my eyes off you. Even now it's difficult."

"You wanted to know if the carpet matched the drapes."

She soured. "Don't make fun of me. I thought I could trust you to take me seriously." When she moved to stand up, Marty grabbed her hand.

"I'm sorry. Tell me more, if you want."

"After that night, I saw *Breakable Goods* twice a week until it closed. By the time the curtain fell for the final performance, I'd been driven by so much fantasy with the hope that your towel would magically fall away, that I had to find a grip on reality." She fidgeted and her hand trembled.

Marty pushed Liz's hair away from her cheek. "Would you like to go out for some air?"

"No, I'm okay." She took a sip from the bottled water. "I never attended another show of yours, but I couldn't get away from you. For the next twenty years, I saw your likeness on billboards, buses, and painted onto the sides of buildings." She gave a nervous laugh. "They were striking glam shots, but when you appeared at the bagel shop, with your hair in disarray and a sweaty upper lip, you looked even more wonderful. I damn near fell out of my chair when you introduced yourself."

"I couldn't miss the opportunity of meeting you."

"Imagine my surprise. I was breathless that you knew who I was, and it's nearly inconceivable that I'm sitting next to you on this stage." Liz looked into Marty's eyes. "I've seen you dressed in breathtaking theatrical costumes, but I like you just as much sitting here in your scruffy shorts and tank top. Your hair has frizzed from humidity, but the color is incredible. A little salt among all that pepper."

"Nina mentioned I could use a little coloring."

Liz placed her hand above Marty's knee. "What a tease you were." She looked down at her hand. "You're all legs." She moved her hand away.

"You don't have to let go." Marty placed Liz's hand back on her leg. "After you saw my performance, is that when you wrote *No Business, Show Business*?" Liz nodded but kept her eyes on Marty's leg. Sometimes her fingers moved against or pressed into the thigh. "Was Abby McNair your infatuation with me?"

Liz raised her head. "Infatuation?" Her voice was shaky. "Crazed and impassioned are better choices for words. Writing you as Abby was the only way I could have you."

"After that book, Abby was your focus in every book."

"She sure was. Twenty years ago, you were the young woman that left me and my hormones scattered in a field of debris. That's my confession."

Marty was speechless. When she'd made the comment, she hadn't thought for a second that she was the cause of an unsettling breach in Liz's sexuality. It saddened her, and the responsibility conflicted with the joy of now getting to know Liz.

"I was twenty-two then," was all she could think to say.

"I'd just turned the same age." She turned her hand and held tightly onto Marty's.

"This is where I need a great line written for me."

Her voice quivered. "Tell me your thoughts. Even if you're angry. I've probably accomplished nothing, but—"

She placed a finger over Liz's mouth and outlined her lips. "I don't know what you expect for reaction, but these aren't normal circumstances for either of us. I want to kiss you again. Right now."

Liz blinked and parted her lips for a breath. "Just kiss me."

A pop exploded inside Marty's chest, and a current of heat sprang from the center of her breast. As their mouths neared, she closed her eyes. Supple, warm lips greeted her. Marty kissed tenderly when she could have easily bruised Liz.

She welcomed gentle bites and slow, short strokes of Liz's tongue. When Liz's tongue slipped between her lips, Marty sucked in a quick breath and pulled away from their kiss. She was still close enough that their lips touched; she wanted them to remain that close.

"It's difficult not to continue." Liz brushed her mouth along Marty's. "Your lips feel wonderful. They're smooth. So soft. I've had many daydreams about kissing you."

Marty wondered if their kiss might have fulfilled a lifelong fantasy, one easily discarded after the first satisfying bite. The thought disturbed her. She wanted to know Liz and explore where their attraction would take them. She didn't want to find herself inside a dark prop box.

Although their shared, hot breaths suggested more than a kiss should follow, Marty forced herself to back away. "I love how you kiss," she said, still catching her breath. "It was nice in the dressing room, but tonight you felt different."

"I let myself feel our kiss tonight. I've wanted you for so many years and now you know my secret."

"I'm surprised and you give me a happy-tingle feeling everywhere, but I have to ask what you want from this."

"I should have asked this sooner: Are you single? That's the first thing I need to know." A satisfied look came across Liz's face when Marty nodded. "Then I'd like to see you in a more intimate setting and see where that leads us, if you're interested."

"We can talk about that. Liz, honestly, you've never been with another woman?"

"No. I've only been attracted to one woman and she's sitting in front of me."

The head of security walked onto the stage. "Sorry, Marty, but the guys are leaving, and I better hustle you two out for the evening."

"We were just leaving," she said, while he helped them to their feet. "Thanks for giving us a few minutes."

When they were outside the Stanwyck, Marty looked at her watch. "It's late. Are you ready to go home?"

"I'm too wired to go home. Can we walk and talk some more?"

"I'd like that." She placed her arm around Liz's waist and they walked toward the central lights of Broadway.

More people had gathered in the heated night air of Times Square, and the mimes played to their growing audience. From the perimeter, they watched the lean actors who were dressed in black tights. Red diamond eyes enhanced their white greasepaint faces, and the remainder of their bodies seemed all arms and legs, save for the fedoras atop their heads.

"They're great."

"They are." Standing behind Liz, Marty held her loosely around her waist. "At the risk of my sounding vain, during your crazed and impassioned moments, did you ever Google me?"

"Once. When I saw your measurements listed on a Broadway database, I closed the window." She pressed the left button of an imaginary computer mouse. "Click. Gone."

Marty laughed. "Why did you X me?"

"When I read your numbers, I decided that the Internet was full of lies."

"That's probably a true statement in many cases."

"Not in your case."

Liz turned and placed her hands below Marty's hips. She slid them upward and followed her figure. When she reached the sides of her breasts, Marty damned Cupid to hell. If she closed her eyes and opened them again, she'd expect to be surrounded by the sleazy bar or back alley scene, but she preferred better for them.

Internally, she became femme beyond femme and wished the show-stopping towel from *Breakable Goods* hung from her. In the middle of Times Square, among the swelter of a midsummer night and flicker of garish Broadway neon, she would fulfill Liz's fantasy. The more she prolonged the thought of dropping the towel, the more she wanted to purr, nuzzle, and knead. Marty looked long into Liz's eyes. Meow.

"You flow perfectly."

Her smile nearly shot across Broadway. Against the damp night, her face turned hotter, and then Liz touched the space between Marty's breasts.

"I want to curl up right here. It's that deep."

Marty removed the burrowing hand and pressed it against her collarbone. She was deep and flowing all right, but not in the context of cleavage and curves. "Why, I have half a mind to take you over my knee and spank you."

A look of astonishment crossed Liz's face. "Holy shit. That was hot."

"Again with that?" She looked around them. "Why? What?"

"You used that southern accent in *Breakable Goods*. Did you do that deliberately, just now?"

Liz moved closer and emanated an unbelievable amount of body heat, even within the sweltering night. Yes, Marty had used the accent on purpose and, cued by Liz's reaction, she consciously put the soft, southern drawl to further test. "My, my. With that look in your eyes, could I interest you in a personalized tour of Charleston? Perhaps a stroll through the French Quarter?"

Playfully, Liz pushed away. "You're not fair. Remember me? I'm the one who nearly stalked you, but instead hid for twenty years and then had you dropped onto my lap, two hours before I signed my divorce papers. My God. Your sound sent me right into an 'I want to fuck you now' mode, and I never knew I possessed that mode until you walked onto the stage." She shook her head. "Now that you've reminded me of it, don't use that voice."

Marty crossed her heart. "I promise I won't use that accent." At least she wouldn't use the character's voice tonight, but she'd retained the southern seed that had been planted.

"Thank you. I wouldn't want to do something that I'd regret."

"You'd regret making love to me?"

"No. I'd regret fucking you. I know I wouldn't have the sense to stop and I'd wake up with the need to run so damn far away that I'd make sure I never saw you again."

"Running would take away this complication in your new life. What stops you?"

Liz's look penetrated Marty. "I'm afraid you'd never find me again."

Cupid hadn't stopped with his little heart nudges. She was thankful there was no song for this scene because her vibrato would be well out of control. "We can't allow that, can we?"

Liz shook her head. "No. We can't. Are you taking me seriously?"

"Yes, but in a matter of hours you've changed from 'I'll be a friend' to someone who wants to ravage me beyond all recognition.

I'm amazed, I'm amused, I'm flattered, I'm scared, but there's a teensy part of me that wants to blush and say 'Who? Li'l ol' me?' "

"Thanks for not saying it with the accent." Liz sat on the concrete, against the George M. Cohan statue that prefaced the seating area. She pulled Marty down with her. "I guess I did throw us together."

"Yup," Marty said and hugged her knees.

"Are you really scared?" Liz asked. Marty nodded and leaned back on her hands. "Why?"

"I just turned forty-two and I'm at a point in my life where I can have just about anything I can imagine. I can explore the Arctic, if that's what I want. Tomorrow, I can insist that someone produce a revival of *Gypsy* and give me the coveted role of Rose, and they will, but I can live without those things."

"What can't you live without?"

"I want to wake up to a woman I love. I want the privilege of serving her breakfast in bed and then starting her bath water. I want to love her, fight with her, have her call me the biggest jerk she'd ever met, comfort her, and I want the knowledge that she feels the same way I do. Hell, I'd even clean her ears with Q-tips if she asked. Not exactly avant-garde, am I? What do you want, Liz?"

She ran her finger down the bridge of Marty's nose. "I like you. I don't know what we're sitting in, on this grimy street, but I like being here with you. I still want to see where we end up." She yawned.

Marty responded with a yawn, and she pointed down Broadway. "The Marriott Marquis is a few feet away. Let's get a room. I think we're tired enough to not screw this up tonight."

After individual showers and then wearing thick hotel robes, it was time to call it a night. Their suite had two beds, and sleeping arrangements seemed obvious. She pulled back the blankets on the opposite bed, after Liz stretched on the king-size bed near the window.

"I agreed that we're too tired to mess this up tonight," Liz said. "I didn't agree to not falling asleep in your arms. Now come over here."

Marty slipped into Liz's bed and their bodies fit easily together. They kissed lightly, twice, and said good night. Liz turned her back and moved Marty's hand up to her breast. Marty closed her eyes and, with her hand gently surrounding her firm breast, was content to sleep.

"I think I've just hit the Broadway lottery," Liz said.

It was a great night at the Marriott Marquis.

Chapter Five

Ten hours later, Marty arrived home. Her prior twenty-four hours were the most satisfying she'd had in years.

She'd picked up some fresh daisies from the local vendor and arranged them in a vase. Now it was time to call Nina and give her the gossip she wanted. Afterward, she'd change her clothes and then head over to Liz's for the afternoon.

When she opened her phone to make a call, the battery was dead. She connected it to the recharger and then grabbed the house phone. The red message light blinked and she pushed PLAY. The voice was her manager.

"How do you feel about beginning rehearsal sooner? Call me."

She dropped onto a chair. What did she think about it? She thought the idea was insane and she immediately returned his call.

"Hey. How are you?" he asked.

"Hi, Adam." Her voice walked the fine line between cordial and sarcastic. "I'm not ready to begin rehearsal, that's how I am. What does sooner mean? Tomorrow? The next day? You told me the end of September. My contract says the end of September. My body tells me the end of September. I'm tired. I have another five weeks before we begin and I'm taking the time off."

"How about this? The contract for The Lawton Theater isn't concrete. If you begin now, you can get the Stanwyck. The acoustics there love your voice."

Shit. He may as well have handed her a million dollars in cash. The Stanwyck talked, but she waited to respond. He didn't need to know she was a sucker for that theater.

"I know you love working there," he said.

Bastard. "Adam, the Stanwyck is my baby, but this show isn't fit for Broadway."

"Obviously, the owners of the theater feel differently. You know how flexible they are. Didn't anyone tell you Marty Jamison brings in the cash? What do you think?"

A week from now? Tomorrow? She wasn't sure she wanted to know how many days separated her from tedium. The show was stagnant. There was no music to learn, no dance numbers. Nothing outside of her lines would tap her creative energy, but two hours alone on stage would surely drain her. Words. The play was words. Could she make the words play?

Audiences loved Marty. She was their siren and a topic of conversation at their dinner tables. With a simple rumor that she had something new in the works, folks clamored to find out where and when. The final presentation had little to do with their anticipation of seeing her perform and there was no such thing as a papered audience for a Jamison show, musical or otherwise. Her name alone sold tickets and filled theaters. Stress? She had damn well better make the words play.

"That's a lot of pressure for an average show." She groaned, but wasn't ready to say no to the theater proposal. "When does 'immediately' happen?"

"September thirteenth. Just two weeks earlier."

"Oh. I thought you meant something outrageous like next week. Okay, I'm in but I'm exercising my contract and bringing in a writer. Find out who wrote this show and maybe we can work out an 'adapted from the story by' deal. We can do better."

"I'll get right on it. Thanks, Marty. You're the best."

"Yeah," she sighed. "I know." She hung up the phone. "I just hope Liz is available." She dialed Nina's number.

"What?" Nina asked when she answered the phone. "You leave in the middle of the night and now you want to talk at the peak of my siesta?"

"Yup."

"Good. That means you have something juicy to tell me."

"Not too juicy." She heard Nina's Bic flick.

"Well? Let's have it. We're not getting any younger. By the way, I picked up some dye for your hair."

"Thanks for the reminder, but I don't want my hair dyed." Already she wanted to preserve things Liz liked about her. "We stayed at the Marriott Marquis last night."

"No kidding? Great. Then it won't piss you off when I tell you I suggested red satin for your teddy instead of yellow. I know. Don't say it. You prefer wearing yellow."

Marty grinned. "Red is perfect, Nina."

"You did get lucky. How nice."

"I didn't. We didn't." She relayed much of their evening.

"Really?" Nina said. "I think that's great, not taking advantage of the situation. Have you had the time to digest any of this? Do you think it'll work?"

"I've had no time to think about it. I just walked in the door moments ago. There's something more pressing than my love life, though. Production for the new show begins September thirteenth. Is that good for you?"

"Sure, but when we set up your dressing room, wardrobe needs to take your measurements again. You've put on a couple pounds."

"I'm not getting fat. I'm due for my period." Marty pulled her shirt up and looked at her belly. She poked at the soft tissue and poked again. Maybe Nina was right.

"You've looked that way for weeks now. Try fitting into your black pants. Then try on your blue bra with the white butterflies. You'll see."

"I'll do just that, but I think you're crazy."

"No. You're getting fat. Now tell me more about Liz. Yesterday you said you wouldn't want to be her first time."

Marty curled up on the chair. "I feel differently now. With the love scenes she writes, sex with her sounds promising, not to mention intriguing."

"Writing and performing are two different things. The best sex is in our heads, or in paperback."

"Yeah, but the love scenes in her last twenty books were written about me. Anyway, we're nowhere close to physical intimacy."

"Right. A day ago, she didn't want your attraction to her to come between your friendship. Just take care of you, sugar. Rachel broke your heart so badly it nearly killed me, too. I didn't like seeing you that devastated."

She scowled, hearing Rachel's name. "I'll be careful. Thanks for caring."

"We're friends. Caring is my job and I like it. Now go and grab those black pants and check out your gut. Call me when we're ready to set up shop. Bye."

"Good-bye, Nina."

Marty hung up the phone and went into the bedroom. She stripped and then grabbed her black pants and the blue bra. When she stepped into her pants, she pulled them up with ease.

"I haven't gained an ounce." Her pride quickly diminished when she tried buckling the pants and couldn't bring the fasteners close enough. "Shit." She tried zipping them first, but the zipped pants were too tight. "Damn it."

She grabbed the blue bra, slipped her arms though the straps, and fastened the back. The tops of her breasts pushed upward and outward, and that bra wasn't a push-up. "Shit," she said again. "Nina knows my body better than I do." Marty looked at her reflection in a full-length mirror. She let the bra fall to the floor. "Maybe I'll start smoking again. Liz likes the taste." She watched in the mirror while she slid the pants down her legs. "I wonder what went through her mind every week when she came to the show." She ran her hands from her hips to breasts. "Not so bad. I can feel a little more weight."

Then she remembered embracing Liz's breast before they slept. Her breast formed perfectly into Marty's hand. She slid her hand over and cupped her right breast. There was more than a handful, and her breast was larger than Liz's.

"Her nipple was hard." She teased hers to life. "Like that. I wonder if she felt the same tingle I'm feeling." She teased her nipple again and followed the path her pleasure had taken. With two fingertips, she traced a line from her breast, down her tummy, and stopped at her thigh. She kept her eyes on the mirror. "The feeling stops right here." She pressed her fingers against pink silk bikinis. "Feels good, doesn't it?"

With fluid, sensual motion, she bent at her waist and touched her ankles. She moved her fingers along the inside of her legs. Midway, Marty unlocked her knees and eased herself to a sitting position. The mirror reflected the slow motion of her legs as she spread them at the knees to frame her torso and face. She leaned back on her palms and viewed what Liz might see.

"Creamy thighs." She brought one knee to her chest and let the other drop closer to the floor. She moved her hand down to rest on the pink cover. Her fingertips grazed the soft labia underneath, and she closed her eyes in response to a heightened tingle. She raised her pelvis in greeting. "The feel of sex." She imagined Liz's cheeks against her thighs. Her hips moved in rhythm against an envisioned tongue. She whimpered.

Pressured internally and on the verge of orgasm, Marty removed her hand and lowered her legs. She listened to her erratic breaths that missed their final gasp. Her chest heaved and she ached for an earth-shattering spasm. As she reached to satisfy her need, she stopped again.

"No." She pounded the floor with her fists and stood.

Marty finished dressing and pulled her hair into a thick ponytail. She washed her face and decided against wearing makeup. Liz had commented that she looked cuter than hell without makeup.

"Cuter than hell. Not a big step, but she meant well. Cuter than hell," she repeated and blew a kiss to her reflection, just because. The house phone rang and she grabbed the bedroom extension. "Hello."

"Hi."

"I was just thinking about you." She sat on the bed.

"Good thoughts?"

"I'll keep you guessing."

"Maybe you'll tell me later?"

"Maybe."

"You're teasing me again."

She was happy that Liz couldn't see her grin. "No, there was no accent."

"I've called to tell you I have to wait for my ex to come over for some things. Can we change our schedule? I'll come to your place and I can sign your books while I'm there."

"That's fine with me. When can I expect you?"

"Around six?"

"Okay. I'll see you then."

They hung up and Marty dropped back onto the bed. A few dishes were in the sink and the carpet could use a quickie from the Hoover. That sounded like fifteen minutes of work and left her with an additional three hours before Liz would arrive.

She went into the living room, grabbed *No Business, Show Business* from the bookcase, and then nestled among soft pillows on the window seat. Years had passed since she'd last read the book. The first thing she noticed was Liz's use of first person. Marty had read the entire catalogue of novels, and this was the only one written from a single point of view and in first person. She opened the book to the dedication page.

"*Dedicated to my woman in red.*" Marty smiled. "I'll be damned," she said, turned to page one, and read aloud.

"*From the moment Abby McNair sauntered onto the stage, she captured me, and she's never let go. Dressed in red silk so tight the fabric became her flesh, each step Abby made, each slide of her hand, each twinkle of her devastatingly blue eyes left me breathing in such an agitated state that my husband asked if I felt ill. Holy shit, I'd said out loud while Abby seduced my mind and body. I'd have given myself willingly to her, on that stage and in front of that audience. Who knew an evening at the theater would drape me in a state of continual desire that would control nearly every movement I would make? Somehow, Abby knew.*"

"Wow," she whispered and turned to a random page.

"*Abby's lips burned through to my soul. Driven by need, I pulled her against me and whimpered as her tongue sliced through my labia. Slowly, her stroke carved a path and she pushed through until her tongue teased my clit with loving kisses.*"

The words renewed Marty's need for release. She closed her eyes and Liz was against her mouth. Liz tightened her legs around Marty's neck and Marty smothered within the embrace. She opened her eyes, closed the book, and exhaled audibly.

"I better wash the dishes."

❖

Liz rang the door buzzer at six fifteen and then greeted Marty with a smile and a small plastic bag from the local drugstore.

"I like when you come over. I always get presents." She peered into the bag and laughed when she pulled out a box of cotton swabs. "Q-tips?"

"Why not? People always get flowers." She pointed to the vase of daisies on the table. "See. They'll be dead in another day. Q-tips are practical."

Marty loved Liz's way of thinking, along with her smile. "I might need them one day." She looked at the box again. "Q-tips. I like that." She set the package next to the daisies.

"I have another gift for you." She reached into her shoulder bag and handed Marty a paperback novel.

"*Taylor Rock*. Your new book. Thank you." She accented her thanks with a kiss to Liz's cheek.

"I've already signed that one for you. So where's your mountain of books I need to autograph?" When led into the living room she instantly headed toward *No Business, Show Business* on the floor near the window seat. She looked at Marty. "Did you read anything interesting?"

"I thought so. It got a little steamy and I stopped to do some housework. Did you seriously have me in mind when you wrote the book?"

"No one else." Liz picked up the paperback and handed it to her. "Turn to page twelve." She sat and waited while Marty searched for the page. "Find the first full paragraph from the bottom of the page."

She scanned from the bottom up. "Got it."

"Read the first two sentences."

"*Wanting the alluring Abby, but sealed into marriage, I chose to see her show twice a week until it closed. When the final curtain came down, I whispered good-bye through a choke of streaming tears.*" She closed the book.

Liz winked at her. "Told ya."

"You really whispered a tearful good-bye?"

She took the book. "Yes and no. I whispered good-bye to you, but there were no tears choking me. That was creative license. Which parts were you reading today?" Her eyes were lethally devilish.

"The glossary," she said, feeling equally playful.

"There's no glossary."

She nodded. "Oh, yes there is. You defined everything to perfection."

"Some things. I had to invent much of your body. I gave you a firm ass and curves that would make gods weep in utter joy."

"You definitely write fiction. My assistant is ready to release me into pasture for my sagging ass." She pulled five books from the bookcase and stacked them beside Liz.

"It isn't important, you know," she said as she took a pen from her bag.

"What isn't important?"

"A firm ass." She opened the first book and signed her name.

"What is important to you?"

"Honesty. Togetherness. I've been so dishonest with me that I need honesty mainlined." She signed the small stack of books and handed them back. "Next lot. You had my number the day we met, and I still lied to myself and to you." She shook her head. "I'm sorry for that. You deserve better from me, and that means you could be in for some trouble."

"Right here in River City." She placed the remaining books on the sofa. Waiting patiently while Liz finished signing the novels, she was confused when Liz tucked *No Business, Show Business* under her leg.

"Why won't you sign it?"

"I'll take it home with me. That's the one book I'll personalize for you, and I'd rather take my time with it."

Marty agreed and returned all the books to their shelves. "Let's see," she said. "Twenty-two signed lesbian novels from the great Chandler. I can get upward of forty bucks a pop for those on eBay. Maybe more."

Liz looked offended. "How dare you!" Then she cocked her head and squinted. "That much? Really?" She opened the book. "Imagine what I could get for one of these."

Marty grabbed the book. "No way." She sat on the sofa. "Of course, we could flaunt our relationship and I'll sign the book, too. Every admirer of Liz Chandler and/or Marty Jamison will bid on this baby. We'll buy copies cheap, sign them, and…" She set the book to her side. Liz sat quietly with tenderness in her eyes. Her cheeks were a little rosy. "No?"

"No."

"What then?"

"While you rambled on about capitalism, I was thinking of you on stage and comparing what I see here."

"What do you see so far?"

"You're larger than life and in full control on stage. From what I can tell in the real world, you're self-conscious and you babble."

Marty grabbed a pillow and hugged it close. "I'm nervous. That's when I blather mindlessly." She rested her chin on the pillow. "Let's see if I can relax. New topic: What prompted a straight, married woman to write lesbian fiction?"

"I thought you'd never ask. A friend told me I was too anal to write anything outside of technical manuals. She went through my bookshelves, found a dusty Danielle Steele novel, and tossed it to me. She challenged me to write a romance novel, but there was a catch. The romance had to be between two women and I had to submit it to a publisher."

"Interesting. So you wrote a novel and a publisher liked the story."

"I thought that was the end of it until the publisher asked if I had anything more. I came up with a quick idea and my lesbian fiction career was born."

"You were an overnight sensation."

"The books were fun to write, and somehow the words flew from my fingertips." Liz reached for Marty's hand. "Then seeing you at the theater changed my writing style."

"Your books became steamier." She let go of the pillow. "What did your husband say about your creative persona?"

"Nothing much. He read *No Business* and looked at me funny, but never questioned me. He was too busy with his girl-of-the-month club."

"And you lived with that? I literally threw my last girlfriend out with nothing but a blanket wrapped around her."

"Really? That's a story I need to hear. Anyway, I lived with his philandering because I didn't care. I was Mrs. Doctor when he needed a wife and I lived comfortably. I was surprised when he eventually asked for a divorce, but I was also relieved."

"Isn't it funny how things happen?" Marty said.

"It would have been nice if things had happened twenty years ago."

"All things in due course. With close friends as the exception, I was in the closet back then. I might have run the other direction if you'd stepped one foot near me. Tell me something. Does anything about me disappoint you yet?"

"Not yet. Should I be worried? Be honest."

"I'm impatient at times, especially if things aren't happening quickly enough." She snapped her fingers three times. "I'm overprotective of what happens in the theater. I'll get mouthy and have to apologize to everyone between Chelsea and Columbus Circle."

"At least you know when you're wrong."

"Yeah, but I wish I had better control of my anger. These days I get nuts only once during a show's run and then everyone breathes freely again."

"Why was it so bad before now?"

"I let my personal life interfere with my professional half. I was living with a woman who cheated on me. Her proclivities for other women went on for about a year, and I couldn't prove it. One day I walked into our bedroom and saw her face first in the crotch of a good friend. I went ballistic." She shuddered. "I still don't like thinking about that afternoon."

"You aren't over her, then?"

"It's been two years. I'm over her, but I don't like thinking about how I'd lost control." She suddenly remembered the new production date for the show. "Oh! There's been a change in our production schedule. We begin mid-September and I need a writer. Would you be interested in some theater work if we can strike a deal with the show's author?"

"Absolutely. Speaking of productions, did you see *The Daily News* today?"

"No. What did I miss?" She went into the kitchen and grabbed the paper from the table.

"It's a gossip piece that might amuse you." Liz took the paper and turned a few pages until she pointed to the column. "Read this."

Marty read silently. *Stage starlet Felice Tate was overheard at Sardi's: "Marty's aging. Her voice is changing, and it's time for her to move over."* She laughed and continued with the author's take. *It seems Broadway's top girl remains at the top of*—she stumbled over the final words—*Tate's shit list.*

Liz pointed to the last spelling of Felice's name. "Look how they inferred a typo. Shit list."

"Felice never stops. At least she's getting some press." She closed the paper and dropped it to the floor. She playfully poked Liz's shoulder. "Are you going to tell me if you have that purple dildo in the prop box?"

"Damn you. Yes. It's there. Now stop saying that word."

She moved within an inch of Liz's ear. "Dildo. Dildo. Dildo."

"What about them?"

"Do you like them? Vibrators maybe?"

Liz turned and looked directly into her eyes. "No toys. I want flesh. A warm tongue. Fingers and hands. A hungry mouth." She pressed her hand against Marty's hip.

"Not even for private penetration?" She touched her lips against Liz's.

Liz moved her fingers across Marty's stomach. "Not even when I masturbate."

"I'd love to watch you."

"We could do it together."

Marty's lip was nibbled and released. "I'd like that." She made a conscious effort to stop her pelvis from moving against Liz's leg.

"Do you know the one thing that would disappoint me about you?"

"What?" She almost lost control when Liz's thumb pressed deeply against her lower abdomen. She wanted to grab the hand and stuff it into the front of her pants. "What would disappoint you?"

Liz moved her hand to the waist of Marty's pants. Her fingers moved slowly, back and forth against the buckle and her stomach. She teased and Marty ached.

"I'd be reduced to tears if I put my hand between your legs and found out that you shave."

"Oh my God," she said and moved away. "I can't take much more. You win."

"I didn't know we were engaged in a contest."

"We weren't, but you still win."

"Good. You're my prize and I want to make out with you."

Liz pulled Marty on top of her. Ravenous, Marty pulled Liz closer. Her hips moved freely against Liz's thigh. She kissed, sucked, and caressed Liz until she gasped for air. Marty's breasts united with Liz's against the limit of fabric, but she wanted their flames to burn through their clothes to complete their union.

Liz's breath was hot against Marty's cheek. "I want to move my cheek against you and feel curly, dark hair tickle my nose. Tell me now. Do you shave? Or will I reach into your pants and feel soft curls surround my fingers?"

Timing was everything, in the theater. Marty waited, yet screamed inside for Liz's hand to dive beyond the buckle and zipper. "Curls," was all she said and Liz's tongue drove straight into her mouth.

Marty fought increasing desire. Liz led Marty's hand to her breast but not under her blouse. When Marty reached between Liz's legs, Liz groaned but gently placed it back on her breast. Liz pressed her thigh against the inseam of Marty's pants and bit into her neck.

"Do you want me?" she asked against Marty's ear.

"Madly." She pulled their mouths together. Shallow breaths forced quick kisses. Oral penetration required space for breathing. She wanted to scream in pleasure from the friction of their bodies that had finally collided.

"I've waited twenty years for you. I want you, but not like this."

She pulled Liz's tongue into her mouth and released it. She pressed into her thigh, held tightly, slowed her kisses, and caught her breath. Marty didn't want sloppy and fevered as their foreplay any more than Liz did, but it sure felt good.

"Now you have me saying 'Holy shit.' That was your version of making out?" She straightened her clothes.

"With you it was my way." She bit into Marty's shoulder. "I love what you do with your tongue."

Marty fanned her face. "If we get this show on the road, I hope to have a couple show-stoppers for you." She stopped fanning and studied Liz. "You look adorably ravished. Your hair is everywhere, your clothes are rumpled, but you have the sweetest look of satisfaction." She reached over and straightened Liz's hair. "The best part is I gave you that look."

"I enjoyed you. I needed to satisfy a bit of desire." She looked serious. "I won't let you down. I don't have a sexual past with women, but wanting you feels natural to me." She straddled Marty's lap. "My guesses are you're afraid that I'm on the rebound from my marriage and that I'll be a clumsy fool in bed with you."

Warm kisses were soft against her cheek. "Those thoughts crossed my mind. Not to mention the 'roll in the sack with a Broadway star and write about it afterward, scenario.' "

"Sounds exciting. Do you think that's what I want?" She nibbled Marty's ear. "A quickie? Get out the big purple? Hmm?" She breathed hot air onto Marty's neck.

Marty pushed her away gently. If she hadn't, she'd have both their clothes off within a few seconds. She looked into Liz's eyes. Among the many things she saw, malice wasn't among them.

"No. You've already told me you want flesh." She studied Liz's features. She was petite in many ways, and her eyes simply looked fabulous. "And curls."

"Curls. Liz want curls." She played back the words and moved away. "Liz want you, but that will keep. It's time for me to say a memorable good-bye."

Had she been right all along? A few satisfying moments for Liz and boom, she's gone? "What? Why? What are you talking about?"

"I'm going to Connecticut tomorrow and won't be back until Sunday."

That settled her. "Good. My heart can't take much more of you."

She pushed Marty's arm. "What if I said I was going to see a cute blonde?"

"I wouldn't feel jealous at all. You want..." Her voice trailed and she twirled a lock of her hair.

Liz blushed. "A lot of it. I am seeing a blonde, though. My editor."

"The quiche eater. She is cute, I'll say that much."

"That's her. We've decided to complete all of the edits for the final book at once. Then I won't have to worry about more deadlines."

"It sounds like a lot of work. Do you think you'll miss writing about Abby?"

"No, and if things work out, maybe I'll have her inspiration all to myself." She stood and put her arm around Marty. "I have to go home and pack a suitcase. What will you do for the next few days?"

"Work out, study the play, chase women." They walked slowly to the door.

Liz playfully pinched Marty's cheek. "No way," she said with confidence. "You've got me."

Marty knew she was right. "I'll keep you in mind. Now give me a hug. I like you and I might miss you a little bit. Will you call me when you have time?"

"I'll try to squeeze you in." After a soft kiss, she closed the door behind her.

Marty sat at the table and looked alternately from the package of Q-tips, to the daisies, from practical, to frivolous, from her life, and then to Liz. She picked up the cotton swabs.

"My life has been constant for the past two years. Neat and constant, like a box of Q-tips." Marty set the box aside and pulled the vase of flowers in front of her. She rearranged a few stems, sat back, and studied the flowers. Some stood tall, while others had a slight bend. "Like Liz, you won't stand for neglect. You're demanding of my time." She looked back at the box and then studied the flowers.

"Few things are perfect. Sondheim writes the perfect lyrics. The Stanwyck's acoustics are perfect. What about love? I thought I'd found love with Rachel, but she shattered me." A white petal fell to the table. Another fell beside it. "I dropped Liz into a field of debris. Maybe we can pick up the pieces together."

CHAPTER SIX

Outside the Stanwyck Theater, Marty propped herself against a pillar and waited for Nina to arrive. Nina would set up the dressing room with Marty's personal items while wardrobe took Marty's current measurements. The sunny street was naturally busy for two o'clock on a Sunday afternoon. Large groups of excited theater patrons gathered for photos of the marquees and then waited for the matinee doors to open. A police officer sat in his cruiser and sipped his coffee.

The narrow road stretched one way, and litter lay scattered in the gutters. A half block to her left and right, paint-stained scaffolding marred the dignity of the theaters, all but the Stanwyck. Near the curb, pigeons warbled and pecked at the ground. She took a deep breath and smiled. It was a great afternoon on 44th Street.

"Good morning, sugar," Nina said when she stepped from a cab. The driver opened the back of the vehicle and pulled out a large trunk. He wheeled it to the door. Nina handed Marty a cup of coffee. "Why are you standing in the sun? You know your skin's sensitive to UV."

She tore off the tab on the coffee cup. "A few minutes won't roast me to cinders."

"It better not. We have a hard enough time getting your makeup right." Nina pulled Marty by her arm to a concrete bench and set a shopping bag at her feet. "Did you try on your black pants?"

Marty stretched her legs in front of her. An early morning massage had relaxed her to the point of wanting a nap. She was content to spend a few minutes watching the pigeons and listening to Nina. "That's another reason we're here," she said and sipped her breakfast.

"Look in the bag," Nina said.

She pulled the bag onto her lap and removed a fold of red satin. "This is pretty," she said and brought out another piece. "You bought yellow after all."

"You look great in both. Wardrobe gave me a go-ahead. Clive is directing and he approved the teddies."

Clive's direction was a major plus to Marty feeling more settled with the show. Beginning when she first stepped foot on a Broadway stage, they had worked together on several of Marty's shows. Their history was good and Clive was like the Stanwyck's owners: flexible and ready to take on a challenge.

"Ready to get measured?" Nina asked.

"I guess so."

Marty wheeled the heavy black trunk and followed Nina through the cinnamon scented hall until they reached the door to the dressing room. Nina opened the door and turned on the light.

"Here you go, queenie. Your palace waits."

She let go of the trunk and sat at the vanity. "We haven't worked this theater in three years. Who was here last? LuPone? The room smells like Patti's perfume."

Nina pulled the trunk through the doorway. "I don't keep track of you gypsies." She unlocked the oversized box and pushed it open. "Come on. Help me."

Marty first took the framed photograph of Joyce Manning and set it on the vanity next to the mirror. With Nina's assistance, they set up makeup and hair products. She pulled out a bottle of hair dye and then returned it to the compartment. While Nina hung blow dryers and curling irons against the wall, Marty stocked the bathroom. They completed the arrangement of the dressing room just as Anna from wardrobe arrived. Marty stripped off her pants and shirt.

"You won't wear your bra onstage. Would you mind removing it?" Anna asked. Marty discarded her bra and Anna wrapped the tape measure around her bust. "Forty," she said.

"Was I right?" Nina asked. "A full inch and a half. Your fat goes right to your boobs."

"Just keep quiet, Nina."

Anna wrapped the tape around Marty's waist and then her hips. "Your waist is twenty-eight and a half, and your hips are thirty-eight and a half." She wrote down those numbers.

"That's almost two inches on your waist and half an inch on your hips," Nina said.

"Still a C cup?"

"Not by much," she said and measured from Marty's shoulder to four inches below her crotch. She wrote down the final numbers.

"That'll change after lunch," Nina said.

Marty scowled at her. "Can I get dressed? It's chilly in here."

"I'm done." She pulled the dress dummy from the trunk and adjusted it to new proportions.

Marty dressed and watched Anna wrap and pin the satin around the dummy. "I'm not overeating that much. I think trying to stop smoking has slowed my metabolism. I'll run or something to get the fat off."

"That might work," Nina said.

"I'll set you up with Nina's yellow and red. You can choose your preference. I found some nice piping for this material," Anna said through the pins in her mouth. "You'll want to take these costumes home with you."

"They'll be gorgeous. Thanks."

"Go study your lines or something," Nina said. "I'll keep Anna company."

Marty grabbed her script and a pencil and walked through the hall. When she reached the wing, she picked up a metal folding chair and dragged it to center stage. Beneath the dim stage light, she opened the script and spoke her first line, but stripped it of punctuation and emotion.

"For thirty years, I conducted my life under the guise of knowing what I was doing."

She wrote in a pause after "years," drew a line through "guise," and penciled in "pretext." She underlined *years* to stress the word. She stood, turned toward the house, and spoke the rewritten line.

"For thirty years" She paused. *"I conducted my life under the pretext of knowing what I was doing."*

"Eh," she muttered, still unhappy with the line. She crossed out "was doing" and added "needed."

"Got a new show going?" the security guard asked from in front of the apron.

"Soon. Hey, can I borrow your gun?"

"Well, I don't know, I…" He pulled his handgun from the holster. "Yeah, why not." He emptied the chambers into his hand, looked down the barrel, and then handed the weapon to her.

Marty took the gun into her right hand. "How does this sound to you?" She looked back into the house.

"For thirty years…" She paused and pointed the gun barrel against her chest. *"I conducted my life under the pretext of knowing what I needed."* She stroked her cheek with the barrel of the handgun and looked down at the guard. "What do you think?"

"It's better with the gun." He took the weapon back.

"I think so, too."

He went about his rounds and she continued marking the script and repeating lines. After two hours, she'd had enough, proving once more that she wasn't a writer. When she headed toward the wing, clapping sounded from the mezzanine. She stopped and turned to the dark house.

"Who's there?" she asked and watched a shadowed figure approach.

"The Lady in White."

Liz's soft voice carried gently toward the stage. Marty waited for her to emerge from the shadows. How was it that she turned Marty into five feet and nine inches of contentment? What of Liz so demanded respect that Marty hadn't gone further the evening they turned warm into blistering? She sighed and tingled with anticipation as Liz stepped into her vision. First a foot, then up to her hips, and then white to her shoulders, the curtain came up and revealed a showstopper. Marty stepped to the edge of the apron. She took Liz's hand when she ascended the steps and walked onto the stage.

"You are wearing white."

"Another hot and humid day. It's much cooler in Connecticut. Trish and I edited until we couldn't take each other any longer, but we finished early." She held Marty loosely. "Hello. Miss me?"

"Never," Marty said and Liz looked up at her with eyes that always filled Marty with delight. "Maybe."

"Show me how 'maybe' feels."

Marty couldn't breathe. She captured Liz's mouth with authority, but Liz's lips moved as slow and delicate as a warm tide. She drifted in and pulled Marty away. Welcomed moisture cooled her lips. She stopped kissing and let Liz's mouth make love to hers. Marty quivered from a tenderness that she'd never experienced.

She broke their kiss and smiled. "How about going away for a few more days? Then come back and kiss me that way again."

"I think I'm spoiling you, Marty Jamison."

"Yeah. Do that. Spoil me."

"Nope. We're going out for a bit. I want to do something daring."

"Aw," she whined, "but you kiss so nicely."

Liz winked. "And don't you forget it."

❖

At the corner of Times Square and 44th street, Liz flagged down a pedicab. "Caution to the wind," she said, entered the confined space of the cab, and paid the cyclist. "Through the park, Bitterman. You know how much I love the park." The driver looked at her indifferently but took the cash and pedaled into traffic.

"You know, don't you? That we're about to die?" Marty said.

As she'd expected, their ride was harrowing. The driver dodged every possible taxi, private vehicle, pedestrian, and at least two police officers on horseback. She held one side rail, Liz white-knuckled the other, and their free hands melded. They laughed, squealed, and promised to attend the funeral of the other, should one of them survive the ride.

"Stop here!" Marty shouted when they reached the curb of Central Park West and Fifty-Ninth Street. "This is fine, thanks." She helped Liz from the cab. "I'll never do that again."

"I'll take you to my favorite place," Liz said. "It isn't far."

Amid the smell of burned pretzels, Central Park bustled with summer sounds: the laughter of children, grunts of tired parents. Music wailed from a new direction with each twist in the walkway, and horse drawn carriages clopped lazily. Aside from an occasional slow cab or automobile, traffic sounds weren't harsh in the park. Hand in hand, they walked to an area near the pond.

"Here it is," Liz said and kicked off her pumps. She climbed to the top of a large boulder and sat.

Marty climbed the massive rock and dropped next to her. They sat beneath a shady tree, facing the pond. "It's peaceful here."

"I want to share this spot with you. Before I moved to the village, I used to come here to work. I've missed my perch. It's always been special to me."

"It's a big perch, that's for sure, and tough on the rump, too. What makes this rock special for you?"

"This is my mini version of the Stanwyck. When I was young, my father often brought me here. Dad was a geologist and he taught me a lot about the formation of this island."

Marty looked around the area. "My guess would be receding water and then land appeared."

"Not even a smidgen close. This outcrop"—she slapped her hand against the rock—"is roughly four hundred fifty million years old."

"Get out."

She smiled. "It's granite, Manhattan schist, and it's the bedrock of this island."

Marty listened, eager to learn something new about Liz and the island.

"Schist was formed under extreme pressure. Long story short, there were once mountains here that may have been as high as the Alps."

"That high?" She looked into the sky and imagined jagged, snow-covered Alps towering above. "Mountains like that were here?"

Liz nodded. "Their pressure formed this bedrock. After erosion by wind and water, a final ice age completed the job of leveling many of the mountains by shoving a mile high glacier through here. That chunk of ice tore a path without as much as an apology, and exposed this bedrock."

"A mile high glacier? That's about four times as high as the Empire State Building. That's some big ice." She ran her hand over a dip in the stone. "How did these small channels happen? They're almost smooth and they're linear."

"That mean old glacier picked up debris along the way. She confiscated and then pushed various sized rocks from the Palisades, for one." She pointed toward the Hudson River and New Jersey where the Palisades were located. "Depending on the size of the rock, they carved these striations." She ran her hand over a dip in the rock. "This larger bow is like your lower back. A lovely slope."

"I'm hoping you'll make my bed rock."

Liz groaned. "Where the city's skyscrapers are built, in the south and midtown areas, granite anchors the structures and that's what gives Manhattan her cool skyline."

"Fascinating. That bitch of a glacier destroyed nearly everything in front of her, but she left us something to work with. I guess that was her way of apologizing."

"Speaking of making amends, do I owe you an apology for breaking into your script study today?"

"Are you kidding me?" She gave Liz's hand a squeeze. "My heart went flip-flop."

"Good. I enjoyed my private show, and you made some excellent dialogue changes. You've also found the humor in the script."

"I'm still struggling with humor, but maybe we'll make a decent show out of that mess. Are you anxious to begin your foray into the theater?"

"I'm excited about writing for you. I was like a school kid in Office Max yesterday. I picked up a notebook and then some red pencils that I'll sharpen to the likes hitherto unknown to mankind."

Marty laughed. "Hitherto, huh? That's some serious sharpening."

"Hitherto," she repeated. "Not only that but hence*forth*, I am your writer, Ms. Jamison. I'm thrilled and honored."

On her stoop, she had claimed she would hand the script over to Liz, and she literally had, but the changes would be a joint venture between Liz and the director.

"If we strike a deal with the author, I think you'll enjoy working with us. There's an incredible amount of affection among theater people. At least that's the way it's been for me."

"Have you ever questioned why?"

"For me, it's because I share a gamut of emotions day after day. They're not necessarily my emotions, but they leave me open to feel more compassion and tolerance in the real world. I also think acting allows me to express myself better as a person."

"When you delivered your put up or shut up ultimatum to me, you were expressive but not tolerant."

Marty blushed and took Liz's hand. "That was the wine talking, but I knew I was on to something with you."

"When I called your cell today, Nina answered. She explained who she was and said you were onstage playing make-believe. Nina met me at the entrance and that's how I found you. I liked her. She called me Wonder Woman."

"I might start calling you Wonder Woman. The way you kiss unhinges me, and I'm curious what might come next."

Liz squeezed Marty's hand and then moved to her wrist. Another squeeze and then she moved slowly up Marty's forearm. Liz stopped at the elbow, but she had awakened each nerve ending in Marty's body.

"Twenty years," Liz said quietly. "I've kissed you like there's no tomorrow, but right now I'm in awe of you. Touching you…no, my entire situation with you defies probability."

"And you don't seem hesitant."

"Not at all." She leaned back on her hands. "Every time we're together, I'm giddy. The sight of you makes me want to do a happy dance. That's how I feel when I'm with you."

"You've written of similar reactions. I think my favorite description was 'she was an expensive support bra for my emotions. Her presence always uplifted me.' "

Liz rolled her eyes. "That wasn't one of my better moments at humor."

"It worked for me. The scene was playful from the beginning. Now, had you written that when your main character was on the brink of orgasm, no."

"With that said, I don't understand why you don't get the comedy within the tragedy of your new show. It's under the surface, but it's there. Wait until I'm officially your writer. I'll write you until you can't stand laughing. Then I'll make sure your character understands the love that's surrounded her all of her life." She looked out to the pond.

Marty admired Liz's self-confidence and they shared that strongpoint. Concerning their play, or their private life, she visualized a healthy relationship on the horizon.

"Come over here," she said and Marty followed to another part of the rock. "Do you see these elongated chips in the rock? Glaciers fragmented chunks of this granite. And look here." She pointed to a nearby section. "This schist is folded. Folded rock. Pressure created these abnormalities, and now they're a part of nature's beauty. We're sitting on your character. She's lost pieces of herself along the way, and now she's folding under pressure—her own pressure."

"Then she is tragic."

"She's not. She's a thing of beauty, too, and understands that her creases and chips are not life threatening. They're her life's battle scars. When her mile-high glacier passes that night onstage, she'll laugh at herself and I'll make sure the audience has fun while she figures everything out."

"A rock and a woman." Marty stared at her. "How do you do that?"

"What?"

"You have an incredible sense of words and how to relate them to other things. You do that all the time when you write."

Liz smiled and shrugged. "It's just word association. Words are convenient. They're best when referred back to and then I play with them."

"What other treasures do you have hidden inside?"

"If you mean talent, I'm also an artist. I've designed all of Liz Chandler's book covers, among others."

"Nice." Marty placed a small twig with a single leaf between her teeth, stretched to her side, and struck a pose. "Could you create me on paper?"

"I already have."

She removed the twig and tossed it at Liz. "Really? If I didn't feel otherwise, I'd say you're stalking me, Ms. Chandler."

Liz shook her head. "No. That would have happened years ago. I obsess privately."

Marty sat up and brushed the dirt from her arm. "Did you create the piece from memory?"

"Sort of. Do you remember your appearance on the PBS tribute to Cole Porter?"

"I sang 'Blow, Gabriel, Blow.' "

"At the end of the song, on the last note, you flung your head back and reached toward the sky with both arms. You held that final note for what seemed like eternity."

Marty smiled. "Audiences eat that up."

"I did, too. You sang that song like both of you were loose and trashy. You were hot and that's how I drew you."

"Let's see: In your mind I'm loose, trashy, and invasive. I'm not so sure that's a great start for me, but I kind of like those labels."

"No, you have two different personas. You're invasive. The woman onstage can be loose and trashy."

"When I belt a great ballad, or even a fun song like 'Gabriel'— those are my best songs."

"Musically, they're your finest moments in the theater. The reverberation of your voice bounces fabulously throughout the house. Unfortunately, television doesn't capture that quality."

"You're my biggest fan." Marty nudged Liz's leg. "Tell me about the picture you created."

"It's an angle shot, as though I had a camera." She stood and approached Marty's left. "Hold your arms high and throw your head back." She adjusted the arms wider. "This is the shot." Over Marty's left shoulder, Liz used her hands to frame the pose. "The vision is downward and shows a portion of your arms, your profile, neck, and then lots of cleavage." She smiled and helped Marty to her feet.

"I hope you'll show the piece to me. Maybe I could use it for an advertisement."

They stepped down from the boulder and Liz slipped her feet into her shoes. "You have quite an ego, Ms. Jamison."

"I beg your pardon?"

"You like hearing those things I say about you."

"I think everyone likes their ego stroked. I happen to get a lot of public attention. Even you admitted having been caught up in at least one of my performances."

Liz took Marty's hand into her own. "What would you do if the attention ended?"

Marty hesitated. "I don't know."

Liz chuckled. "You aren't prepared if your starstruck admirers should find another Marty Jamison type to fawn over, just like your character wasn't prepared."

"Well, if it's any consolation, I don't own any guns."

"How did wearing her shoes feel for that moment?"

"I wanted another chance. I felt empty inside. I wanted to rewrite my script."

Liz opened her ringing cell phone. "It's Melissa from Barnes and Noble. I have to take this call."

Marty walked over to the concession and purchased a bottle of water and a pretzel. She sat on a bench and thought about Liz's hypothetical statement.

When she'd taken over the lead for *Bourbon Street*, praise came quickly and from every direction. With its nearly constant barrage, fanfare had become a staple in her life. Friends honored her as a guest at the finest parties in Manhattan, she sat at the best tables in any restaurants, and performing garnered a phenomenal monetary payoff. If audience approval stopped tomorrow, what did she have beyond singing, dancing, and acting? She wondered if she should ramp up her act and not allow her competitors the edge. The thought of losing her audience left her queasy.

"Did you sell out at the store?" Marty asked as Liz approached and sat next to her.

"I wish. No, she reminded me of a reading I've scheduled for tomorrow. Would you like to come and listen?"

"I'd love to hear you read." She handed the pretzel to Liz. "What time and where?"

"I have some things to do uptown, so meet me at the Barnes and Noble on Fifth Avenue at five o'clock."

"Okay. Now back to the character. You placed me into her shoes because."

"To make you better understand her problem. She's lost and needs help in recognizing what she's done to her life."

"I have to admit I didn't like the feeling."

"Good. Now you just have to trust me to help you get your role right."

Had double entendre snuck back to haunt her? Marty smiled at her life. She wasn't the character onstage. She was the happy actor who sat beside a lovely new love interest.

Life was good in Central Park.

Chapter Seven

Two hours before meeting Liz at the bookstore, Marty stared into her closet of dresses. She'd never attended a reading and was clueless what to wear. Casual? Daring? Elegant? Shorts and a tank top? She called Liz for a proper wardrobe.

"Casual. You're attending a reading, not a Broadway opening."

She opened a different closet and chose a white skirt, a bright blue blouse, and then a single strand of pearls for an accessory. White sandals completed her outfit.

"There," she said to her reflection in the full-length mirror. She pulled her hair out from under her collar and then opened an additional button on her blouse. "What's a little extra flesh among a group of women? I think I'll look acceptable for Liz, without distracting from her afternoon."

Marty grabbed the door handle to Barnes and Noble and suddenly stopped. Had she read Elizabeth *Mathieu* on the sign in the window? Maybe this was the wrong Barnes and Noble? She walked back to the display window and photo of Liz. Clearly, the last name was Mathieu. Puzzling. Why would she use another name? She read the placard aloud.

" 'Barnes and Noble presents author Elizabeth Mathieu, reading from her series *The Adventures of Lily and Billy: Tree House Troubles*.'

Her what?" A copy of the book lay open and another was propped against the announcement. On the cover, a small boy climbed a tree and a girl peered out the window from above him. "Really? Liz writes for children? Yes, really. It's right in front of you."

Marty entered the store. Once inside, the scent of paper filled the air around her. Then she figured every mother and early grammar school child between Fifth Avenue and Harlem had invaded the bookstore. More children arrived and scurried around Marty; some bumped into her, spun her around, and headed toward the back of the store. When she composed herself, a hand touched her shoulder.

"Ms. Jamison?" A woman asked.

Marty turned around and wished she'd worn a shoe with decent heels. She faced an attractive woman who was at least six feet tall. "Yes."

"I'm Melissa, the store manager. Liz said you'd be here, and I wanted to help you find your way through the throng. As you can see, she's quite popular with the kids. Come with me." She led Marty into a small office. Liz waited inside, dressed in faded denim blue jeans and a white T-shirt with an annoying happy face painted onto the middle. "You still have ten minutes. Come out when you're ready." She left the room.

Marty smiled at Liz. "I'm pleased to meet you, Ms. Mathieu. Why didn't you tell me you wrote children's books?"

"I think surprises are nice." She handed her a copy of the book and lowered her eyes to Marty's cleavage. "I don't think you'll need those today. I doubt you'll find many adult women in the audience."

Marty quickly fastened the button through her embarrassment. "I thought—"

Smiling, she looked back up at Marty. "I know what you thought. I'm sorry the reading won't be what you'd expected."

"I think it's wonderful that you write for children." She looked at the front of the book. "Is this your artwork?"

"Yes. I've done the complete series of ten. Like it?"

"I do. And Mathieu?"

"Maiden name. Come on." She opened the office door and Marty followed the quick pace. "It's time for you to see me onstage. I love these kids."

Marty stopped and leaned against a table that was stacked with new releases. Packed tightly together, children filled the seats and several stood around the perimeter. Their loud voices stopped when Liz walked to her chair. The sudden hush surprised Marty. The children's eyes followed each move Liz made.

"Hello. I'm so happy to see you again." She waved and the kids bombarded her with their own greetings. "Okay, you know what to do." They cleared the area of seats and sat on the floor in a semi-circle around Liz. New participants caught on quickly.

Melissa joined Marty. "They're all underprivileged. She gives them a free copy of her new releases, on their promise to come back and read to her."

"To her?"

"She also sends copies to all of the children's wards of each hospital in Manhattan. I think she visits the kids, too."

The next hour and thirty minutes unfolded to Marty's delight. Each child read once, sometimes agonizingly slow, and Liz encouraged them to take their time with the words. At the end of each chapter, she asked questions about that section. The children remained attentive for the entire program and they, including Liz's nurturing of them, enchanted Marty. At the close of the reading, Liz signed their books and received her own gift of a hug from the children. When the last child kissed Liz's cheek and left with her mother, Liz met Marty at the table.

"You are one incredible woman," Marty said. "You're voluntarily aiding their education. How many people would do what you've done?"

Liz smiled. "I'm sure others contribute in different and greater ways. Aren't the kids great? I can tell who reads more at home and who doesn't, but still they come and give it their all. Maybe my input will do some good in their future." She looked around the large room. "I need to say good-bye to Melissa. Can we share a bottle of wine afterward?"

"Yes."

❖

When they reached the closest outdoor café, humidity had left them sticky with perspiration. Instead of wine, they ordered iced coffee. Liz fanned her face with a napkin.

"I'll bet it's ninety degrees right now." She patted the seat next to her. "Sit beside me." Marty moved to the chair and Liz rested her hand on Marty's thigh. In spite of the heat outside, Marty still felt the warmth of Liz's hand. Liz leaned against the back of the chair and watched pedestrians.

Marty studied Liz. She looked comfortable in her happy face T-shirt tucked in perfectly, and Marty felt overdressed, but she smiled. She was the femme to Liz's deliciously soft butch. Liz could wear flannel for all Marty cared.

"You're wonderful with children."

"I think we should go steady," Liz suddenly blurted.

Marty laughed. "You mean, like, you give me a ring and I put yarn around it? That kind of going steady? High school stuff?"

Liz looked at her left hand and grimaced. "Are you telling me I have fat fingers?"

"No. They're sleek, like the rest of you."

"I want you to be my girlfriend. That probably sounds silly, but I like the feeling the thought gives me."

Silly? Yes, going steady was silly. Marty was in her forties, well beyond the quaint charms and claims of puberty, but of course she wanted to wear Liz's ring. The idea thrilled her so much that she might even consider playing spin the bottle. No, she'd definitely play spin the bottle with Liz.

"Tell me how the thought feels."

"Like a cauldron of cuddly contentment." She sipped her coffee and rolled her eyes. "My editor would probably have a field day with a description like that, but that's how I feel." She looked over at Marty and grinned. "How about it? Wanna be my girl?"

Marty hesitated. "I don't know." She looked around the table and under her napkin. "I don't see a ring."

Liz grabbed Marty's hand and placed it on the table. She leaned down, inches away from Marty's hand. "It's naked, that's for sure."

She drew a line over the spot where a ring might rest. "Let me see what I can do about that."

"The diamond district isn't too far away," she suggested in jest.

"Champagne taste." Liz pulled at her outdated T-shirt. "I'm a poor girl." She took her other hand from her pocket and leaned close to the table again. Slowly, she pushed the cheap prop ring that she'd found on the street, onto Marty's pinky.

"It's perfect." Marty adjusted the ring.

Liz sat up looking proud. "I scrubbed it cleaner than Johnson and Johnson, so don't worry about that, and I won't be upset if you don't wear it. I just wanted to feel closer. I have to go away tomorrow. Knowing you'll be here when I return makes leaving easier."

Disappointment filled Marty. "Where are you going?"

"Phoenix. I have a family wedding to attend, and then I'm scheduled for a group of book signings on the west coast."

"When will you return?"

"Two weeks, just in time to begin working with you."

Marty looked down at her ring and then back at Liz. "I like the ring. I like that you want to be closer and I'll miss you while you're gone. I was hoping we could spend fun time together before we started arguing over dialogue." She smiled.

"Unfortunately, that's impossible, but I'll call you when I can." She placed money on the table. "Let's go. I have to finish packing."

Liz snapped the final suitcase and set the luggage near the door. She joined Marty on the sofa and cuddled against her.

"Look at us," Liz said. "It wasn't long ago that we sat here and you grilled me on my sexuality."

"I'm glad I was persistent." She pushed Liz's hair away from her cheek.

"Me, too. Would you like any souvenirs from my journey?"

"No," Marty said. "Just come home and fill the space inside of me again." She pressed her lips onto Liz's hand.

"Abby used that line in *No Business.*"

"I know." She continued a slow pace of kisses up Liz's arm.

"Stop." She pulled her arm away.

Marty looked up. "What's wrong? I'm feeling affectionate and I'll miss you."

Liz pulled Marty into her arms. "We can do better than sweet arm kisses. That stuff is for sappy romance novels."

Liz's lips—soft, rough, and soaking—sought every exposed portion of Marty's neck and face. Her breasts were kissed through their covering fabric and Liz didn't stop there. Down, lower, painfully slow, Liz's mouth came to rest on Marty's exposed knee. Liz pushed the skirt away and ran her tongue up Marty's thigh. When she reached the hilt, she stopped. "Curls." She nuzzled against the unexposed hair.

Marty groaned. "Don't tease me. Touch me."

Liz pushed Marty's legs apart. She slid her hand up Marty's thigh and stopped short. "Say please."

"Please." Marty whimpered and jumped when Liz's fingers touched against the silk of her bikinis. She tingled beyond recognition and pressed against Liz's hand. "Oh dear God. Please make love to me."

Liz moved her hand away. "Soon. I don't want us to be about the invasion of pants."

"I get that. I really do, but do you have to be such a tease?"

"I could have not touched you."

Marty released a deep breath. "I guess I know what I'll be doing tonight."

Liz's eyes widened. "Tell me about it."

"No." She looked at her ring and then at Liz. "A ring and promises of tomorrow. Are you trying to make an honest woman of me?"

"I never thought you were dishonest. Will you really, uh, you know, tonight?"

Marty stood and smoothed her skirt. "No. I'll wait for you."

After a few more smothering kisses and a gentle hug good-bye, Marty went back to her apartment and snuggled into bed. She fell asleep, while remembering Liz and the children laughing and reading.

Chapter Eight

Two weeks passed slowly and quickly. Marty slept soundly on Monday night, knowing Liz would be home on a late flight. She would grab a few hours of sleep, and then they'd meet at the theater.

On Tuesday morning, Marty's phone rang at seven o'clock and she sloppily grabbed the extension on her nightstand. "Hello," she mumbled.

"Time to get up, sugar."

"Why, Nina? Why are you calling me at this hour?"

"I'm looking out for you. Get up, get dressed, and I'll meet you outside."

"Why?"

"We'll walk to the theater. It's a hot morning and you'll burn some calories. Brush your teeth, pack a change of clothes, and grab an apple. I'll meet you outside in ten minutes."

"I can't eat fruit after I brush my teeth."

"You'll be thankful that you have that apple. Now get dressed."

"But—"

"Nine and a half minutes," Nina said and hung up.

Marty placed the phone on the cradle and sat up. She ran her hands through her hair and over her face. She rubbed her eyes. Liz flashed through her mind, and her mood elevated to that of full exhilaration. She sprang from her bed and followed Nina's instructions to the word.

❖

"I'm not all cruel," Nina said on the stoop outside the apartment building. She handed her an iced coffee. "I know you need your caffeine."

Grateful for the drink, she took a long swallow and then performed a lively dance down the steps. "Much better. Good morning, Nina," she sang.

"Nice to see you're bubbling after my rude awakening. That's all I've got. Now tell me your news."

"We haven't walked twenty feet and already you want to know if I got lucky?"

"If you'd returned my call yesterday, I wouldn't have to ask."

She looped her arm with Nina's and picked up the pace. "I was working at home all day. No, I didn't get lucky, but we had a wonderful day."

"From what I can tell, the woman has some serious like for you. She gets a high approval rating from me."

Some serious like. Marty smiled in wonder. Her life had changed with a single glance through the window of a crowded bagel shop. It had been two years since she'd thrown her ex out for her final fling with infidelity, and no woman had caught her attention so quickly since then. Thinking back, Marty had never felt anticipation for anyone, the way she felt it for Liz.

"Nina, do you believe in love at first sight?"

"Me?" Nina took time to think about her answer. "For me? No. It takes a long time for someone to stick in my craw."

Marty laughed. "You make love sound wonderfully romantic."

"I'm too coarse to do the gushy thing. Is that what Liz is for you? Love at first sight?"

"I don't know," she said. "I can only say she makes me go 'oh yeah' inside."

"It sounds like fun," Nina said.

"Fun? I'm reveling on the greatest human emotion and it reduces to fun for you?"

"Yes. Fun for you and fun for Liz."

Perhaps it was that simple. "It is fun. I'm crazy about her."

With their brisk pace, they soon arrived at the corner of 38th Street. They gathered with others at the crosswalk and waited for the dotted red hand of the crosswalk signal to turn white. Marty looked across the avenue and noticed Liz walking the final steps to the entrance of Bank of America. She wanted to flag her down, but thought better of making a spectacle of herself and embarrassing Nina. She'd see her soon enough at the theater. Just as the light turned white, she looked over her shoulder and back at the bank. A tall man greeted Liz with a kiss to her cheek and they entered the bank.

"Let's go," Nina said and pulled her along by her arm.

A twinge jabbed Marty's stomach. It signaled fear. Her gut reaction instantly shrouded her with the same feeling of inadequacy she'd experienced when she caught Rachel with another woman. She took a deep breath and refused to get crazy over a woman she'd just met. A few kisses do not a girlfriend make. She looked at the ring on her pinky. It's not like they had professed undying love. Aside from that, Liz had friends and family. Maybe she was kissed by a friend.

Marty beat her feet on the pavement a little heavier. Her confidence had diminished when she caught Rachel cheating on her, but that was two years ago. How does self-confidence suddenly hurl itself under a bus—again?

"Do you think Liz could be using me?"

"That's always a possibility, especially in your line of work, but I have good character judgment. I doubt she's anything less than the real deal."

When they approached the theater, the sight of the building threw her into a better frame of mind. The Stanwyck waited patiently for her. Nina pointed to the marquee and read. "Marty Jamison, Opening Soon. There's a vague marquee, if I ever saw one. No title to the show?"

"Not yet." She wrapped her arms around a pillar and squealed. "Hello, gorgeous."

"You're crazy." Nina shook her head and walked toward the entrance. "Let's go. You have plenty of time to shower and get dressed."

Marty kissed the pillar and followed Nina to the dressing room. "There's no romance to you, Nina."

After a refreshing quick shower, she reentered the dressing room. Liz greeted her with a smile, and any feeling of inadequacy had run its course through Marty.

"Hello." She gave Liz a bouncy squeeze. "I am so glad you're home."

"You're in fine spirits. Now kiss me, or I'll—"

Her lips quickly landed on Liz's mouth. No less invigorating than it was on any other occasion, there was promise in their kiss. Then Marty felt guilt.

"Wow," Liz said when Marty pulled away. "Did someone turn off the kiss switch?"

"I did. I have to tell you something, and I feel like crap about it, but you can clear things up for me."

"What's wrong?"

"Here's an injection of honesty for you. On my way here, I saw you outside Bank of America and you walked inside with a man. When he kissed your cheek, I felt…I don't know. Left out, I guess. Are you seeing someone else?" Marty watched an additional self-confidence point fly out the window.

"No. He was my ex-husband. Paul and I still have some matters to take care of and money is one aspect."

Now she felt worse than crap. "I'm sorry. You did say your divorce was amicable."

"Yes, I did, and you told me you were over your girlfriend." She sat and pulled Marty down with her. Liz rested her arm on the back of the sofa and let her hand rest on Marty's shoulder. "What's happened with that?"

"I am over her."

"But you've not shaken the jealousy."

"It's not jealousy. I doubt I'd ever feel that about a man. It's more than that. I'm trying to trust a stranger."

Liz moved her hand from Marty's shoulder to the sofa. "I'm a stranger now?"

"No, I don't think of you as one, but you are, technically. I'm opening my life to you because I want you here. I want to trust you. Maybe I jumped the gun with you."

"Regrets?" Liz asked. "Are you giving me the heave-ho?"

"No. God, no. No way do I want that. I saw you with him. I worried that maybe you were seeing someone and what's wrong with that? You don't owe me anything."

"True. I don't owe you anything." Liz's hand was gentle on Marty's shoulder again. "Relax. You're babbling and you don't play martyr well."

"Then stop me."

"Okay, listen to me. I like you, Marty, and I want more of you. I don't know how far we'll get, but I swear no person will come before you. My affection is yours. What's more, and maybe this'll make you shake in your pretty silk drawers, what's more is I hope liking you turns into loving you. It's that simple for me, with you. Simple and *semper fidelis*."

Marty didn't respond right away. In her heart, she believed Liz. She believed everything about her. Maybe that's why she concerned herself with the lack of a conventional timeline. She understood what had been common to her: meet the woman, date the woman, kiss the woman, know the woman, and then maybe sleep with the woman. All her life she'd restricted herself to those familiar dance steps. That control wasn't so when Liz's heavy kissing binge had knocked nearly all practicality out of Marty. Thankfully, they controlled impulses that would have turned kisses into a satiated night of hot and wet.

Stripped of the limitations of a graduated timeline, Marty felt dropped into the quick pace of a romantic musical. With a few lines of dialogue, their show moved forward. A timeline was a kind of script, in the end. Wasn't it? Scripts were constantly changed.

Liz turned and leaned against Marty. She loved her scent. She buried her nose against her hair and then nipped at her ear. When Liz sighed, Marty suddenly had to squelch her desire to stand up and belt a heart-pounding, sappy ballad to explain the current scene.

"No response?" Liz asked. "You know, I could have worded that speech differently. I could have said 'get your head out of your ass and let me care for you, you damn fool.' Would that have worked?"

"That would have worked a lot quicker. Turn around." Liz shifted again in Marty's arms. "I want to trust you, and I welcome thoughts of maybe falling in love with you. Would you now kiss this fool?"

"So demanding."

Before their lips touched, Nina entered the room.

"Oops," Nina said. "I hate busting in on your rendezvous, but the production team is waiting for you two."

Liz moved away. "Let's go make your star shine." They followed Nina to the stage.

A table was set up at center stage and there sat Clive—the director, and Marty's frequent understudy—Allison, and no one else. There was no producer, no musical director, no choreographer, and no chorus line. Their setup looked more like an interrogation than the makings of a Broadway show. Marty couldn't help but laugh. Her show was a long way from opening night.

She touched his shoulder. "Hey, Clive. It's been a couple of years for us."

"Glad to work with you again," Clive said. "Pull up a chair."

Marty then kissed Allison's cheek. "It's good to see you, Allison."

"Likewise," Allison said and opened her script.

She introduced Liz and sat beside her. "Well," she said and stretched her legs. She loosely folded her arms on the table. "Does anyone know who the hell bought this property and decided to sucker me into signing? Not to mention, I don't see a producer sitting here."

"It's my understanding that a temporary producer will arrive today or tomorrow," Clive said.

"A temporary producer? Is that like a little bit pregnant?" Allison asked.

Clive shuffled through some papers. "I think I have the owners' and producers' names here."

Marty looked at him. "Good. I have so much respect for you that I should have your children. I'd like you to tell me why you signed on to this show."

Clive looked up from his papers. "It's a funny story. It won't be easy for you, but I see a Tony with your name on it."

"Uh-huh. We shouldn't be on Broadway. We should be in Poughkeepsie or Hartford. Hell, even they're too good for this play."

Clive smiled. "Whatever house we play to, you'll be queen. If you speak it, they will come." Marty groaned. "My reputation is at stake, too. We have some great stuff here and all of us will work with Liz to make the rest of it great. We're on your side."

"You say that like we're a full company." She sat up and looked at each person. At least she trusted them. Bert, the stage manager for her previous show, wandered out from the wing.

"Hey, Jamison." He nudged her arm. "Ladies," he said to the other women. He nodded to Clive. "I'm on loan from the St. James while they renovate. So what do we have here? This is the Chandler show. Right?"

Marty looked at Liz. "Chandler? How odd is that?"

"That's the name," Clive said. He scanned a page with his finger and stopped. "Right. Paul Chandler. Dr. and Mrs. Paul Chandler."

Liz squeezed Marty's leg and she snapped her head toward her. Eyes wide, Liz turned crimson with embarrassment. "I think that's my ex-husband."

"What?" Marty looked back at Clive. "Are you sure you have that name right?"

Clive checked his papers. "Uh, yes. Paul Chandler. His wife's name is Liz." He looked at Liz over the rim of his glasses. "You're our producer?"

Marty swung her head back to Liz. "What do you know about this?"

"Nothing. Well, yes, maybe something."

Marty pushed her chair away from the table. After a quick breath, she spoke rapidly. "Excuse us. I need to have a conversation with our writer. Can we have a few minutes?" They walked outside.

"I'm not feeling good things," Marty said. "You're co-producer of this show? Why do I suddenly mistrust you?" She paced in front of the entrance.

Liz was calm with her response. "I have nothing to do with this production. At least I don't think I do. Paul and I talked years ago about backing a show, but it was just talk."

Marty's mind scrambled with adrenaline. "You were with him at the bank. You kissed him. I think you're still seeing him. Are you trying to set me up? Is that your plan?"

"Hold on, now. Paul kissed my cheek. I did not kiss him. I told you why we were at the bank and this producer gig is a huge coincidence. I had no idea Paul made any type of theatrical investment."

"And he never mentioned the show before your divorce?"

"We haven't talked about investing for years."

Nina came out of the theater. "The natives are restless. What's going on? Are you okay, Marty?"

Marty was curt. "Ms. Chandler is our producer." Liz shot a look of disbelief at her. "It seems we have a conflict of interest."

"*Ms.* Chandler?"

"Oh," Nina said. "Then you are the other half of Dr. Paul?"

"It's probable." She raised her voice. "There's no conflict of interest."

"I'm seeing the picture pretty well. You even had me in your apartment and talked fluently about the script. It was almost as though you'd read it a dozen times before that day. You were gung ho on the future of that play."

"Was I? And before that, I invented a divorce, I knew you'd be at the café the day we met, I all but threw myself at you, and all for the sake of making a fast buck? I don't think so. Do you think I know anything about producing a show?" Liz crossed her arms and waited.

"No, but I wish you would tell me what you do know."

Nina turned Liz to face her. "Are you and the good doctor in cahoots?"

"No." She turned back to Marty. "We're not. I wouldn't do that to you. Haven't you been listening to me?"

Confusion and anger overwhelmed Marty. "I have listened, and you sucked me right into your scheme. Is this one of those surprises you like so much? What's your stake in all of this? Kiss the girl and make her cry?" She snapped her hand toward Nina. "Cigarette, please."

"Oh, my God," Liz said. "Why are you suddenly irrational? Go home, Marty. Take a sick day, for Christ's sake. While you're there, read *No Business*. That's my stake. That's my heart."

Nina lit a cigarette and handed it to Marty. Without a thank you, she took a deep drag and closed her eyes. Nicotine swam vigorously throughout her bloodstream and gave a rush she needed.

"I don't have the book any longer." She looked up at Liz. "You have it. Another bit of convenience for you." She dragged on the cigarette and blew the smoke out quickly. "It wouldn't surprise me if Felice Tate showed up as a part of this."

"There's no talking to you," Liz said. "You're unreasonable."

"Liz," Nina said and turned Liz's face toward her. She spoke gently but with conviction. "You're dealing with the livelihoods and the emotions of professional and private people. If you and your husband are trying to hurt Marty, you'll not succeed. She's like granite and has a powerhouse of people who will appear at her beck and call. They can easily turn this little pile of annoying garbage into the biggest damn mistake anyone has ever made. Do you get my drift?"

"Yes. I understand. I especially understand granite, and Paul is my *ex*-husband," Liz stressed and looked at Marty. "My *ex*."

Marty didn't acknowledge the comment.

"Whatever," Nina said. "Now tell me, are you involved with any of this?"

"No," she said, "at least not at the moment, but I'll find out what's going on."

"Okay," Nina said. "I need to talk to our girl. Would you go back to the stage and tell Clive that we'll be there in a few minutes?"

Liz grabbed the door handle, looked back at them without expression, and entered the theater.

"This is incredible," Marty said. "I need to call my attorney and see if I can buy my way out of the contract. I'm not comfortable."

"Don't call him. It isn't necessary and it's unprofessional. Think of this show in the same way you thought of your first show. You were lost somewhere in the chorus, but you felt like the star. You're that star now. Make it happen and don't whine."

"I'm not whining. I—"

"You're whining. I believe Liz. If you saw her eyes the way I did just now, you'd believe her, too. Finish your cigarette and we're going back inside."

"I want to believe her. Do you think I'm wrong in feeling manipulated?" She took the last drag and mashed out the cigarette.

"No, but you'd be unreasonable not to give her the benefit of the doubt and then find out the truth. This isn't the end of the world." She pulled Marty into a hug. "I want what's best for you, and all of that is waiting on stage right now."

She stayed in Nina's embrace, needing that moment of trust. "Okay." She released Nina. "Let's get to work."

Before she reached the stage, Marty thought feverishly to formulate a plan of attack for the show. There seemed a matter of self-preservation for the actor named Marty Jamison. Her answer came quickly. She would attempt to hijack the production as her own and hope the others wouldn't throw her out on her ear with a "Jamison's gone mad" statement to the press, and then tag her with a lawsuit.

Liz remained a problem and stood out like a sore thumb. How could Marty trust her? Out of all the people she did trust, Nina was the only one who had her complete faith, and Nina placed her trust in Liz. What reason did Marty have to follow Nina's lead?

Twenty novels suddenly came to mind. Each book highlighted Abby McNair. And Abby was Marty. The only sense in the scheme was that no scheme existed. The doctor and Mrs. Chandler couldn't possibly have planned a half-baked plot and then waited twenty years to implement their plan. Logic forced her to give Liz the benefit of the doubt.

When she arrived onstage, all heads swung in her direction. She stopped next to Liz and rested her hand on her shoulder.

"I have something to say," she said to the group and leaned down, close to Liz's ear. "We'll talk about this later." She stood erect, clasped her hands together, and enjoyed their echo while it rang throughout the empty house.

She walked a slow circle around the table. When her gears shifted to working mode, adrenaline flowed briskly through her veins, and there wasn't a darn thing that would stop her from getting this play right. She took a moment to study the face of each person at the table. Talent sat before her. A small group, but they were her ways and means. Bert winked at her. Marty walked another half circle around the table.

"What we have here is a show poorly written, next to nothing for a budget in normal theatrical terms, and a script of Felice Tate's caliber. What's worse? Not a single song." She waited for the others to stop laughing, and smiled with them. "We're so screwed that we need to rethink this entire script and make Marty Jamison a happy actor. The good news is, I respect all of you. Now, I have more news. It may not intentionally be true, but this show is a test for my reputation and now for yours as well."

She stopped her pace and was hesitant to say her next thoughts, but she took a deep breath of support.

"I'd like control of this production." Marty waited a significant amount of time, in case there were immediate objections. In particular, she looked at Liz who gave no opposition. "I will not dismiss any input you give me, and I will not play the out of control, spoiled actor who doesn't get what she wants. Clive, you have my full support on direction. Liz, you have me on writing. Bert, you're always my man." She took another breath. "Allison needs to pray we get this right, too. The bottom line is this: I get the final say on everything. This isn't for me, personally. I'm doing this for the name on the marquee. I can survive a flop, but I don't want Marty Jamison going down in flames. If we can't bring this to her standard, I'll step back and let Clive have the reins." She looked at each of them. "How do you all feel about that?"

Clive answered first. "By circling us like a starving wolf, you're acting like the diva you don't want to project. There's no way in hell I'll give you control of direction, but I'm willing to listen to your input."

Kicked right to the curb. It was worth a shot, anyway. "Okay."

"I think it sounds deliciously decadent," Allison said, "but I agree with Clive."

Marty looked at Liz.

Liz nodded. "You have my trust. We'll work together on the script."

Marty appreciated and understood the gentle slap to her cheek. "Good. *Semper fi.*" She pointed to her copy of the script. "Liz, if you look at my notes, I've written some dialogue changes. I'd like you to consider those changes and I want us to begin there. Give us the low-down on your initial script study." She sat at the table.

Liz cleared her throat. "The first thing I want all of you to know is I'm probably the Liz Chandler whose name is associated with production of this play. I didn't know until a few minutes ago. I'll get those details straightened out. As I'm the producer, I'd like Marty to receive that same respect." She pulled a dollar from her pocket and placed it in front of Marty for retainer. "Consider yourself hired as co-producer, and that might be all you'll see with our budget."

Marty shoved the dollar into her pocket and was, for the most part, settled and feeling that they just might create something unique and wonderful.

While Liz made her presentation, Marty thought about Paul Chandler and the connection that Liz still had with him. An amicable divorce. She supposed it could happen. Marty understood ruts. She understood comfort zones, but she also understood the need to initiate a final break. She had broken up with a lover after eight years.

Either Liz thought she could survive a lifetime with him and wallow in comfort, or she didn't want to hurt him. *Semper fidelis.* Always faithful, but it hadn't applied to Dr. and Mrs. Chandler with their bevy of lovers. Through all of their marriage, though, Liz was most unfaithful to herself.

She decided Liz possessed an old soul that was capable of feeling and giving love, and she wanted to find love within Marty. More signs pointed in that direction and away from conspiracy. She was also a thoughtful soul, maybe playfully selfish. Who else would think of the possibilities behind giving a gift of Q-tips? She chuckled to herself. Liz was determined to prove herself. Sprawled in the grime of Times Square and continuing a conversation with Marty, she could be nothing less than determined. She laughed and all eyes turned to her.

"Sorry," she said. "Go on."

If Nina believed Liz, Marty would at least take the time to listen. She wanted Liz as the innocent that she'd met only a few weeks ago.

"So my final analysis is"—Liz waved the play in the air—"this is salvageable junk. With the right touches, we can turn this show into a dramatic comedy."

Marty nodded. "Good. Thanks."

"I agree," Clive said. "Let's get working on a read-through."

Nina was smart. Her presence wasn't needed and she quietly left the stage halfway through. So did Bert. Without interruption, Marty read the original script from beginning to end. She stammered, stuttered, and spit poorly written sentences for an hour and a half, all the while drinking her way through sixteen ounces of water. Everyone else yawned through those ninety minutes and, upon completing the read-through, her mouth was still gummy. She grabbed Liz's bottle of water and took several swallows before closing the script. She folded her arms on the table and pulled a saccharine smile. "Discuss," she said, and Clive spoke first.

"You need to lighten up. You missed your timing with lines that are tremendously funny. Whatever this conspiracy theory is you have going, it affects your concentration. My first suggestions are ditch the diva, bring Marty back, and then stop fighting the show."

"Okay," she said, this time embarrassed by Clive's comment.

Clive flipped through his pages. "I've marked each line where I want you to study your delivery. I think we can keep those lines. Also, I've marked sections that can be improved upon."

"What about deletions?" Marty asked.

Liz chimed in. "I have some. Small stuff. We need to concentrate on continuity, too. I heard no smooth segues into the next joke, moan, or what have you. That's an easy fix but will also depend on your timing. It would have been nice if the author had given us a digital copy, but I'll take care of that tonight."

"Great," Clive said. "About your timing. You have a great line here when she accidentally fires her only bullet." Clive read from the script, "*I don't need another bullet.*" He paused. " '*You're killing me.*' You need to insert a beat between the sentences. Even in its present condition, study the script and hone your timing."

"I think the end of the last line would be funnier if you changed it to '*I've got you,*' " Allison said. "Marty says the other all the time."

"Yeah, that's good," Clive said. "Try it. Give it to me gently. Your character says it to her reflection, and I want you to say it like you're in love with that reflection."

Marty looked at Liz. "Okay," she said and slid easily into Clive's directive. "*I don't need another bullet.*" She took the beat. "*I've got you.*"

"Perfect," Clive said.

"Maybe not," Liz said and looked square into Marty's eyes. "Say the last sentence again."

With all the sweetness that she could muster, she looked into Liz's eyes and repeated the new line. "*I've got you.*"

"It's your best line…if you do it correctly." Liz's timing was perfect. She took off her reading glasses and rubbed her eyes. "Can we take a break?"

"I'm ready," Clive said and pushed away from the table. "Let's take half an hour."

Liz stood and pushed her chair to the table. "We'll make headway with this soon." She turned to leave and Marty called to her.

"Wait. Let's talk for a minute."

Liz stopped. She looked over at Allison and then to Marty. "I think we should keep this on a professional level while we're here. Don't take it personally. We'll talk afterward."

Don't take it personally. Marty hated that line. It was one of the last sentences she'd heard from Rachel, and the words had the ability to send her into a whirlwind of pissed off. She carefully curbed her reaction.

"Liz," she said, and watched her take the steps down from the stage and walk toward the main entrance. "Fine." She dropped the script onto the table and startled Allison.

"Are you all right? Your thoughts seem scattered. You're tense, too."

Marty took a deep breath and smiled at her. "I'm okay. I'll be okay. Thanks for asking." She motioned toward the wing with her head. "Go on, take a break."

Marty looked around her and then stroked the back of the seat Liz had sat on. She repeated the line, "I don't need another bullet. I've got you," and took her exit, stage left.

She wandered through the hallway and out the main exit of the theater. Nina was there leafing through a copy of *Fashion* magazine. Marty stretched across the bench and rested her head on Nina's lap. Hot sun drenched her and took away the chill she'd felt from Liz. Nina set the magazine to her side.

"The new Versace line is terrible. Nothing new there, I guess," Nina said and placed the magazine over Marty's face. "You're already pink from this morning. If you blister, don't come crawling to me for makeup."

"I promise not to call."

"Did you talk with Liz?"

"No. She's angry with me."

"You'll work it out. How's day one going? Getting it together?" She nodded. "We've devised a plan of attack."

"Here comes your girl." Nina lifted Marty's head from her lap. "I think this is where I'll make my exit."

Marty sat up. Liz approached and sat next to her. There was no indication of the stern businessperson who had walked away minutes ago. She even surprised Marty with a kiss to her cheek and then she took hold of her hand.

"There's no sense in me acting like a twelve-year-old," Liz said. "I have nothing to do with Paul and this script. I mean there's no setup. Not from me."

"I want to believe you. There's just too much strain surrounding the play, and it's overwhelming me. The reality is I'm stuck with this, no matter how many times I go to sleep and hope to wake up to a different show."

"When we finish today, I'll call Paul and find out what he knows."

"Do you think he can make a dinner invitation tonight? I'd like to talk to him, too."

"I'll ask him." Liz ran her hand over Marty's shoulder. "Relax. We'll figure out our direction with the show and you're a good student. Oh, I had a call on my cell from our—from Paul's and my financial advisor. He can probably give me the lowdown, but I can't get him on the phone."

"Maybe he'll call back. Let's get back inside and do some more brainstorming."

When she stood, Liz pulled her back down to the seat. "Not so fast, kitten."

She couldn't help but smile. "Kitten? That's what you called me the night you kissed me after the show."

"I think you'll always be kitten to me, but I've been thinking about timelines, and now I agree with you. We need to build trust."

"I'm glad you said that. Suggestions?" Liz ran her fingers over the back of Marty's hand. Funny how the touch evoked a feeling that moved slowly up her arm and then tickled her throat.

"I could easily make love to you at any given time. My suggestion is no sex. Not yet." She winced at her own suggestion.

Marty winced at the same time. "Probably the best way. Well, you have the purple—"

She covered her ears. "No."

"You have big purple, and I have..." She paused. "A mirror."

A confused looked came over Liz. "Mirror? What does that mean?"

"Never mind."

"No, really. What about the mirror?"

"Maybe I'll tell you one day." She stood. "Let's get back to work."

"Marty," Liz said and stepped closer.

"Yes?"

"I mean that. I could make love to you now, all day long, and through the night. Even yesterday."

A quick sexual upheaval surged through Marty. Liz teased with her business-like, no sex announcement, but savagely rewrote and dangled her desires where Marty could see them. She wanted to turn the pages, devour each word, and not skim the narrative to get to the "good" part. She wanted to experience each meaningful word Liz threw down and into their lives.

"I'll have a hell of a time wanting you, but I can imagine every move we'll make. Each touch."

"Every kiss," Marty said.

"Each whisper and bite."

Marty laughed gently. In an attempt to gain an upper hand, she teased Liz. "Curls."

Liz blinked. "Oh," was nearly inaudible.

The remainder of their day was reasonably productive. After intensely listening to the proposed changes, Marty read the entire script again and stressed her vocal chords. That the show had no songs turned out to be a good thing for her. She closed her script for the final time that day.

"That was better," she said with minimal satisfaction. "I'm having trouble keeping the two voices separate, but I'll get that worked in if my throat doesn't give out. How do you all feel about the changes?"

"Not bad. An improvement, anyway," Clive said. "Let's sleep on it and see what happens tomorrow. What do you say we call it a day?"

"Same time tomorrow," Allison said and headed toward the wing. "Good night."

With agreement from Liz, their workday ended, and she looked forward to dinner.

CHAPTER NINE

Hand in hand, they walked leisurely toward their Chelsea apartments.

"What's it like for you to hear me on stage after all these years?" Marty stumbled over her feet when Liz yanked her closer.

"You're still a turn-on. I wanted to damn our agreement of no sex. I couldn't look at you while you read. Instead, I buried my nose in the script."

"I noticed, but I'm not sorry that my voice tickles your happy places."

"Marty!" She said nothing for another few yards. "I wanted to sit in front of you with your arms and legs wrapped around me. I literally felt your body heat against me."

"The truth comes out. Were we wearing clothes in your scenario?"

"I thought we agreed not to do this."

"We aren't having sex. We're referencing sex."

"Somehow I think there's no difference for us. All things make you desirable, some less than others. Maybe we should change the subject."

"Okay. Shoot me a topic."

"What props or set dressing will we need for the show?"

"The only costume is my teddy and a pair of slippers. As for props, we need a gun, some bullets, a script, a bottle of whiskey, a tumbler. The set is a bed, a makeup mirror, and an armoire. Basic bedroom stuff."

"Not much to work with," Liz said. "We should glamorize the set. Your character is somebody. We should make her wealthy, of course. At least comfortable."

"We'll talk with the set designer about those things. He'll come up with something fun."

"Here." Liz pulled out seats at an outside café. "I'll call Paul." She opened her cell phone, pressed a speed dial number, sat back in her chair, and then reached for Marty's hand. Marty sat quietly and listened to their conversation.

"Hello, Paul…Yes, the transactions were acceptable…No, I still need to do that. Hopefully tomorrow." Liz rolled her eyes and covered the phone. "A sweet guy, but I'll be happy when this is completely over." She uncovered the phone again. "That's fine… Great. Listen, Paul, are you busy tonight? I need to talk to you about something…A theatrical script with our names on it…Yes, really. Can we meet you for dinner, say eight?…Good…Marty Jamison… Have I landed her for the role? You could say I'm still in the wooing stage with landing Marty." She winked at her. "Okay, we'll see you there. Good-bye, Paul." She closed her phone. "He'll make some calls and see us at dinner. We aren't far from your place. Let's freshen up there."

Inside the apartment, Liz grabbed the dead daisies, threw them into the wastebasket, and set the vase into the sink. "I told you that would happen." She walked back to the table and picked up the box of Q-tips that Marty hadn't bothered to put away. "And look here. Just as fresh and sterile as the day I bought them. Practical. I did well." She beamed.

Marty took the small container from her hand. "They're fresh, and so are you." She dropped the swabs onto the table and held Liz by her waist. She traced her lips with one finger and continued down Liz's neck slowly, watching as she outlined her collarbone.

She looked into her eyes. "Kiss me lightly so that our lips barely touch. A long kiss. Show me how gentle you are." Marty closed her eyes and waited. "Make my heart sing."

Liz's breath blew warmer the closer she came. A delicate touch of lips joined Marty's, their mouths featherlike. Their lips touched here and then there. Mindful of each new position, of each new bow and dip that shaped Liz's mouth, Marty could almost feel the minute lines on Liz's lips.

"Let me wet your lips." Liz's tongue passed lightly over Marty's mouth, first her top lip and then the bottom. "Now wet mine," she said, and Marty returned the act.

Moisture lessened their friction. Their mouths glided, unrestrained. Marty wanted more pressure, to take their kiss fully, but feared interrupting their tender union. Marty felt carefree, she felt cared for, and she felt their kiss clear to her heart.

"This is wonderful," Liz whispered.

"Wonderful." As if on cue, they separated their mouths and held each other tenderly, comfortably.

"I guess we have the patience to practice restraint after all," Liz said.

Marty stroked Liz's back and then she held her, content to know her that way. Marty took a small step forward on her timeline.

"We better get a move on if we're to meet your husband on time," Marty said, breaking the spell.

Liz glared. "Knock it off. He's my *ex*-husband. Say it. Say 'Paul is your ex-husband.' "

"Paul is your ex-husband." She smacked Liz's backside and led her into the bedroom. "My bathroom is here. You can use that one and look through my closet for something dressier." She walked in and pulled a fresh face cloth and towel from the cabinet. She turned to hand them to Liz, but she wasn't there.

"Is this it?"

Marty walked back into the bedroom. "Is this what?"

Liz studied the full-length mirror in front of her. "Is this the mirror you mentioned?"

Marty's face flashed hot. She walked behind Liz and watched the two of them in the reflection. "Yes."

"What do I need to know about this mirror that makes the two of you so friendly?"

Marty moved her mouth close to Liz's ear. "You don't need to know anything, but you might want to know something." She rubbed her nose against scented hair and shoved the towels into Liz's hands. "Now wash up. We're on a schedule."

Liz didn't move. "Wait." She grabbed Marty's hands and pulled her arms around her waist. "Look at us. Don't we look attractive together?"

Marty studied their reflections. Liz was a few inches shorter and her shoulders were narrower than Marty's, but before she could answer, Liz turned abruptly in her arms.

"You need to believe in us. I don't even want you to respond to that statement. I just want you to think about my words. Now let's freshen up."

"Okay," Marty said to Liz's directive and watched Liz enter the bathroom.

❖

They arrived at the restaurant at eight fifteen and the maître d' escorted them to their table. Paul stood and greeted Liz with a kiss to match his previous kiss. Marty shook hands with Paul and felt the soft, immaculate hands of a surgeon. He ordered a bottle of wine.

Paul was good-natured. She suspected he had a pleasant bedside manner and his light sense of humor would be a plus to his doctoring. He was courteous to Marty and attentive to Liz.

"Paul," Liz said, "we're working on a show that says you and I own the property. How could that happen?"

Paul set his wine glass down. "Okay. I made a few calls and this is what I know." He turned to Liz and dropped his hand onto hers. "Do you remember years ago when we talked about investing?" She nodded, pulled her hand away from Paul's, and instantly took hold of Marty's hand. Paul stopped talking, looked at their hands. "Are you two an item?"

"Yes, Paul," Liz said.

Marty grinned and wiggled her eyebrows at him. He smiled and kept his hands to himself.

"Anyway, I told Bill, our advisor, to keep an eye open for something in the entertainment field. He didn't forget, but I did. The play you're talking about was recently made known to him. The writer wanted peanuts, a one-time payment with her name credited as 'adapted from a play by such and such,' and our advisor saw it as an Off-Off-Broadway show. He thought we'd make a few dollars. He contacted some people and offered a small budget, after trying to contact me for several days." He looked at Marty. "How the play ended up in your hands is beyond me. I'm surprised someone of your caliber is involved."

Excellent bedside manner. "Thank you, Paul. Remind me to fire my agent," she joked. "No, this is my fault. I didn't fully read the play before I signed the contract."

"Is the show a problem?" Paul asked.

"It's just not my style."

"Paul, I'm involved as a writer. We're working with peanuts and everyone deserves better. We're also into a major transition with the work and we need money. With Marty in the starring role, investors are bound to get their money back and plenty more. Can you contact Bill and find out who is backing us?"

"I can do one better." He pulled a pen from his jacket pocket and wrote on a business card while he spoke. "I wish I could help, but you know our money is tied up elsewhere." He handed the card to Liz. "That's his private number. Call him." His phone rang and he checked the caller. "It's the hospital. Excuse me." He stepped away from the table.

"So we're back to square one, with nothing but a lousy script."

"We'll have fun with it. There's always fun in producing any show." Marty drank from her glass. "Clive was right. I need to lighten up."

Paul returned and placed a hundred dollars on the table. "I'm sorry. I'd love to have dinner with you two, but I have to get over to the ER." He held his hand out to Marty. "A pleasure to meet you," he said. "Liz, keep me posted on this, and good luck to you. To all of us, I guess. I'll look forward to opening night. Good night."

Liz scooted her chair closer. "I guess it's just us," she said and sounded happy for their situation.

"If I didn't already tell you, you look yummy in my dress." She poured more wine. "I'm sorry I didn't trust you. The coincidence seemed too great for you not to be involved in some sort of scheme."

"Make it up to me?"

"Name your price." Marty swayed to the music the band played. She looked out to the dance floor.

Liz took Marty's hand. "Dance with me."

"I'd love to." Liz led her onto the dance floor. "Thank you for telling Paul we're a couple."

Liz's eyes softened. "You're welcome."

They moved slowly. Hoofing on Broadway was a bunch of fun, but Marty enjoyed the simplicity of their quiet, personal dance even more. "Do you like dancing with me? Am I okay for you?"

"Eh. You could use some lessons."

"Smartass." She yanked Liz against her and warm fingers snuck into Marty's cleavage. "What are you doing?"

"Copping a feel."

Marty looked down and watched Liz's fingers move slowly against the curve of breasts. She was super-heating Marty again, and then Liz pulled her hand away.

"I wish you'd taken your time." Marty took hold of the hand that had touched her breasts.

"You're so smooth and soft. I wonder when I'll finally have you."

"Have I told you lately that I like you?"

"Not since before you nearly ripped my head off outside the Stanwyck."

"I like you, Liz Chandler." They danced a few more steps. "I was thinking about the way you get along with children. I'm surprised you and Paul had none."

"I regret it. Call me selfish, but the thought of giving birth petrifies me. Paul and I talked about adopting but never followed up, just like our theater talk. Well, I didn't follow up."

"It sounds like you and Paul talked about many things and then let them go."

"I guess if we'd been interested in each other, things would have been different. Now I'm all talked out. Now I'll do. That's another thing, Marty. I won't put things on a back burner with you."

"In the future, if we made some sort of commitment to each other, what if I decided I wanted to have a baby?" She saw no terror in Liz's eyes.

"Is that what you want?"

"I don't know," Marty said. "Maybe. I've thought about it, but never voiced those thoughts. The topic could come up."

"I'm not opposed to motherhood, I'm opposed to pain."

"There's always adoption, too." They danced quietly until Marty broke their silence. "Owning a box of Q-tips would come in handy if we had a baby."

"Yes, it would."

Her feeling of nesting felt short-lived when a commotion caused her to look toward the door. There, with her never subtle entrance, Felice Tate sashayed behind the maître d'.

Liz turned to see what had happened. "If Felice keeps swinging her hips that way, she'll throw her back out of alignment."

Marty took a quick glance around the dining area. "The only open table is next to ours."

"We can leave if you want."

"I wouldn't dream of it. Let's see what amusing quips she comes up with tonight."

Liz groaned. "Can you believe that classic Diane Keaton getup she's wearing? Even Keaton had the decency to stop."

Felice looked to the dance floor and immediately saw Marty. She waved, said something to her entourage, and then to the waiter. He nodded and went about his business.

"Let's have some fun. Ask Felice to dance with you," said Liz.

"I should ask her. She looks kind of cute in that outfit." Liz smacked her arm.

"I beg your pardon." Marty looked back at Felice. "You like that look?"

"Not the shabby look Felice is wearing, but I like when a femme sometimes dresses masculine. It makes me go oomph."

"Really?" She pouted. "Maybe I should make a visit to Men's Formal Wear."

Marty's eyes widened. "There's an interesting idea."

The thought of Liz wearing a perfectly tailored suit floored her. If Liz showed up at her door in silk pinstripes, her hair loose, and a fedora tipped perfectly to eye level, Marty would reduce to a warm puddle. Liz would see kitten all right. Kitten may even perform puppy tricks. Roll over. Beg. Down on all fours. Oh yeah, kitten would easily beg.

"Go on. I want to see the look on her face when you escort her to the floor."

She looked toward Felice. "I don't want to leave you sitting alone, and I don't want to play Felice's game."

"On the contrary. I think you'll have her peeing in her boxers. Go ahead. I'll bring the younger guy out to dance with me."

Marty warmed to the idea. "Okay. If Felice wants press, I'll get her some."

They reached their table just as a waiter placed a bottle of iced champagne near the center. "Compliments of Ms. Tate," he said.

"Good evening, lovebirds," Felice said.

"Hello, Felice," Marty said and Liz had already introduced herself to her dance partner. "Excuse us, gentlemen." She took Felice by the hand.

"What? I'm not dancing with you, Marty."

"Aw, come on Felice. You're dressed for the part. The press you'll have in the morning will be priceless." She grabbed the hat from Felice's head and placed it on her own head. "I'll lead."

Felice perked up with the mention of PR. "Just one dance?"

Marty didn't take the time to respond. She guided Felice to the center of the floor and proceeded to lead her into the sexy rumba, a perfect dance for Felice's hip wiggling. Light applause came from other patrons when the celebrities joined hands.

"It had to be a rumba," Felice said as she moved her hand a full circle around Marty's waist. They repeated the dance's footwork and Marty dipped Felice.

"Kind of sultry, isn't it? I'm afraid you'll squeal if I attempt to look sensuously at you, and this would be a perfect time for us to kiss."

Felice's eyes widened. "Don't."

She grinned, pulled Felice up, and danced casually. "I'll give you a break, but you missed another opportunity for the gossip page."

"I'm not into women."

"Good. Liz would have my hide, anyway. Let me ask you a question. Why do you have that group of middle-aged men at your side all the time? I know they back you, but they aren't good for you. They don't care about you."

"They get work for me. I do okay."

"I've seen your shows and you can do better. You're talented and that talent isn't staged properly."

Felice laughed. "It's hard to believe you care."

"It's even tougher for me to believe. You're a pest, otherwise."

"Now that's the Marty Jamison I would expect to hear."

"I've never been quoted as having said anything bad about you."

Felice raised her eyebrows. "Tater tot?"

Marty snickered. "Okay, yeah, there's that, but it's more of a nickname. Personally, I'd like to spank the hell out of you and then find you some decent support instead of those men sucking down your champagne."

Felice shook her head. "Right. New support and next week I'm cast as the new replacement for Roxy Hart in *Chicago*."

"Probably not, but you'd have a good shot at nailing a spot as a cellblock dancer."

"That's just what I want. Start at the bottom. No thank you."

"That role is not the bottom, Felice. Not on Broadway."

"Despite what you say, I do have my following." Felice was resentful. "You're afraid of me, aren't you? That's what this 'Marty cares' speech is all about."

"Not for a minute."

Felice didn't need to know otherwise. That would have been too much free ammunition for her. Still, Marty felt a need to offer advice to the pixie from Pittsburgh. The music ended and she kept hold of Felice.

"Listen to me, Felice. Don't waste your talent filling the pockets of those men. You'll regret it. You're at an age where the right part will launch you into a fantastic career. Maybe more than you'd ever imagined. Find the opportunity. Do *not* let this time pass without taking control."

Felice was indifferent. "Thank you for the advice, and I'll keep it in mind. You dance a nice rumba, by the way."

"You do, too." She released her and watched her walk from the floor. Felice suddenly stopped. She walked back to Marty and looked square into her eyes. "Is there something you want to say?"

Felice moved close and reached for her hat. When she touched the brim, she put her arm around Marty's waist and pulled her close. She used the hat to shield their faces from the crowd. Applause broke out for their gesture.

"They think we're kissing and I'll get better press."

She smiled. "Good job. I'll just be pummeled by Liz."

"Oops, sorry," Felice said and took the hat away.

"Not so fast. If you play, you pay." She leaned over and kissed Felice full on her mouth. She grinned and released her as cameras still flashed. Felice stormed off the dance floor to even greater applause. Marty returned to her table and Liz, who wore a look of amusement on her face. "She'll see those pictures on the front of *The New York Post* tomorrow."

"You're evil," Liz said. "Otherwise, you didn't look exactly pleased out there."

"Felice isn't one to listen to sound advice. I truly don't like watching those men use her." She shrugged. "That's her choice." She kissed Liz's hand. "Let's skip dinner and go back to your place."

Liz threw her napkin on the table and Marty grabbed the bottle of champagne from the ice. She held it toward Felice and winked. "Thanks. Good night."

❖

Marty popped the corked champagne bottle and Liz yelled from the bedroom, "Just pour one glass. We'll share. Bring it back here."

When she arrived in the bedroom, Liz wore a floor length orange negligee. She handed a yellow one to Marty.

"It's late. Stay with me tonight."

"That was my intention." She sat against the headboard and patted the space next to her. "Sit with me."

Liz curled at her side. "I'll put you up in the guestroom."

She nearly choked on her champagne. "Like hell. I'm sleeping with you. It'll be our Marriott redux and a terrific test for our celibacy. Anyway, you don't have a guestroom."

Without hesitation, Liz took the glass and finished the contents. She placed the glass on the nightstand. "Good. I've wanted to cuddle with you all night. Let me watch you undress."

"Bad girl." Marty pushed from the bed. When she reached for the nightgown, Liz snatched it away.

"I don't think you need to wear this."

"You're wearing one." She climbed onto the bed. On hands and knees, she crawled over to Liz and then straddled her. She pinned Liz's hands to the wall.

"I told Felice if she plays, she pays." She moved her breasts closer and then backed away when Liz nearly trapped the dress with her teeth. "Cha-ching," she said and took the nightgown.

"Tease."

With her back to Liz, Marty slipped out of her dress and let the nightgown fall over her head and shoulders. She pulled the blanket back and slipped between the sheets. Liz turned off the light, snuggled, and stroked Marty with featherlike touches. Tender fingers moved from Marty's shoulder and then grazed her back. A warm palm slid over her hip and the same fingertips scrolled to the back of her knee.

Marty swung her leg over Liz's hip and pulled her closer. She moved her fingers freely through folds of Liz's hair. It was cool to the touch. Strands flowed evenly and fell quietly into soft waves. Liz's breaths were steady, their sound left pure within the quiet space of her lips to Marty's ear. Marty touched her lips to Liz's forehead and a breath turned into a sigh.

"What are you thinking?" Liz asked.

"I feel protective of you. I want to take care of you." She eased her arm around Liz. "You fit nicely in my arms and in my life. I don't want to imagine you not being there."

Liz breathed a sound of contentedness. "Each time you say something new, I feel as though I've opened a magnificent Christmas present."

"Do you like Christmas?"

"It's my favorite holiday." She looked into Marty's eyes. "Love flows. There's no stopping it."

"No stopping it," she repeated and her heart smiled. "I want to make love to you."

Liz ran her fingers over Marty's cheek. "I want you, too."

"But we won't," she said and then kissed Liz softly.

"We made a pact."

She ran her hand over the curves of Liz's back. "I'll stay content holding you and listening to your sleep sounds."

"We're like granite. We can bear the load." Liz closed her eyes. "Good night, kitten."

"We're Gibraltar." Marty mentally tiptoed up the timeline and thought, *Closer to loving you, every minute I'm with you.* "Good night."

CHAPTER TEN

O ne week into endless readings of the script, Marty's throat felt like she'd swallowed razor blades. Allison fed her warm tea with honey, and Nina stuffed her with cough drops. Liz and Clive accommodated her by working on additional dialogue problems. Their reworking the script gave her time to relax and care for her persistent throat condition. She talked in a whisper if she wasn't reading.

One consolation was that a much better show came to fruition. Liz and Clive were diligent in their pursuit of perfect dialogue. After three days, they knew the lines better than she did and perhaps with more enthusiasm. During one reading, Marty and Clive sat in the house and listened while Liz read the live character and Allison read the subconscious character. The new dialogue was funny, but still flat in some areas. Liz and Clive went back to working the words and sent Marty to her dressing room.

In her room, Marty opened another cough drop and popped it into her mouth. If nothing else, her sinuses were clear. She stripped off her top and then stretched belly first onto the daybed. Nina slathered warm gel onto Marty's back and began a soothing massage.

"Tell me all about it, sugar," Nina said. "What are those mean ol' people doing to my girl?"

"No more than is expected from them. We're making great strides, but we're nowhere near a final script. Maybe we'll have it right in a few days."

"And how are you feeling about everything?"

"I still don't think I can carry the entire show. I'm overwhelmed and nearly a physical wreck. I'm out of my comfort space. Every morning, when I think of coming back here, I want to puke. That's not me, Nina. That's not Marty Jamison."

"What are your alternatives? Can you hire another actor to costar? How about Linda Wyman? She's done fine understudy work for you."

"Linda's working another show. I've talked to Allison about sharing the bill, but she's just found out she's four months pregnant and we'll need to replace her. When she and Liz read the script, their performance came through as extraordinary *tête-à-tête*. Our play works with two people." She crunched her cough drop and a hit of eucalyptus plowed through her nose. She sniffed. "Another problem is money. Liz can't get hold of the right people for additional financial backing."

Nina stopped her massage. "Are you crying?"

"No. It's these damn cough drops." Then she weakened. A gush of tears fell from her eyes and she sobbed against her pillow. "I can't do it, Nina. I feel horsewhipped."

"Come here, sugar. Things aren't that bad," Nina said. Marty turned and gratefully accepted Nina's shoulder. "In all our years together, you've been tough. Only once have you cried in front of me. Do you remember that time?"

"The night Broadway's lights dimmed for Joyce. Hers was the longest minute of darkness that I'd ever felt." Her eyes stung with the memory.

"Joyce taught you a lot about the business. She tucked you under her wing without a darn bit of fear that you might overshadow her."

"She taught me everything."

Nina grabbed a tissue from the table and handed it to her. "Joyce saw a lot of herself in you. Spunk, no bullshit, ready to do the show and do it right. She made darn sure the show went on."

"Ever the trouper. I still miss her."

"Sure you do." Nina nodded toward Joyce's photograph. "She loved you like a daughter and she believed in you."

"She was my lifeline." She dried her eyes and looked back at Nina.

"She's always looking down on you, sugar. If Joyce were here, she'd tie you down on stage and keep you there until you owned that part. Let her know you haven't forgotten her. Go out there and do whatever it takes to get that show right."

"You always know the right things to say to me."

"That's why I'm here. Make Joyce proud and win me a Tony. I need a new doorstop for my bathroom."

Marty laughed and stole a final cry in Nina's arms. When she settled, she blew her nose, popped another cough drop, and put on her blouse. "Okay. I'll give the damn play everything I've got."

"That's my girl," Nina said.

❖

For the remainder of the week, Marty worked meticulously to set her pace and commit lines to memory, even with constant changes thrown to her from Liz and Clive. When Liz made a sudden departure to Connecticut for the weekend, Marty studied alone and on the stage.

The set was originally sparse, with nothing more than a dressing table, a chair, a bed, and one armoire. Bert and the set designer had seen to Liz's request of glamour. Soft pillows, flowers, pastel fabrics, and a special pillow requested by the set director adorned the bedroom. Nina contributed an overstuffed, five-foot floor cushion with red silk on one side. The other side was yellow. Depending on which costume Marty wore, the pillow would show the opposite color. The cushion was there for the reenactment of a scene from the character's previous show.

If Marty had a favorite scene among the messy play, that was her favorite. She loved the sensuality of Nina's pillow against her body and she'd make darn sure her audience would experience the same feeling if they sat as far back as the rear of the balcony or Brooklyn. Marty loved that pillow.

"It's *purr*fect," she told Nina.

Bert brought out a prop bottle of Jack Daniel's. He placed a crystal tumbler next to it on the dressing table of cosmetics and perfumes. Clive wanted the character to drink something more elegant, but Marty insisted on feeding her cheap whiskey. Jack Daniel's fit the character's mood. A prop pistol was stashed inside the armoire and atop the bed lay an old script. She arranged the items to how she would pick them up.

By the middle of the second week, she was ready to go with a full rehearsal without the script. If Liz and Clive made additional changes, she memorized them immediately.

Soundmen wired her so her throat would no longer tear to shreds. That in itself was a major step toward her feeling more comfortable in the role, and she'd stop whining about her throat. She could finally do away with those damn cough drops, too.

Overhead lighting was sufficient for their current needs and they'd wait until next week to use the full technical crew. Marty felt one hundred percent into the show and she bubbled again.

"I can't wait to get into this teddy." She stepped into the red garment. "I love these spaghetti straps."

"The low cut shows some cleavage. I think that's hot," Nina said and pulled at the material around Marty's waist and breasts. "I think you've dropped a couple of pounds. Anna may have to take this in soon."

"Really? I'll let her know how it feels." Marty adjusted the crotch of her nightwear. "This is wide."

"Anna didn't want you to wake up one morning and see your pubic hair all over YouTube. I don't think Liz would appreciate it either."

"Good thinking." She let out a breath of satisfaction. "I'm excited about running through a dress rehearsal. I think we've finally gotten it together."

"Great. Now sit down and let me put your face on you." Nina moved the band of microphone that a soundman had attached near Marty's hair. "Oh shit," she said. "Do you think we announced your pubic hair to everyone?"

"I don't know why I didn't see that coming." She shook her head. "Can't do anything about it, if we did."

A knock came to the door. "It's Liz."

"Come in," Marty said.

The door squeaked open and Liz closed it behind her. "Are you almost ready?"

"In a few minutes." She took hold of Liz's hand. "I missed you this afternoon."

"I'm here now. Sorry about my escape, but I had to do another bank job with Paul. He says hello." Liz brought her arm from behind her back and handed her a single white rose. "Break a leg."

"Thank you." She took a deep smell of the robust flower.

Nina repositioned the microphone and patted Marty's shoulders. "Done. I'm going out to watch the show." She left the dressing room.

Marty stood. "I'm nervous. This feels like an opening night." She stroked Liz's cheek with the flower petals.

"I think you'll do well." She smiled. "I can't wait to watch you do the pillow scene. That should be yummy."

Marty wrapped her arms around Liz and held her loosely. "I'll do the scene especially for you." She leaned closer and placed baby kisses around her ear.

"I love when you do that. It vibrates all the way to my toes."

"Steamy."

"Hot," Liz said. "I want instant gratification when you nibble." She bit into Marty's earlobe and pulled back quickly. Horror shone through her eyes and Marty braced for the worst. "Is that your microphone?" Her voice cracked into pubescent. "Are we live?"

"I'm not sure, but we'll find out soon enough."

"Jesus Christ." She turned completely around and stomped out of the room. "I can't believe I have to go out there and face everyone."

Marty kept up with Liz's brisk pace. With the direction they'd taken, their turn forced them to enter the house via the stage. When they entered the wing, Liz pulled back the curtain and stepped onto the apron. Marty held back the drape and heard whistles and applause. Liz stopped, took a bow, flipped them the bird, and then flounced down the steps to take a seat.

"Now there's a trouper."

"You ready, Jamison?" Bert asked.

"Yes."

To open act one, the character rolled around in bed, unable to sleep. Marty walked onto stage, scooted under the blankets, and sank into an uncomfortable mattress. With her back to the audience, it disappointed her that she wouldn't see the curtain rise. That was always her favorite moment.

"Here we go," Bert said and Marty closed her eyes. At the flowing sound of the pulleys, her body reacted as though she stood inches from the curtain. Her flesh prickled with the meanest sting and felt wonderful.

On Allison's cue from the wing, Marty fell into character. She rolled fitfully, tossed blankets, fluffed a pillow, and then rolled toward the house. She sighed heavily. Her eyes snapped open and she sat up.

She grumbled, "*A woman can't get any sleep when she's contemplating suicide.*"

Clive yelled from the audience and pointed to his ear. "Cut. We have a sound problem."

"Damn it," Marty said. She sat cross-legged on the bed and looked toward the house. "It worked fine a minute ago." Liz shrunk into her seat.

A soundman came to the stage. "Let me see your mic."

She reached for the microphone, but it wasn't attached. She looked up at him. "Maybe it's in the hallway or my dressing room. Sorry."

He trotted off stage. "Test. Test," soon rang through the auditorium. He returned and reattached the instrument.

"Let's try it again," Clive said.

And she did. She put all of herself into the first act. If she'd had any indication that the missing microphone would foretell the direction the act would take, she'd have crawled under the blankets and stayed there.

Words. She worked them the best she could, but they refused to stir interest even in her. They were lifeless. She felt like a babbling idiot, not that that was much of a stretch at times. She'd have preferred

Allison and Liz going back and forth. The lines were funny, then. When Allison ran through them with her, they were in tears with laughter. Not now. Not with the singular sensation of Marty Jamison, who had signed on the dotted line and magically assassinated her career with one script. Marty didn't need another bullet.

Exasperated, embarrassed, and damn angry, at the end of the first act she placed the prop gun onto the vanity and looked into the makeup mirror. She delivered the final line, not with the affection that Clive expected, but with sarcasm.

"I've got you."

She waited patiently while the curtain fell unbearably slow. When it hit the floor, so did she, and she knocked the handgun from the vanity and across the stage. She didn't bother to pull up the comfy pillow. Marty removed her mic. She stretched her legs in front of her and bent forward. When she reached her ankles, she held her palms to the floor. Her position relieved tension that may have otherwise released a flowing monologue of a single word. A loud string of "fuckfuckfuckfuckfuck" would have been the only highlight of act one, and she truly felt those words.

She stretched and breathed. She heard no sounds other than the air that escaped her throat. After four deep breaths, footsteps tapped the stage and she looked to her left. Bert stood next to her.

"Hey, Jamison." He sat facing her and set the tumbler and bottle of whiskey in front of him.

"Hey, Bert."

"How you doing, Marty?" he asked and poured three fingers' worth of liquor from the bottle.

She pushed upright and looked at him. It was the first time she'd ever heard Bert call her by her first name. When she noticed his look of concern, her chest tightened and her eyes spilled tears without a single sob to justify them.

"Hey, now," he said. "You aren't the strong woman I know. Did you leave her under the blanket?"

She shook her head and Bert handed her the glass. The strong aroma of alcohol entered her nostrils. "I thought this was dyed water," she said with an even tighter throat.

"My private stash," he said. "Take a drink."

Marty wiped her cheeks and took a large gulp from the glass. The whiskey burned all the way down her throat and took her breath away, but the fast swallow calmed her immediately. Alcohol fumes burned when she inhaled. She cleared them with a hard exhale. Getting drunk might not be a bad idea. She took another swallow and handed the empty glass back to Bert.

"That's rough stuff."

Bert tapped the bottle. "More?"

"One more." She looked over at him. "What did you think about the act?"

Bert poured more whiskey. "It's a tough show for you."

"You hated it." She slapped his leg. "I did, too. The whiskey, this is good. Thanks." She emptied the glass again, and that drink went down more smoothly. "I'm acting like a baby over this show, but it's not working no matter what I do."

The effects of alcohol quickly hit her brain and she welcomed the numbness as it grew from the inside and traveled outward. Nina's mega pillow beckoned. Although the floor was warped and mobile beneath her hands and knees, Marty crawled across the stage, climbed on top of the pillow, and kneaded like a content kitten.

"Meow," she said and then curled into comfort. "This is good, too."

"What's your game plan?" Bert asked.

"I'm gonna lay here and let Jack Daniel's have his way with me. The rest of the game is bullshit." She heard more footsteps and opened one eye. Liz approached the pillow. Marty closed the eye. "Uh-oh. Here's the boss. Don't let her hurt me."

"Give us a minute, Bert?" Liz said and sat on the cushion next to Marty's feet.

"Sure," he said. "I think she's on our side, Jamison. I'll talk to you later."

Marty opened her eyes. Bert gathered his bottle, glass, and microphone and then left the stage. Allison made an entrance behind him.

"Is she okay?" Allison asked.

Marty raised an arm. "Present," she said and dropped her arm back onto the pillow.

Liz pushed Marty's hair from her cheek. "Our star's just a little tipsy right now. Take the rest of the day off, Allison. We'll see you tomorrow."

Marty curled closer to Liz and reached for her hand. With both eyes open, she gazed at Liz. Liz smiled, but her hair, so severely pulled back, looked like a migraine waiting to happen. Maybe the smile wasn't real but stretched into life from a tight ponytail. She wore her reading glasses perched atop her head and looked scholarly.

Marty stifled a giggle. "You didn't come here to ask me to do act two, did you? I won't do it. This entire production is a shambles and I'm seriously thinking of finding a new profession." She reached for the handgun and haphazardly spun it on her finger. "I should have been a cowboy."

"No. I'm here because you're right. We need a costar."

"Yup. Oh, did I tell you yet? I quit."

Liz's eyes widened with alarm. "You can't quit."

"I'm the great Jamison and I'll do as I like." She snorted a laugh. "Are you going to sue me?"

Liz looked away and then back. "I suppose if I have to, yes, I will."

Marty snuggled into her pillow. "That's scary. Lock me up and throw away the key. Bring me my bread and water and don't let me drop the soap." She thought about her words. "No. Cue the fallen soap. Heh."

"This is serious. You're contracted to perform and I—"

Marty closed her eyes and her words slurred. "Relax, Shandler. I hereby r'linquish my"—she took a deep breath and exhaled slowly—"finding a way to make the show work. You and Clive now have full creative control. And me? I'm taking the rest of the day off." She buried her cheek further into the pillow. "Nina did good."

Liz pulled Marty to her feet. "Come on. Let's go into the dressing room. Nina and I will get you dressed and then I'm taking you home."

CHAPTER ELEVEN

Three hours later, Marty awakened on Liz's sofa. She opened her eyes to Lichtenstein's bathing beauty. She sat up, stretched, and looked back at the crisp lines of the artwork.

"I like that picture." She looked out the window. It was still daylight, but the sky was about to dump an evening shower on the city. She walked toward the kitchen and heard Liz's quiet voice come from the bedroom.

"I'll have to discuss this with Marty and Clive. I'm not much in the position for packing a bag for the Bahamas."

Marty stopped and looked toward the bedroom. *The Bahamas? Liz and Paul in the Bahamas?*

Then Liz laughed softly. "Yes, of course I do, Paul. Everything is working out nicely. Don't worry."

There came the sickening feeling that swallowed Marty whole. Her mind raced with anxiety. *She's still seeing him. How did I let my guard down? Liz thinks I'm passed out and not hearing a word of their conversation. Had they actually pulled one over on me? What's their plan?* She shook off the thought.

What's wrong with me? Am I plagued with making wrong decisions? First Rachel, then the play, and now Liz.

"No, they're reasonable people. I'll talk to them…I think that would be lovely…Okay. I'll let you know tomorrow night. Good night, Paul."

What would be lovely? A cozy getaway for two, at her emotional expense, didn't sound lovely. Reasonable people? Yes, she considered herself a reasonable person, and Nina's words came back to her. "I believe her."

It was difficult not to charge into the bedroom and demand Liz tell her what was going on. Instead, she browsed a bookcase and waited for the call to end. Soft rain tapped the windows. Thunder rolled lightly. Maybe she'd call it quits with Liz.

When Liz entered the room, she appeared happy and nearly skipped her way to the sofa. Marty didn't feel the same exuberance. She felt used and unnecessary.

"Hello," Liz said. "Was your nap refreshing?"

She tried sounding upbeat. "Sure. I see your afternoon went well."

"It did. While you slept, I signed *No Business*, took a warm shower, and sent flowers to a friend."

Marty forced a smile. "Sometimes a girl needs flowers."

"She sure does." Liz sat next to her. "Then I had an annoying call from Paul. I need to talk to you about my weekend."

Her attention took particular hold and she was all ears to the story Liz might concoct. Marty draped her hand over Liz's shoulder in an attempt to look casual and then sound casual. "What made your call annoying?"

"Paul and I have property in the Bahamas. We've been trying to sell the place and now we have a buyer. The problem is the bank in Nassau needs signatures in person. Paul wants to fly down Friday morning. We'll sign the papers and I can return home Friday night at the latest. What do you think about that? I know the show's in a bad place, but I have to get these things completed."

At least she mentioned their destination and her story sounded legitimate. "I guess you should go. Call Clive and get his input."

"I'll call him later." Liz toyed with Marty's hair. Her tone changed from businesslike to tender. "We let you down. Clive and I never saw today's train wreck coming. I'm sorry."

"I was a spectacle, all right. The dialogue isn't funny with one person. The character is ridiculous, and she'd be better off if she shot herself in the head."

"Paul asked about our progress. I lied and I told him things were going smoothly." Liz bit her lip. "He doesn't need to know the gory details." Then her eyes lit up. "Why don't you come to the islands with us? We'll stay the weekend and we can brainstorm ideas."

Marty didn't answer, but gave Liz a sour look. "While you're gone, I'll put a call out for auditions. I think we need a girl younger than me, someone who is fresh. Clive and I can hold auditions all weekend and we can start new on Monday."

"Can you find someone that quickly?"

"In this business? Hell, yes. We'll be swamped with enough women to fill the theater." She thought for a moment. "I'll also try to find more financial backing, although it'll be tough since the show isn't a big damn glamorous musical. No word from your elusive advisor?"

"None." Liz bit playfully into Marty's shoulder. "Know what? I didn't get to see your pillow scene in the second act. I'm disappointed."

"I doubt you missed anything."

"What's wrong, kitten? You sound angry with me. Is it the show?"

Marty couldn't hold back any longer. "Ream me a new ass, but I heard portions of your conversation with your—with Paul."

"And?"

"I feel pushed aside. My ex did that to me, and I don't want that experience again."

"Oh," Liz said. "Well, I have to go. Did you never sort out the emotions you felt with your ex?"

"She cheated, I threw her out, end of story."

"That answers my question."

"I—"

"No." Liz put her fingers to Marty's lips. "Just listen to the rain with me. It's a nice sound."

"I'm about to call it quits and you want me to schmooze Mother Nature?"

"Quits? You aren't a quitter. Please, just do this for me. We'll talk in a minute."

Soft waves of water splashed against the windows. Another bout of faint thunder rolled and disappeared. Marty wouldn't mind taking off for sunny islands, but it didn't seem appropriate with Paul in tow. Her mind flashed back to the day she met Liz. Steel drums echoed island music and Liz's hair blew wildly. Marty's life hadn't been the same since that afternoon in Times Square, and she was thankful for every minute. Almost every minute. At that particular minute, she was pissed off but kept her trap shut to humor Liz.

"Rain happens," Liz said. "The sweet part is it nourishes and strengthens our planet and fills it with flowers. We have to accept the rain, even if bucketfuls fall on our heads."

"Well, *kumbaya*," Marty said. Frustrated, she looked up at Liz. "Talk to me in real words. What's on your mind?"

Liz snickered. "What? Not feeling the mood?"

"Don't laugh at me. No, I'm not feeling the mood, and there's more to your words. You writers like painting a pretty picture. Just skip to the lecture."

Liz nodded. "Not a lecture, but you may not like what I have to say. You've had life coming down on you from all directions, and that's created havoc for you."

"I'm handling things."

"Considering all that's happening around you, you've managed reasonably well. I've disrupted your existence and the show has kicked you around, but I refuse to let your drama interfere with my emotions. I'm falling in love with you and I like the feeling. For me, that's the flowers after the rain."

"This rain of yours, is it my inability to deal with what's happening around me?"

"It plays the lead role. We have something wonderful building, but your jealousy will quickly cause one minute of lights out on Broadway for us."

"I'm not jealous of Paul. I can't describe what I'm feeling, but it isn't jealousy. Something isn't sitting right with me."

"How does abandonment sit with you?"

Abandonment had never crossed her mind, but the word was precise. She'd felt abandoned by Rachel.

"I can't blame a glacier for my emotional striations. Those scars happened quickly and read more like an erratic EKG."

"Let's talk about the root of your feelings." Liz leaned against the end of the sofa, a position that left Marty with a lesser feeling of pressure.

"No. My time with her is one I want to forget."

"But you haven't and your memory of her isn't good for us."

"I'll try not to let it interfere."

Liz used her foot to playfully nudge Marty. "Too late."

"How can you be so lighthearted? This is a serious discussion."

"Yes, it is, but you aren't discussing, you're avoiding. I'm trying to help you. I don't want you to call it quits. We're worth more."

Rachel and her little snack of the day looked so smug when Marty had ordered them out of her apartment. She could ignore her feelings, couldn't she? No, she couldn't. With a thought of Rachel, Marty reacted with such internal anger that she wanted to chew glass. Was Liz worth feeling the anger and agony of that afternoon?

"Marty?" Still, Liz waited, giving every opportunity to open a dialogue. "I want you to leave. I need to think about what I should do about us." When she pushed up from the sofa, Marty grabbed her hand.

"No. I'll talk." Marty bit her lip, thinking of where to begin. "I'm a confident woman. I haven't been a saint, but I've made things happen without hurting other people."

Liz sat with her. "You have a good name in this city."

"Yeah, well, how silly was Marty for thinking everyone should act the same way?"

Liz sat up and shook her head. "Stop there. When you talk about yourself in the third person, you don't own the problem. You give it to someone else."

"It isn't easy for me to admit failure."

"What failure?"

"My relationship with my ex."

"What was her name?"

"Does it matter?"

"Yes. A name makes her real, too."

Marty's stomach twisted. She hadn't mentioned Rachel's name out loud to another person in more than a year. She'd made the memory a private hell. All she wanted was to tend to unfinished business and she had a name for that business. Before she had thrown Rachel out, she should have delivered a dozen or so slaps to her face. Those missing slaps were the only regret she had in her life.

Marty twisted her hair with her fingers. She stared at the floor and then looked up at the Lichtenstein phone caller. The bubbled caption stood out. "OHHH...ALRIGHT." Marty looked over at Liz.

"Rachel. Her name was Rachel," Marty said quickly to get it over. Her words then came more easily. "I thought I'd done something wrong for her to want other women, but I was there for her emotionally, physically, and I was supportive of her career. She was a talent agent. I didn't know a constant bevy of women had her mouth wandering all over most of Manhattan and half of New Jersey. I found that out later. How hard is it for people to remain faithful?"

"For some it's unheard of. How bad was it for you?"

"After two years of living together, she asked if I would consider an open relationship. That left me with the worst feeling of unworthiness, that there was something I wasn't giving her. I told her sleeping around was sleazy. If she wanted other women, there was no point in us remaining together. She promised she wouldn't and I trusted her." She suddenly felt embarrassed. "Oh. I'm sorry I said sleazy. I know you and Paul saw other people."

"Don't worry. I'm not the issue."

"But that's where you become the issue. You didn't leave Paul and you had other lovers. I'm afraid if we're together, you'll want other lovers the same way Rachel wanted them."

"Paul and I weren't sleeping together. We were roommates. We had the paper that said until death do us part, but that paper was sexually worthless for us as a couple. We didn't hide anything from each other, and my extracurricular activities during that relationship have nothing to do with how I'll feel and act with you."

"Do you understand my hesitation? The possibility of infidelity scares the hell out of me."

"Of course I understand," Liz said. "Why did Rachel sleep with other women?"

"I—" She stopped. "I never asked her and we haven't talked since. I'd assumed it was because she was a player."

"So you don't know if she slept around because of her desire for a variety of women, or because you lacked something that she needed, and now you're carrying the weight of inadequacy."

"I wasn't in the mood for conversation that afternoon."

"You have an issue to resolve. Maybe you should have that conversation with Rachel." Liz reached out with her arms. "Come here, please." Marty slid across the sofa and into welcoming arms. When held there, everything felt perfect. She rested her head against Liz's breast. How soft Liz was. "You know what I'm thinking about?"

"What?"

"I'm thinking about your shows, the songs you sing, the books you read."

"I love your books. You're a hopeless romantic."

"You are, too. Romance is everywhere in your life. You thrive on it and you need it to feel happy."

"Yes, I do."

"Do you feel romantic with me? Do you want me to love you some day?"

"My best footwork in years was stopping in the bagel shop to meet you."

"Then you need to trust us and believe in yourself. I'm not going anywhere, and we're in no hurry."

Marty held tighter. She was tired of dancing the chorus line. It was time to costar with Liz. Not tomorrow, not next month, but now. She sat up.

"Liz—" The door buzzer stopped her.

"I'm expecting papers from Paul. I have to get the door." She kissed Marty's cheek. "Hold that thought. I'll be right back."

Swell. Marty didn't appreciate being pushed aside and especially during a critical moment. Paul again. He's here today and not gone tomorrow. Let's all go to the Bahamas, and oh, wouldn't that be fun? No, it wouldn't. Liz talked a pretty game, but Marty needed to take a stand, no matter the pain she felt. Liz would have her weekend on the island, but when she returned home, she wouldn't have Marty.

She walked into the kitchen just as Liz turned away from the door. She was all smiles and held a vase shrouded in white paper that sparkled with colorful stars. She stepped closer and placed the vase in Marty's hands.

"I wasn't expecting anything from Paul," Liz said. "These are for you, my star, and they're from my heart. Sometimes a girl needs flowers."

Marty was speechless and thankful her entrance hadn't run off into a monologue of obscenities directed toward Dr. and Mrs. Chandler. She hated her new role of jumping to conclusions. She felt the proper thing to do next was dive out a window, but that feeling quickly subsided. Marty hadn't received flowers from a special woman in several years, and suddenly she was the most fortunate woman alive.

"Really?" she asked tearfully. "You ordered flowers for me?"

"Of course. You're my girl." She reached for Marty's finger and touched the ring. "Remember?"

Marty smiled. "Your girl." She placed the vase on the table and tore open the paper.

Liz stood behind her and rested her chin on Marty's shoulder. Marty anticipated a lovely and lively summer mix, or an eccentric bouquet of Q-tips, but when she removed the paper, the floral arrangement surprised her.

"They're different than a normal bouquet, but they're special beyond belief," Liz said.

"They're…lovely. This is wonderful, but the florist has only baby's breath here. Did they make a mistake?"

"No, that's what I ordered."

Marty turned in Liz's arms. She felt better when Liz's smile and tender eyes came into view. Falling deeper into love with each minute of happiness and each moment of anxiety, Marty knew love wasn't about the proper flowers. Love included acceptance and understanding, even when things weren't perfect.

"Why just these flowers?" She gazed into Liz's eyes that shined with promises of tomorrow. What she saw and felt made her heart pound. "What makes them special beyond belief?"

"Baby's breath is a symbol of pureness and innocence."

She heard a sentence that sounded like it ended with a comma and not a period. Liz wanted to say more, and Marty wanted to hear the missing value. "What more does baby's breath mean?"

"Read the card."

She shook her head. "You tell me," she said, but Liz was slow to respond. Marty's heart pounded with anticipation. "Please." She held her breath.

"The flower symbolizes everlasting love. That's what I want to give you. It's out there and waiting for us."

Her heart jumped rhythmically to the simple serenade. Her hands had never trembled upon hearing words of love, but now she couldn't stop them from shaking over a hint of it. She couldn't utter a word and Liz's eyes reflected the alarm of a child who had just spilled a glass of milk. Liz's exhale sounded like defeat.

"You look as though you're about to turn away from me. Please don't."

Marty took a quick breath through her lips. Still, she said nothing. When tears blended into Liz's eyelashes, Marty caught them against her fingers. "Are you sure you aren't confusing me with the woman you watched week after week? Maybe Abby?"

Liz suddenly exuded the look of a confident woman. "No. The woman on stage would have known the proper romantic line to say. Abby said all the things I needed to hear. She was the perfect Marty, and you aren't perfect. I'll love the woman that isn't so far into my fantasy that she immediately sweeps me from my feet and carries me into the bedroom without questioning my judgment. You were speechless and then you questioned me. Your hands feel like quivering jelly."

"Like jelly."

"Like jelly. Like my knees."

It didn't take a pinstripe suit to reduce Marty to a warm puddle. An honest moment worked just as well. Funny, how a timeline could curl at the edges, roll up, and explode into oblivion, once it was ignored. Not that she'd given it much attention.

They held each other gently, swayed slowly, and Marty's sparkle flourished inside.

"You're right," she said. "I don't have the perfect line, so I'll reach right inside and grab what I'm feeling. I've wanted you close since the moment we met."

"Me, too. Are we crazy?"

"Probably," she answered and they laughed. Marty moved back and held Liz's hands. "We've never had a real date, so we haven't been conventional. Why bother now?"

Liz turned her back and leaned against her. "As a romance writer, I could fill your head with promises of the moon, the stars, and the sun, or I could sweep you away to parts unknown and turn you into my love slave."

"That wouldn't be slavery."

She turned back around. "What I will promise is all of me. Head to toe, occasional endless nights, unlimited affection in my heart for you, and"—she walked her fingers upward from the center of Marty's chest and playfully pinched her chin—"I'm sure there will be times when I'm nothing more than a bitch, but I'll be *your* bitch."

"Mostly a pretty picture," Marty said. "This is where I insert the reality of my Rachel issues that have surfaced."

"I'm not trying to sugar coat what we could have. She left some wounds that I'm willing to chance, but you need to help with that, too."

"Infidelity squeezes my heart so badly that it nearly suffocates me. Most of all, I feel inadequate. I don't know if I'll be enough for you."

"I understand. I also understand that you want to wake up to someone who loves you, so you have to give yourself to someone. I want to be that someone." Liz smiled sweetly and yanked Marty against her. "Your ass is falling, but you're far from inadequate.

You're warm and loving. You're talented, fun, you listened to my story about old rocks and giant ice cubes, and you make a great cup of coffee. What more can I ask for?"

"For me not to say dildo?"

She poked Marty's ribs. "Yes, for you to stop saying that word. You're a pest, too."

"You make me incredibly happy, when I'm not equally terrified." She leaned over and kissed her lips. "I'll work on things."

"I had that in mind all along. Now, don't think I'm an angel. If I decide to write more fiction, you'll wonder who I am and how you fit into my life."

"I won't settle for neglect." She ran her fingers through Liz's hair. "Do you think you'll write more?"

"Maybe I'll try my hand at writing material for a certain Martina Jamison. I hear she's worth a dollar or two."

Marty smiled. "At least one."

"Okay, enough mush for now. Call Clive and get the new show rolling for us."

Marty sat at the desk and Clive answered his phone immediately.

"Hey. It's Marty."

"You okay?"

"I'm fine," she said and Clive wasted no time getting down to business.

"Good. Let's begin damage control. We need money and a costar. What are your thoughts?"

"If you can set up auditions for Friday and Saturday, I'll handle the money."

"What happened to Liz's advisor? He knows who should be responsible for this mess."

"He's not answering her calls. All we have is us."

"Bastard. Okay, I'll get on auditions as soon as we hang up. I'm thinking mid-twenties, dark hair, but we'll dye someone if we have to. Who do you have in mind for backing?"

Marty laughed. "I could do a Dillinger, although his wasn't a favorable finale. I don't know. I'll find cash somewhere."

"Okay. I'll make calls tonight and we'll begin auditions Friday. I'll set it up for ten in the morning."

"That works." Liz walked to the phone, motioning her desire to talk to Clive. Marty got up from her chair. "We're set then and we'll see you tomorrow. Liz wants to talk to you." She handed the phone over and kissed her cheek.

Thinking Liz brought home a copy of the script, she searched the room and kitchen, but came up empty-handed. "Script?" Liz pointed to the bedroom.

When she entered the room, the play was open and at the center of the bed. Marty stretched onto her stomach and let her feet dangle over the side of the bed. She grabbed the script and read changes that Liz had already inserted to accommodate two actors. A feeling of relief washed over her and she even smiled. The only thing missing was half a dozen songs.

"Like the changes?" Liz asked when she entered the room. She stretched onto her back next to Marty.

"So far, they're fine with me."

"Many of the lines will remain the same. We'll just have to figure out the distribution."

Marty dropped the play to the floor and faced Liz. "How will I fill my time while you're gone?"

"I'm sure you'll be too busy working to give me a single thought. I'll have to call Nina to see what naughty things you're doing."

She softly taunted. "Naughty? Me?" She pushed up on all fours and playfully kneaded the blankets. Liz's eyes softened and her chest rose quicker with each breath. Marty leaned closer. "Meow."

Liz had a heavy dose of serious in her eyes. "You know what you're doing to me, kitten. If you come any closer, we don't turn back."

Marty straddled her. She leaned down and bit into her neck. "Maybe we should stop pretending." She pushed from the bed and further teased. "If memory serves"—she opened the front of her blouse—"I'm wearing a lovely red teddy underneath my clothes." She fingered the top of the satin beneath the blouse. "Tsk tsk," she said and dropped her shirt to the floor. "Such lazy girls, you and Nina."

She pushed her pants to the floor and then kicked them aside. One strap of the teddy fell over her shoulder. She gathered her thick hair and held it near the top of her head. Marty tilted her head and slowly ran her hand along her neck, over her breast, and down her tummy until it rested on her opposite hip.

"You made that same move in *Breakable Goods*. Do you think I'll let you get away with it?" Her eyes took on a defiant look of desire. "I'm not kidding. One more word and that teddy is history." She sat up and reached for Marty.

Marty stepped away from Liz's reach. With her hand on the other strap, she pulled it down until the top of her teddy fell to her waist. "Curls." Liz came toward her. She took hold of Marty's hand and slid it from her hip to between Marty's thighs. Marty groaned when Liz pressed harder. She pulled Liz against her and moved to the rhythm of Liz's press. "I play, I pay."

"I play, too." Her eyes were no less interested. Liz pressed her tongue into Marty's mouth and an explosion of warmth blasted Marty's thighs.

When Liz revealed her body, Marty took in all of her. Toned arms reached forward. Tan lines brightened the delicate white of her breasts. Small, dark nipples were inviting. Marty's gaze moved further down Liz's tummy. A thin waist led to full hips and then to a cover of dark hair. Sleek legs held fleshy thighs.

Liz slowly pulled at the sides of Marty's teddy until it fell to the floor. Her eyes followed until she whispered a single word: "Curls." Marty reached for Liz, but Liz stopped her and motioned toward the bed with a head jerk. "Now," she said. Marty moved quickly to the bed. "Hands and knees."

Marty bit her lip. She rolled to her stomach and arched slowly onto all fours. A warm hand followed the curves of her back and down along her hip. She murmured and moved with each stroke. She hung her head. A warm hand cupped and then squeezed her breast. Bites against her flesh aroused her even more. She leaned into and sometimes away from Liz's teeth. Marty reached between her legs, but Liz stopped her.

"That's for me." She moved Marty's hand away.

Tender kisses replaced the legion of bites on her back and then Liz eased Marty fully against the bed. "Why did you stop?"

Marty rolled to her side and Liz was there with a soft smile waiting. Her eyes melted Marty and it didn't matter that Liz had ceased touching her. What mattered was Liz's presence. She ran her fingertip down Marty's nose and then the backs of her fingers against her cheek.

"I want *you,* Martina Jamison," Liz said in a tender voice that Marty had never before heard. "I don't want to handle you like a wrestler." She kissed Marty. "I want the bashful babbler from Queens."

"Why her and not my stage persona?"

"The girl from Queens takes you down from the pedestal that people have placed you on. Not that you act like a star." She nudged her. "Usually, but you know you have that power. I want her because she brings me closer to the woman who believes in God and the same woman that babbles when she feels nervous. Those are the real things."

Marty lay there, smiling, gazing into Liz's eyes. Her words struck with the same power that "I love you" would wield. She wondered if Liz saw the skyrockets that shot off inside her. Did she hear the popping of champagne corks? Did pretty colors of confetti cover her, too? Could she hear the rumble of Marty's heart mimic today's distant thunder?

"And there you are, speechless again."

Marty focused through the tears in her eyes. "My heart's about to burst into a lizillion shimmering pieces." Liz's hand pressed against Marty's chest. "Can you feel it?"

"I do," she said. "*Liz*illion? I think you've honored me."

Marty kept hold of Liz's hand. "Most women want the woman on stage. Once they have her, they leave her in the prop room or just leave. I can't tell you how much more deeply you've just touched me."

"I've told you I'm playing for keeps."

"Sometimes it's difficult to believe."

Liz kissed her again. "I'm all about time with you. Maybe one day you'll trust our production and let our curtain go up all the way."

"*Semper fi,*" Marty said and ran her hand over Liz's shoulder. She scanned her breasts. Her eyes and hand followed the delicate curve of Liz's waist. "Do you want me?"

Liz took Marty's roving hand and placed it against her breast. "Ravenously."

Liz's full weight pressed onto Marty. No longer willing to settle for delicate and refined, Liz moved quickly downward. Marty looked past her knees. No mirrored fantasy teased her. Liz was there, parting Marty's legs. She ran her fingers along the inside of Marty's thighs, and Marty lifted her hips against her touch. She flinched when the weight of Liz's warm breath covered her. Marty reached forward and ran her fingers through Liz's hair.

"Curls," Liz said and pressed her lips lightly against Marty. "I've waited too long for you. Curls," she said again and jammed her mouth against Marty.

Marty fell into ecstasy. With her own might, she moved against Liz with matched pressure. She could have come right then but Liz stopped and nuzzled her cheek into Marty.

"Beautiful, thick hair. So curly and soft. I want to stay here forever. I belong here."

Marty pulled Liz into her arms. She kissed her welcoming lips. They rolled together, each touch more demanding than the last. Marty's mouth dampened Liz. She suctioned her mouth against her breast and Liz pulled her tighter. Liz gave freely. Marty took everything.

"What do you want?" She moved her mouth to Liz's hips. Painting a wet map as she moved, Marty drifted farther down. She pulled at Liz's dark pubic hair with her lips and bit gently into her flesh.

Liz moaned loudly. "Do that again."

Marty sank her teeth into Liz again. Before she gave final pleasure, Marty pushed to her knees. She wrapped her leg over Liz's thigh and pressed into her.

Liz moaned and moved with the rhythm. "Oh, Marty. I feel you. You're wet."

Coarse hair chafed and moisture blended. Marty moved slowly, building their desire until Liz's sounds and tightening abdomen signaled Marty to stop.

"No, you don't," Marty said. "This is how I'll have you."

She sank her tongue into the wet flesh she'd abused. She lavished Liz's labia and clit. Motion stirred groans. Groans stirred Marty when Liz's smooth lips slipped from her oral grasp. She welcomed the taste of her, but abandoned her own pleasure. Her tongue against Liz's clit, Marty eased two fingers inside Liz. Slow strokes inside, slow outside, Marty watched the rhythm of Liz's body push into orgasm.

"Marty," Liz squealed. "Don't stop."

She wrapped her legs around Marty's neck. Smothered against soft, fleshy folds, Marty became a part of them. Thrusts strengthened and Liz came loudly with a final catch in her throat.

Liz reached. "Come here," she said through strained breaths.

Marty held her. "I'm here, babe. You were beautiful. You make the sweetest sounds when I touch you."

Liz moaned. "I've never had an orgasm that strong. That was a showstopper." She covered Marty's cheeks and lips with warm kisses and delicate bites. "I want to feel you come with me."

"We'll work on that." Embraced within Liz's arms, Marty kissed her lovingly.

Liz rolled Marty to her back. "I want to make my kitten purr."

"Please do."

Liz pampered Marty's breasts with hands and mouth, each touch warm and strong. Each bitten nipple throbbed within Marty's thighs and Liz took them relentlessly. She blanketed Marty with kisses. Each kiss, each pass of her tongue were questions that Marty responded to. "Yes."

"You're creamy white," Liz said and bit into Marty's ass. "My porcelain kitten."

Liz knew each place that aroused Marty. With all of the written promises found within her novels, page three or chapter five came alive. Marty bent her leg. Teeth sank into her calf. With her leg pushed high, Marty's limber body moved freely. Fingernails scratched fluidly from the back of her thigh to the tips of her toes, and Marty twitched with desire. Liz's lips glided fully against Marty's ass. She writhed against bites that left burns, and she craved more. She rolled to her back and pulled Liz tightly against her.

"Curls," Marty breathed against Liz's ear. "I want your mouth against me."

"I'll devour you."

"Yes." Marty licked at Liz's mouth.

"Show me what you want."

Marty bathed Liz's mouth with strokes of her tongue. She nibbled her lips the way she wanted hers nibbled; she sucked them into her mouth and released them. Her tongue reached deep inside.

"That's what I want." Marty reached between her legs and groaned.

Liz moved Marty's hand. "Mine," she said. Marty soon felt velvet lips caress her thigh. Fingertips moved slowly, sometimes catching on hair. She looked down when Liz rested against her thigh. "You're beautiful, kitten," she said and stroked Marty's labia with her fingers.

Marty jumped from Liz's touch. Her legs wide, cool air clashed with warm breath, until Liz parted Marty's lips. Marty arched toward Liz when her warm tongue glided through her.

Marty whimpered. "Oh."

Wildfire tore through her, never doused but stoked more by another wet passing of Liz's tongue and then another. She rocked against Liz, building, taking, greedily accepting lick, after tickle, after bite. Marty clawed at her thighs.

"More. Make me come," she said. Her knees suddenly pushed to her chest and Liz's tongue dove inside her. Liz's nose pressed against Marty's swollen clit. Wildfire combusted, scorched, and then consumed every cell of Marty. She cried out with a groan and squeal. Her breaths choked her until a final thrust quenched her.

"No, no more," she said, but Liz continued.

Marty's mouth was dry. She attempted to swallow, but Liz swallowed Marty and quickly worked her into a second orgasm. Flames licked through until Marty lay limp, exhausted, abused, and satisfied beyond her belief. Liz stretched against Marty's side and draped her leg over Marty's hip. Her kisses were strong and then tender against Marty's mouth.

"What are you thinking?" Liz asked.

Still sensitive, Marty tingled in reaction to the figure eights Liz drew around her breasts. She reached with one hand and unfastened the pins that no longer secured Liz's hair. A flow of hair fell to Marty's shoulders and she ran her fingers through it. Delicately, and with a hint of thank you, Marty said all she could with a single, lingering kiss.

"I'm thinking how incredible making love was and how much we've shared in such little time." Marty turned to face her. "I was afraid of this, of being your first time."

Liz laughed softly. "I've been making love to you for twenty years. How could I not get it right?"

Marty looked lovingly into her eyes. "No one has ever touched me with such familiarity. Show me that again." She pulled Liz into her arms. "Promise me that."

"Again and again and again," Liz said and stole tiny bites from Marty's neck. "Finally, I have you. We were fabulous, kitten."

Stillness. Their sighs turned to whispers, then giggles and more kisses. Marty hoped Liz would never let go of her. "I'm feeling awkward," Marty said when their giggly tenderness subsided.

"Why?"

"I don't know what to do. If I thought you were a one-night stand, I'd say thank you, ma'am, and send you on your merry way." Liz nodded against her shoulder. "If we'd been together for a while, I'd ask you to take a shower with me."

"Ugh." She shook her head. "Sexy showers are too ordinary before and after sex. We aren't run of the mill. Are you embarrassed?"

She ran her lips over Liz's cheek. "Hell no. I've been doing this for years."

"Then relax, kitten. Hold me like you'll never let me go."

That worked. She knitted her legs with Liz's and held her tenderly against her breast. Comfort. Happy. Loving. Sexy. On a lush mattress or sitting on the ground at Times Square, Marty knew all those feelings with Liz beside her, and she wanted more. She welcomed caring for her and thoughts of loving Liz slapped her brain silly. Marty wanted to whisper, "I love you" into her ear. Maybe she was Marty's once in a lifetime feeling when everything smacks quickly into place and love happens with the accuracy of splitting atoms. Nothing could manage or beat that power. Or maybe there was one thing that could harness Marty's feelings.

"I'm not a one-night stand, am I?"

"Yes, you are," she said and instantly ground Marty's heart into the floor. "Janis Joplin said it's all the same day, so you're my ongoing one-night stand."

Marty's heart found its place and spread a smile across her face. She held Liz a little closer. "I'm still feeling awkward. I've never slept with another person this early in a relationship. Maybe we should do something," she said, but couldn't think of any place she'd rather be. "Got any ideas?" Liz nodded against her breast. "Hit me with one." Liz shook her head. "Why not?"

She sighed and nestled closer. "I'm enjoying your scent too much."

"Dolce and Gabbana." Liz shook her head again, and Marty's face radiated heat. "Oh no. You don't mean—" Liz nodded and Marty felt a smile against her breast.

"Yeah," she murmured, "and I still taste you on my lips." She looked up at Marty. "How you would taste was the one thing I couldn't imagine. Now I'll never forget it."

More words were needless. This time, their bodies eased together and their lips met lovingly. Exaggerated caresses and kisses spoke for them, and they made love slowly, until the earliest of daylight leaked through the windows.

CHAPTER TWELVE

"Did we make love all night? Or did I dream that?" Marty asked with a lazy voice and kissed Liz's neck. "We must have. You smell like sex. How is it your neck smells like sex?"

"We were wrapped around each other like pretzels. I wish we could stay here all day."

"You're gonna kill me."

"I think we slept a half hour. It's getting late." She nuzzled into Marty's hair. "We need to make tracks to the Stanwyck."

"To hell with work. Let's cuddle and snooze."

"We can't. Come on. We have about thirty-two seconds to get showered, dressed, and to the theater."

"I'm not even sure what day it is."

"It's Thursday."

Marty rubbed her eyes and yawned. "I'll be worthless." Liz pulled her toward the shower stall. They stepped inside and Liz turned the faucet. A sting of cold water hit them from two directions. "Shit," she yelped and washed her face vigorously. "I'm outta here." She stepped from the shower and dressed.

❖

Disgustingly radiant throughout the ride to the theater, Liz happily rambled through the likelihood of producing and writing her first Broadway show, and studied her notes at the same time—not to mention her obvious joy at having bedded the featured performer. She was a giddy, but strong glacier that moved forward and Marty couldn't understand why Liz wasn't sitting there as the same vacant lump she had become. Marty was useless without sleep. She was stiff as New York bedrock, and the last thing she wanted to do was make phone calls and siphon money from friends.

Marty groaned as the cab pulled up to the Stanwyck. "God help me. Clive scheduled auditions for today. There's at least a hundred women swarming the door." She felt the electricity of their air, but secretly wanted each woman Tasered so she could go back home and sleep.

Liz closed her notebook and shoved it into her bag. She leaned across the seat and looked out the window. "Wow. All Jamison wannabes," she said too cheerfully. "Good business decision from Clive. We're down two weeks."

Marty snapped her attention from the window to Liz. "Was that directed at me?"

"No. All of us screwed up. Relax. Today isn't a good day to be sensitive."

"I'm not sensitive. I'm exhausted and I have all of those women to consider."

Liz nudged her. "You could do worse."

"You're an unsung comedienne." She found a mirror in her shoulder bag. Dark circles rimmed her eyes and she snapped the mirror shut. "Oh, hell." She put on her sunglasses and stepped out of the cab. Clive came out of the theater and waved them over. Without kissing the pillar, but instead giving it a slap, she put on her best friendly smile and greeted the group of women. "Good morning," she said. "I'm glad you could make the audition. Break a leg."

"Take their portfolios and send them to the stage," Clive said to Liz and pulled Marty aside. "Sorry about this. It's better that we start immediately and only for today."

"You're right. I'll make my money calls and you two can handle the mob. Get Allison's input, too. I'll join you in an hour."

"Right," he said and joined the energetic group of women.

Standing alone, Marty watched the parade of women who were eager to work with her. Liz seemed in her element, collecting folders and sending the candidates into the theater. She wore the title of producer instinctively. Marty yawned and then headed to her dressing room.

"I need coffee," she mumbled and dropped belly-first onto the daybed.

"Uh-oh," Nina said. Marty heard the coffee pour and the carafe replaced. "Sit up, sugar."

Obediently, she sat up and took the coffee. "Thanks."

"Uh-huh." Nina reached for the sunglasses. "Let's see what damage you've done." She eased the glasses away from Marty's face. "Oh my. Sealed the deal, huh?"

"Endlessly." She managed a smile.

"You're getting too old to pull all-nighters."

"Tell me about it." She took a sip. "I need to make some calls."

"Do you want me to cover that mess around your eyes?"

"Work a miracle, please."

Nina laughed. "How's Liz looking?"

"Fresh as the day she was born. She makes me sick." She poked some numbers on the phone. From deep inside, she located a buoyant sound to her voice. "Yeah, hey, Greg, it's Marty Jamison." She closed her eyes while Nina worked around the conversation.

"Good to hear from you. What's going on?"

"I'm calling to ask if you'd be interested in making an investment in a show we're doing."

"A new show already? Wow. You're a workhorse. What's the show?"

"A simple, two-woman play. Not a musical."

"Not a musical? Two women? On Broadway?"

"Yeah. That was pretty much my reaction, too. We have a stingy budget and need money. Will you take a piece of the show?"

"Sorry. You know I love you, but without music? That's not a lucrative investment. If you get something else cooking, give me a call."

"Okay. Thanks, Greg." She closed the phone and gulped the rest of her coffee. "I have nine other contacts and all of them will turn me down."

Nina refilled the empty cup and handed her an envelope. "It isn't much, but it might help."

Marty opened the envelope and withdrew a check written out to her name. "Ten thousand dollars? That's a lot of money."

"I have faith in you, sugar. You're in a tight spot and maybe that'll keep you flush for a day or two and maybe I'll make a buck. If the show bombs, I'll eat the investment."

She handed the check back to Nina. "I can't take your money. There's too much risk."

Nina pushed her hand away. "You need the cash. Besides, I don't want to screw up my tidy checkbook by voiding a check."

"Okay." She gave her a hard hug. "Thank you. I'm sure we'll put it to good use."

"Go on now. Make your calls and find us a jackpot. I'm going out to watch all the little Marty Jamisons tout their wares."

Marty made her second call, then the third, and then the fourth. No deal. She wracked her brain for the slightest memory of a favor owed her, and then she set Nina's phone onto the vanity. Everything in life, even eggrolls, came with a price. She picked up the photograph of Joyce Manning.

During her final performance, Joyce had complained of fatigue and chest pain. When the closing curtain came down, she had said her last thank you and good-bye to her audience, and then to her cast members and crew. She smiled defiantly through each word. No one, not even Joyce, was aware of the gravity behind her words.

"I've had a great run and I couldn't have done it without any of you. I love you," Joyce had told them.

After the longest standing ovation in Broadway's history, Joyce collapsed on stage. Marty had been sitting in the second row. She jumped from her seat and hoisted herself onto the stage. She knelt next to her. Joyce never regained consciousness and died from a torn aorta shortly after the close of her show.

"It's not about us." Joyce had once told her. "It's about the whole show."

Her tears splashed onto the glassed picture frame. She ran her hand over the photograph and wished she could reach inside and hug her.

"I miss you every day. I couldn't save you, and I can't turn time back, but I can honor you and all that you taught me." She kissed the photo. "This one's for you, Joyce."

Marty set the picture down and grabbed Nina's phone. After a few swipes of her finger, she logged into her Chase Manhattan account. With a deep breath for bravery, or maybe to sooth her idiocy, she transferred several thousand dollars from her savings to her checking account. Account balance: six hundred thirty-two dollars and fifty-seven cents. She pushed the logout link and let her breath out. She looked back at Joyce's photo.

"Keep an eye on us, sweetheart," she said and left to join the others.

❖

Marty burrowed into a seat next to Clive. A hefty woman performed a monologue onstage and Clive wrote "no call" next to her name. She looked down the list and they'd already heard eighteen women. He'd marked only one other with "maybe."

"How'd you make out?" Clive asked.

"I managed a few bucks. That'll help keep us above water until we fold on opening night."

Clive looked at her in horror. "What? Don't even think like that. With the right costar, we're gonna knock 'em dead. Your investors will be fat and happy."

"We'll see," she simply answered. Too worn out to care, she only wanted to breathe more freely once they'd secured a costar. "Where's Liz?"

"She and Nina are at the entrance. They'll eliminate some women right off and send the others in to us." Clive stood. "Thank you," he said to the latest actor. "Next, please."

Their day progressed. At least Clive and Liz's day progressed. Marty dozed off and on in her seat, confident of Clive's ability to weed out the contenders. Clive chose players on instinct, not necessarily on their portfolio of credits. Occasionally, he asked Allison's advice. When a sneeze startled her fully awake, she rubbed her sleepy eyes and looked toward the stage. The group of women had dwindled.

"Thank you," Clive said. "We'll be in touch tomorrow if we need you."

Marty watched him draw a line through her name. Liz, with all the energy of a double espresso, shuffled between the rows of seats and then sat next to her. Nina sat behind them.

"We have a wrinkle in the plan," she said. "Well, not a wrinkle, but an interesting turn of events."

Marty sat upright. "Let me guess, Felice is here to read for the part."

Clive smiled. "It wouldn't surprise me. The woman has some enormous balls."

"What's the news?" Marty asked.

Liz grinned. "Bingo."

Her eyes widened. "You're kidding me? Tater tot? Tell me you're joking."

Liz shook her head. "Clive, I've closed the auditions. I want Felice to play opposite Marty." She looked over at her. "What do you think about that?"

Marty looked at Clive. "You're letting her get away with closing your auditions?"

Clive nodded. "Why not? Maybe she's on to something. The show needs a boost and frankly—"

"Marty Jamison isn't enough." Marty laughed and wished Bert would show up with his handy dandy bottle of rotgut whiskey. "Why am I surprised? Felice has been breathing down my neck for months, and this is the perfect time for her to prove herself."

She gave herself a moment. She'd told Felice to get her act together, and fate flung a definitive moment into both of their laps. Felice was smart, wanting to read for the part. Marty was adult enough to stay professional. She shifted in her seat and then focused her attention to the stage. After a deep breath and then an exhale slow enough to set a world's record, she scratched a destiny notch onto her timeline.

"Let Felice read last. The women before her deserve their chance."

Clive's interest was renewed. "Okay, let's have the next reader." He looked back at Liz. "In the future, talk to the director before you close auditions. In the meantime, let's see how Felice does."

While the remaining women read, Liz scribbled feverishly over her script. She tagged dialogue with the opposite character and she drew a sketch of a split set with similar features placed opposite. On the top left, she wrote "Marty." On the right, she wrote "Felice."

"Counting your chickens?"

"They're just names, kitten."

"Just names?" She assumed "kitten" was to soften the blow of using Felice and she was uncomfortable now with Liz's claim of producer. "You can be more honest with me. You'll let Clive audition these women and then you'll flex your muscle, won't you?"

She continued with jots and deletions. "Only if Felice proves herself deserving of the part, and I hope she does. She's exactly what the show needs. Her envy over you will have people knocking down doors to get tickets."

Marty scowled. "Oh, well, of course. Sometimes I forget I'm a commodity."

Liz looked up at her. "If Felice is our choice, Clive and I will discuss it with you."

Marty turned her eyes front and scanned the rounded backs of the seats until the stage came into her view. She fixed her gaze on the drape that occasionally moved on the right. She knew Felice caused the motion of that curtain. *She's exactly what the show needs,* Marty's brain repeated. Liz's statement evoked the evolution of Broadway divas. Out with the old and in with the new. Not gonna happen. Marty wouldn't give Felice the opportunity to upstage her. Her eyes remained riveted on the wing, and then she laughed.

"You know what? Bring her on. If that curtain rises with Felice Tate on the other side of the stage, God bless all of us."

"Atta girl," Nina said from behind and patted Marty's shoulder.

Marty wanted to scream. Not out of anger, but out of fatigue and for her resiliency that had decided to shirk its duties. She fought to keep her emotions in check. Her current situation, everything that had happened in recent weeks, called for a good yell that would shake the shingles from Battery Park to Harlem. Meanwhile, she'd await the final candidate.

Growing impatient, Marty stood. "Clive, wrap this up and get to Felice."

"Felice is next," Liz said.

Before the current woman finished her monologue, Marty grabbed the revised copy of the script. She left her seat in row five and proceeded backstage. There, at the wing, Felice stood and she faced the stage. Marty stepped quietly and stopped inches from her. She leaned so close to Felice that she almost became a part of her.

"Boo," she said.

Felice swung around and tripped over her feet. She smashed into Marty and both landed on the floor with Felice on top. Felice looked scared to death.

"Damn it!"

As Felice was about to push herself up, Marty grabbed Felice's arm. "Looking for another kiss?"

"You wish." Blushing, if not mortified, Felice got up from the floor and helped Marty to her feet. "You scared the hell out of me."

"I whispered. Are you that skittish around me? It seems that wouldn't be a natural Tate trait." Marty picked up the script and handed it to Felice.

"I'm scared to death, walking in here and half expecting you to put your money where your mouth is."

"You've been dancing all over me in the columns, and now you're—"

Felice glanced at the front page of the play. "This is the show? What's all of this scribbling? Oh, how professional your team is."

If Felice hadn't strummed her smartass chord, Marty would have more readily accepted her presence and encouraged her to read. Instead, the true Felice emerged, and Marty wasn't in the mood for her.

Marty glared. "That mess could be your ticket to Broadway, Ms. Tate. You'll read from that script, and I suggest you begin soon."

Felice protested. "That's not fair. The others read what they'd chosen."

"Yes, they did. Doesn't it make more sense to read from the script you'll work from? You're the only one given this opportunity. If you don't get out onto that stage now, I swear I *will* take you over my knee and spank you." She looked at her nails and then back at Felice.

Felice flushed. "That's harassment. I could—"

"You could what? The way you shoot your mouth off around town, no one will take you seriously." She guided Felice to down center stage and pointed to Liz and Clive. "They'll determine if you're good enough. If they agree to use you, they'll discuss it with me."

"Really?" Felice laughed. "Marty Jamison will welcome me with open arms. Please. I'm a snowball in hell, standing here."

Marty turned to the house. "Clive, Felice changed her mind. I think you should call back—"

"I have not!" Felice yelled to Clive in her own determined way and turned back to Marty. "Just let me read."

"Break a leg."

Marty walked off stage and waited in the wing. She'd prefer Felice wouldn't get the part, strictly for selfish reasons. Emotionally, the situation was fifty-fifty for her. For Felice's public barbs, she could dangle this job in front of her, make her eat her words, and maybe request an apology. No, she didn't want an apology. She was just tired and cranky. Felice was a good sidekick. Marty rubbed her eyes, trying to awaken more while she waited for Felice to begin.

Felice cleared her throat and stood silent. She looked over at Marty and then back toward the house. Marty sighed. Felice seemed lost on that bit of stage, and if she didn't get on with her reading, Clive would thank her and tell her to go home. Felice motioned for Marty to come out to the stage.

"What's your problem now?" she asked, but then noticed Felice's irregular breathing pattern. "Are you okay?"

"I think I'm going to throw up."

Marty laughed outwardly. She softened, took hold of Felice's arm, and eased her to the stage floor. "Just breathe."

Clive walked to the apron. "Are you okay, Felice?"

"Yes. Can I have a minute before I read?"

"Yeah, sure. Liz is writing up something new and we'll get it to you in a minute. Just relax." He returned to his seat.

"What does he mean?" Felice asked.

"I'm not sure, but we'll find out soon enough. Are you feeling better?"

"A little. I didn't think I'd be nervous around you. It's easier talking crap about you than showing you I'm a qualified actor."

Marty rubbed Felice's arm in a motherly way. "I'm aware of your talent. Since I received this script, everyone around me has said you need to play opposite me. I've laughed and I've groaned about it, but I'm ready to accept this situation as a given."

Felice looked mildly astonished. "You'd actually work with me? After everything I've said?"

"You'll grow out of the naïve wannabe star and concentrate on great acting. Everyone goes through that phase and some make it to the top. Now you have the chance to convince them that you're the only woman capable of handling the role. I'm handing you step one, Felice." She watched Liz approach the stage. "If they give you the thumbs up, you're mine."

"Oh shit," she said, now fully astonished. "I'm not the same caliber as you. I'm just mouthy and having fun. Auditioning was a joke. I wanted to annoy you."

"Really?" Marty snorted a laugh. "Look, you were brave enough to come. Since you disrupted the process, you should at least read. What do you have to lose?"

Liz approached the apron and held papers toward them. "Clive wants you to read together."

Marty glanced over the paper and handed one to Felice. "This is new dialogue."

Liz nodded. "And it's just the beginning. As soon as we heard you two bickering, we needed a fresh approach. Have fun." She smiled and returned to her seat.

Marty leaned over to Felice. "Are you okay to do this? You won't lose your lunch, will you?"

"I'm afraid I'll make a fool of myself. I almost idolize you. Why do you think I make comments? It isn't just about press. It's about me wishing I had half the talent you have. I don't belong here." Felice stood. "Thank you," she said to Clive, "but I've decided not to read for the part. Good-bye." Felice walked toward the wing.

Marty fumed, caught Felice by the hand before she disappeared into the wing, and pulled her back to the stage. "Wait one damn minute, Tater tot. You disrupted this audition, your presence *closed* the audition, and now you chicken out? That's bullshit. You'll read for this part if I have to work your legs like a bellows and blow the words out of you."

Felice shoved her hands onto her hips. "Tater tot. That's so cute. Can't you come up with something more original?"

"You're trying my patience." She picked up the page that Felice had dropped to the floor. She shoved it back into her hand. "You have the first line."

Felice looked at the paper and, with a lilt in her voice, said, "*Fine.*"

Marty wished to God she could just go home and go to sleep. Lips pursed, she tapped her toe, and waited, and waited. Felice cocked her head.

"Just read your line," Marty said impatiently. Felice said nothing more and then Marty heard Liz and Clive laughing.

She tried to curb a giggle. "That was my line."

Marty stopped her toe in mid tap. She looked at her page of the script. In Liz's handwriting, the dialogue beneath the subconscious character's name had a single word. Fine.

She let go of the script page and watched the paper sail quietly to the floor. She looked up at Felice and Felice backed away. Marty didn't know what expression Felice saw, but there was fear in her eyes. Marty held the look for another moment, just because she could. Then she abruptly turned and faced the house. "I want Felice opposite me," she said. Allison let out a whoop and Nina clapped.

Felice let out her breath and then sucked in another. "Oh my God, I can't—"

Marty shook Felice's hand. "Welcome to Broadway. We have an unnamed play that's pretty much nothing more than a massive jumble at this point."

Visibly shaken, Felice looked around the stage, up and into the catwalk, and then her eyes followed the proscenium arch. "I don't believe what's happened. I'm playing Broadway."

There were goose bumps on Felice's arms and Marty's flesh prickled in response. For her, watching Felice was like watching herself all those years ago. She felt Felice's wonderment. The magic of the theater had never ceased.

"The pay sucks. We're on scale."

"Coffee money. I'll manage," Felice said. "I guess this is where I thank you."

"You're welcome." To Marty, those few minutes with Felice proved just as amazing and amusing as when Liz poured her heart out on the same floor.

Clive and Liz approached the stage. They congratulated Felice and sent her to wardrobe. A bottle of black dye, or a wig, was in order.

"We have some things to run through with you," Clive said.

Careful of the footlights, Marty sat near the edge of the apron. Was it bedtime yet? She sighed sleepily. "I'm listening."

Liz began. "Basically, the show remains the same. Your character wants to commit suicide and she talks with her subconscious. Instead of Felice playing the consoling, younger subconscious character, she'll play the whimsical smartass. In essence, she'll play herself."

Marty blinked. She narrowed her eyes. What did she just say? She and Felice would play themselves? She looked to her right, at Clive, and then left at Liz. Marty guessed where they were about to go and she wasn't pleased. She leaned forward, placed her hands on their arms, and pulled them arm against arm. Marty rubbed her hands over her face and then through her hair. She bit her lip. Marty made every imaginable gesture, just to keep from flipping out. If they understood how she steamed inside, they'd be halfway to Buffalo. Still, she was professional enough to listen, just in case she was wrong.

Liz and Clive continued back and forth. Talk of new ideas, box office numbers, and how the show had magically transformed from a drama, to a comedy, and now to a…to a what? A biomedy? That sounded like a remedy for indigestion. Somebody please make them stop and she could go home and get some sleep.

"What do you think?" Clive asked. "I think Liz has the right idea."

Marty looked at Liz.

"We're talking a sold out house every night," Liz said. "Before the show ends, you and Felice will own this town. New York will eat out of your hands. With a good start tonight, I can have a new script by the time I'm back from the Bahamas."

Clive wrote in his notebook. "I'll get a press release out and we'll get the marquee changed today. Maybe we can get you and Felice scheduled for a *Live at Five* interview on NBC. I'm thinking Sue Simmons for the interviewer."

"We'll prime the Tri-State Area," Liz said.

They continued with their rapid-fire ideas. While their personal dialogue banged like pots and pans in her brain, Marty's head geared up to explode. To counter their moment, she turned diva.

Marty held her hands up. "Stop it." Silence. She waited the proper beat. "First of all"—she zeroed in on Liz—"you need to brush up on your *Who's Who* in theater. I already own this town." She smiled and nodded. "Oh yeah, and don't you forget that." Liz's smile disappeared. "Second, I will not allow either of you to pimp my private life to the masses. Third," she repeated the word more forcefully, "*third,* if this comes down to my having to perform *your* way, somebody better start writing some damn music to keep this songbird happy."

"We don't have the cash flow for songwriters and an orchestra," Liz said.

Marty shot an angry look at her. "Find it. You and the good doctor *own* this show. You should be busting your ass and gathering financial support. You so aptly worked your producer hat today. Produce some cash for us." She swept her eyes to Clive. "I'm serious. You want to make a joke of me? Then you had better drown me with the key of B flat. If I don't have at least one song in my hand by Monday, I'm out of here."

Liz found her producer hat again. "I'll have you in court."

Marty laughed. "For what? My contract says a dramatic, one-woman show. That's not what you've got here. I'll counter sue. And you know what? I'll win. Take that thought to the Bahamas with you. End of story." Marty stood and exited stage left. She stopped and waited behind the drape.

"Talk to her," she heard Clive say.

"I'll give her a few minutes."

Allison spoke up, irritated. "You guys threw too much at her. Your idea is damn brilliant, but you know how stressed Marty's been. I'm surprised she didn't tell both of you to go to hell."

"I think she did," Clive said.

Although a temperamental diva had always lurked close to the surface, Marty'd kept that part of her at bay on most occasions. Today was an exceptional day. Her heart thumped wildly against her chest. Exhilarated and with enough spontaneous energy to scale the proscenium arch with her fingertips and back again, she did the second best thing. In a light-footed jog, she wound through the maze of hallways and into the early afternoon sunshine.

Marty darted across the street and up to the streaming havoc of Times Square at noon. After a quick right turn and a pace powerful enough to expend some anger, one street later she arrived at Europa Café. She shoved the door open and stopped abruptly at the counter.

"The usual, Ms. Jamison?" the barista asked.

"Please. A shot of espresso, too."

Marty paid him and then sat in a seat that faced Broadway. Her heart continued its strong rhythm against her chest. She looked out the window and stared at the globe on the JVC billboard across Broadway. She fiddled with the straw in her drink. What irked her most was Allison's statement that it was a brilliant idea. The more she thought about that statement, she understood that their new take on the show truly was a smart move.

In *Gypsy*, when Rose realized her daughter's act had ended up in the dregs of a sleazy, vaudeville burlesque show, she made the moment work. Rose forced Louise into performing a strip number. "You aren't really gonna strip. All you're gonna do is walk around the stage…and drop a shoulder strap," Rose had said. Reluctantly, Louise gave the audience a little and they begged for more. Louise was an instant success.

Without Felice and the new direction of the show, "dregs" closed in as the operative word for their play. With Felice on board and new ideas, there could be nowhere to go but up. Marty felt personally defeated with that admission.

She stared at her colossal, silkscreened likeness that hung next to the JVC globe. "You do own this town, but you're not above giving a little."

She grabbed her coffee and walked casually back toward the theater. When she came across the bagel shop on 44th street, she went inside, sat down, and then pulled her cell phone from her pocket. "Here's another one for you, Joyce." She called Liz.

"Where are you?" Liz asked.

"I'm sitting in the seat you were in on the day we met."

"Really? Is that a good memory or one you'd rather erase?"

"It fluctuates. Had you asked me fifteen minutes ago, I'd have wanted to erase that day."

"Then I'm thankful for the interlude. Are you coming back or do I have to send the hounds for you?"

She sensed a smile at the end of Liz's sentence. "I'll be there in fifteen minutes. I'd like all of you to meet me in my dressing room. Will you arrange that for me?"

"Of course. Are you okay? Clive and I hit you with a lot."

"We'll talk about it when I'm there."

Marty finished her drink and then walked leisurely to the Stanwyck. She'd been numbed and angered by the day's rapid progression and outcome. Still, she laughed to herself. Felice Tate.

Her costar. She could deal with Felice, but found the rest difficult to swallow.

When she entered her dressing room, Nina, Felice, and Liz sat on the day bed. Clive appeared comfortable in the bulky chair, and Allison sat at the vanity. Allison stood and offered the seat, but Marty waved her down.

"Do you need me, Jamison?" Bert asked.

"No, Bert. Liz or Clive will be in touch with you. Good night," she said. Bert waved as he left the room. She remained at the threshold. She couldn't hear as much as a breath from the others. "Thanks for meeting with me. It's been a hell of a day for events, and this is what I have to say about today's happenings." She looked over at Liz. "In all of your creative spontaneity, you failed to consult with me and my feelings, especially with turning the show into pot shots at me."

"They won't be pot shots."

"Yes, they will be. You should have let Felice read and then all four of us would have sat down and discussed your new ideas. I won't fault you for that because you're new at the production helm." She turned her head to Clive. "Clive, you knew better."

Clive sat up. "I'm—"

"Let me finish. I'll do the show. I agree with Allison that your new idea is brilliant, but I'm taking some time off. All of us agreed to begin rehearsal early, and gee, hasn't that been fun? However, my contract clearly states that rehearsal officially begins in another ten days. She looked back at Liz. "Our writer and producer will be in the Bahamas for the next few days and we have no script, so my presence isn't necessary. Clive can attend to things that won't need my input."

"Don't forget," Liz said with a bite to her voice, "you're on retainer as producer."

Marty slapped her with a broad smile. "I produced a bunch of bucks in less than an hour. How've you done?"

Liz turned red. "I can have a new scr—"

Marty looked away from her and continued. "Nina, would you get me a paper and a pen, please." Nina hustled and then handed her a notebook and pencil. Marty wrote a phone number and name down. She tore the paper off and handed it to Liz. "Betty Tomlinson composes terrific music. Tell Betty the songs are for me and she'll jump on her piano." She wrote on another page and handed it to Felice. "That's where I live. I'd like you to come over tomorrow at noon, if Clive releases you for the day." She looked at Allison. "Thank you for defending me today."

"You're welcome," Allison said.

"Okay, gang, there you have it. I'll be back in this theater in ten days. If Liz comes up with a script before that, give me a call. I'll see what I'm doing at the time." Marty smiled. "One more thing, but this is only a suggestion. I'd like the show titled *I've Got You* and I want a big ol' exclamation point at the end of the title. Make sure it's on the marquee, too." She waved. "Have a good weekend, everybody."

As she walked down the hall, she heard Clive talking.

"This'll cost a fortune. I'll make some calls for money. Just get that script into her hands soon."

When she stepped back into the summer sun, she turned off her cell phone and felt relief. At her next stop, she would fall happily into her bed and a much needed sleep coma.

Chapter Thirteen

After five hours of wonderful sleep, Marty stood under a long, warm shower. She sang every show tune she could think of until she dried off, slipped a T-shirt over her head, and pulled on a pair of shorts. She twisted her hair into an upsweep and clipped it to the back of her head.

At the front door, she shoved her keys into her pocket, put on a pair of sandals, and grabbed her cell phone. She left her apartment and walked until she reached Liz's place. She hit speed-dial number one on her phone.

"Hello, sleepyhead. How was your nap?"

"Refreshing. I'm outside. Can I come up?"

"Yes," Liz said and they met at the apartment door. "You look wonderful."

"I feel wonderful, but we need to talk about what happened today."

Liz closed the door. "Right to the point, huh? No hello? No kiss?"

Marty sat on the sofa and leaned back. "Come here, babe." Liz was next to her within seconds. "You feel good."

"How about that kiss?"

Marty gave her a warm, tender kiss. "I care for you in a whole bunch of ways. Do you believe that?" She ran her fingers through Liz's hair.

"I do. You're about to read the riot act to me, aren't you?"

"Not too badly. In fact, you might enjoy it." She dotted Liz's cheek with soft kisses and slow passes of her tongue.

"I'm sorry, Marty. I got carried away with the possibilities of you and Felice."

"The same way I'm getting carried away?" she asked and kissed her way to Liz's throat. She bit gently and then again. Liz moaned softly.

"No. I like this more."

"You've turned this show personal for Felice and for me." She opened two buttons on Liz's blouse and found unrestrained breasts. She ran her fingertips across curved flesh, intentionally missing her nipples. Liz squirmed when Marty opened the remaining buttons and removed the blouse. She clasped Liz's breasts. "You didn't stop to think how we might feel."

"You're right. I didn't think." Her breaths shortened.

Marty took one breast, as much as she could, into her mouth and released it. "Knowing me on a private level interfered with your professional approach."

"I suppose it did. Take my other breast."

She ignored the request. "No, no supposition there. I need to keep separate my private and personal lives, regardless of what the show may bring my way."

"I'll be more careful."

Marty pulled Liz's lounge pants over her hips. She knelt on the floor and ran her fingers through the dark trim of pubic hair. Liz leaned against the back of the sofa. Eyes closed, her chest raised and lowered with each shallow breath. Marty parted Liz's legs. She could have stayed another full night looking at Liz's body, to explore each outward curve and enter warm, fascinating places. Marty propped Liz's feet on the sofa. Liz gasped when Marty touched sensitive flesh.

"I need to punish you." She kept her eyes on the center of Liz's thighs.

"Don't tease me."

"Like you've never teased me." She rested her finger against Liz's now wet flesh. Liz moaned and pushed forward. "Is this what you want?" She pressed slightly inside.

"Yes."

Marty smiled and moved her finger slowly upward to Liz's clitoris. At the slightest pressure, Liz jerked. "And this?"

"Oh, yes. A lot of that."

She took her hand away and leaned forward. She lifted the front of her T-shirt and pressed her breast against Liz.

Liz groaned loudly and moved her hips side to side. "What are you doing to me?"

Marty moved back and lowered her shirt. She took Liz's hand and placed it against the flesh she had just teased. "I'm punishing you."

Liz's eyes snapped open. "You want me to—"

"I want to watch you. If you don't let me, I'll bring big purple over here."

"No. Don't. No big purple." She began a slow and steady massage.

Marty smiled. She kissed Liz's inner thighs while she watched the tempo of her hand and thighs quicken. "That feels good, doesn't it?"

"Yes."

"Lesson one." She kissed the hand that stroked. "When my name is on the marquee, you'll confer with the actors."

Liz's breath caught. "Please touch me. I need to feel you."

"Lesson learned?" She asked, caressing Liz's hand with her cheek.

"Yes. Confer with the actors."

"Lesson two." She licked the back of Liz's hand. "Never close an audition without consulting with the director."

"Lesson learned. Please touch me."

"You'll be a good little producer?"

"The best," she said with minimal breath.

Marty slid her finger inside Liz. With a loud, quick, and sharp grunt and then another, Liz came until nothing remained but the sounds of her raspy breaths. Her feet dropped to the floor and she rolled her head to the side. Her eyes remained closed.

"I killed her." Marty smiled. While Liz fell asleep, Marty took another long look at her body. "Come on, babe. Off to bed with you." Liz was a ragdoll moving into Marty's arms and into the bedroom. "I'll set your alarm. What time?"

"Five," she murmured and pulled the sheet over her.

Marty pushed some buttons on the alarm clock. Liz nestled into the pillow and Marty kissed her forehead. "Sweet dreams," she said and Liz grabbed her hand.

"Sleep here. Liz wants kitten here."

Marty smiled. She had calls to place, but they could wait until morning. Still in street clothes, Marty stretched onto the bed, and Liz backed into her arms.

"Good night, Liz."

Just after noon on Friday, Felice rang the visitor buzzer to Marty's apartment. They met on the landing outside.

"Hello, Tater tot. I'm glad you came."

Felice shook her head. "I don't know what made me think you might call me Felice." She glared at Marty. "Can I get a little more respect from you?"

"Sure. Will you curb your penchant for slamming me in public?"

"What? Not call you old and yesterday's news?" She laughed. "You've been a wonderful target."

"You're just an obnoxious little pissant." She looked away when she heard a slight gasp from Felice. She straightened her smile and turned back.

Felice grabbed Marty's arm. "I'm what?"

"I invited you over because I want to spank the brat in you." She pulled her toward the steps but let her go when Felice showed the slightest sign of panic.

Felice stared at her. Then she laughed nervously. "You're messing with me, aren't you?" Marty didn't answer, but reached for her arm again. "Aren't you?" Felice backed away.

She couldn't get enough of seeing Felice's frightened look again. It teetered between "Oh, shit" and "Is this woman nuts?" She let her wonder for another few seconds, and then she nodded.

"I'm playing with you. Do you have time to walk down to the piers?"

Felice let her breath out. "Sure."

Through the row of brownstone apartments, they strolled casually toward the Hudson River. Felice was talkative and interested in what had developed yesterday.

"I'm not sure why Liz and Clive apologized to me, but I felt I should accept," Felice said. "Can you steer me around there?"

Marty smiled. She owned a terrific opportunity to tell her any silly thing that she might believe, but didn't take the time to think of anything witty. She looked over at her costar. Felice was twenty-five and looked much younger without makeup and clothes fit for a Woody Allen tribute. She looked too vulnerable to toy with.

"You've just landed a costarring role with me. That's usually reserved for someone who's done some work on Broadway." Felice smiled. "I get a lot of creative control with my contracts, and I would discuss with you any changes that might take place. Liz and Clive had a moment of temporary insanity and let their egos sound off. In short, they should have approached us together."

"We're the boss?"

"Absolutely not. It's all about respect. It's not about turning diva, like I did yesterday. That happened because of many other circumstances surrounding our show. They understand why I walked out."

"They told me it's been rough going since production began."

"Exactly, and yesterday they got caught up in the fact that the one person I'd laughed about costarring with me actually gave them an approach to make the show work. Did they explain anything about our miserable play?"

"Yes, and thankfully. I didn't dare ask. I'm nobody."

"That's where you're wrong. You are someone, even Off Broadway." Marty looked over at her. "Are you still afraid of me?"

"Not as much." Felice smiled. "At least I don't feel like I'll throw up. That's got to mean something."

"Good. I want you to be comfortable."

"I still think I'm a better actor than you."

"I have no doubt you feel that way."

They crossed the West Side Highway to access the piers. Several small boats sailed the river, and a Circle Line cruise ship chugged through another round of the island. Across the river was New Jersey, with her own set of piers. The afternoon was comfortably warm and they took a seat along the railing.

"To steer you around some more, the original show was insane, and I won't bother with explanation. We needed a second actor to play my subconscious. Eventually, we held auditions and then you barged in."

"I don't know what gave me the nerve."

"Imagine my surprise. I haven't had the time to talk with Clive and Liz, but the gist of what they want is giving your character lines similar to things you might say about me."

"I'm playing me?"

"Not exactly, but they expect the audience to read us as Marty and Felice. The idea is cheap and a little sleazy, but it'll work."

"And you don't mind?"

"I was beyond pissed off at first, but not now. Frankly, there's been so much bullshit with this show that I welcome the idea if only to get things going. I had initial negative feelings, but I think we could have some fun. Can you sing?"

"Yes."

"Great. Can I ask you something personal?"

"It depends on how personal."

"Who are the men that escort you around town?"

"Two of them are my uncles and the other is a friend of theirs. They manage me."

"Are you happy with them? Do they have you on contract?"

She hesitated. "I get work, but only part time. No contracts. I trust my family."

"Are you uncomfortable talking about them?"

"Yes, because it's Marty Jamison who asks. You don't need to hear about my failed acting career. It's embarrassing for me."

"You haven't failed and don't be embarrassed. Off Broadway runs some great shows and I recall an Obie nomination for you. That's their equivalent to a Tony. It's a big deal. You need the right people working for you. What are your plans as far as acting?"

"I'd like to continue. I'm a good actor. My day job is boring and I balance boredom on stage. That's the fun part of my evening and weekends."

"What's your day job?"

"I manage a medical office."

"Would you rather act more?"

"Yes. I've never full out pursued acting because it felt too big. You know what I mean?"

Marty nodded. "Yes, and I also hear a confidence problem. I've seen your stage work and you're a natural for the job. I get the feeling your uncles know that, but keep your talent at bay. That way they still cash in on you. If I called a couple agents and managers, would you consider dumping the three stooges and sign with someone reputable?"

Felice looked shocked. "You'd do that for me? Finding good representation is tough. Of course I'm interested."

"I was counting on that answer." She pulled a paper from her pocket and handed it to Felice. "I called some people this morning. The first two are agencies and the other two are local managers. They're good people and always hungry for new talent. I've put in some good words for you, so give them a call."

Felice took the paper. "You mean real work? Maybe revivals?"

"I can't guarantee Broadway, but somehow you've managed to wiggle your way in the door for now." She nudged Felice. "How does that make you feel? You were screwing with me and landed the role."

"I'm scared, but excited."

"When I stepped onto my first Broadway show, I thought I'd bust a gut. I was your age and scared to death. Another actor took me under her wing and I want to pass that favor to you."

"I'm surprised you don't hate me, after all the things I've said about you."

"You've made me laugh a lot, Felice. Just be sure to talk with some of the people on that list."

They sat quietly. Marty felt good inside and wondered if a friendship might develop for them. They seemed comparable to herself and Joyce in that respect. Of course, she'd miss Felice's entertaining jabs.

Marty's phone rang. She found it at the bottom of her handbag and checked caller ID. "Our writer extraordinaire," she said. "I have to take her call."

"Hello."

"Hi, kitten. Paul and I have a glitch here and I wanted you to know first."

Magic. Marty's abandonment issues instantly rose to the surface without hearing the news. Liz's intonation was enough to alert the demon. She shifted in her seat and kept her eyes on the river. She said nothing.

"Marty?"

She answered with indifference. "I'm here."

"The bank screwed up and I'm stuck here until Monday. I'll call Clive and tell him not to expect me until Tuesday, but I'm working on a script and should have it completed by then."

"How nice for you. The sun, the beach, Paul."

"I can't help—"

"Isn't it wonderfully convenient for you? Things just drop into your lap like rain."

"You know what I said about rain."

"Yeah, well, I'm not in the mood for analogies. Maybe I'll see you at the theater on Tuesday. Hopefully, a hurricane doesn't demolish Nassau's airport."

"That was uncalled for, Marty. I suggest—"

"Tuesday, Liz." She closed her phone and Felice stopped her from chucking it into the river.

Felice shook her head. "You'll regret that," she said and took the phone from Marty's hand.

"Introducing the phone to the Hudson or my comment about the hurricane?"

"Both, you jackass."

Marty glared at Felice. "Where do you get off calling me a jackass?"

"It's hurricane season and she could well get caught up in something horrifying. Jackass isn't strong enough for you."

She didn't respond, but quickly regretted her comment to Liz and now worried about the weather. She'd never wish harm to either of them. An hour on a hot tarmac would be nice, though.

"Don't be an idiot. Call her back. You still have to work with her."

"You're not so afraid of me after all." Marty took a deep breath. She looked at the phone in Felice's hand. "Hit redial." Felice pressed the button and handed the phone to her.

Marty walked several yards from Felice and stood against the railing. Liz answered after four rings and there was a cool reserve in her voice.

"What can I do for you, Ms. Jamison?"

The edge to Liz's voice was foreign, but deserved. "I'm sorry. I reacted. I didn't think."

"Are you making a conscious effort to destroy what we're building?"

"No. I was out of line." Silence. "Say something."

"I will. I have the show to worry about, and I'm by no means happy while stuck in Nassau. You have something to deal with and until you do, I won't be wrapped up in your drama."

"Liz—"

"There's no debate, Marty. I've wanted you for twenty years and here you are, larger than life itself, but you're allowing your past to tarnish what we could have together."

"I know."

"Obviously, I have to wait a little longer."

"Patience is a virtue for you." She wished she hadn't said those words.

"Maybe a curse. I'll find out, won't I?"

"What are you saying?"

"Beyond a professional level, I won't see you."

The words crushed her. They left Marty skewed, and she wished she'd never met Rachel. "Wait. No, Liz. Can't we just take things slower? We should have done that from the beginning."

"We're miles beyond that pale. I don't like telling you that I won't see you, but you need to shed a few tears or find some type of closure with Rachel, before we can consider a loving relationship."

Her eyes stung. Somewhere, there was an answer. She'd find it if it killed her. "Then don't tell me you won't see me. Tell me we'll talk about this when you return."

"I can't say that with meaning. I know how you feel about me, and if I didn't feel the same for you, I'd never wait another year. I just hope you won't take that long."

Marty's timeline reappeared on crisp white paper, but it didn't begin at zero. She saw multiple negatives to get through.

"I'll see you Tuesday. I should have a completed script by then."

"Yes, of course. I know you're right about Rachel, but not see you?"

"I feel it's best that way. Maybe you should contact her. That could mean all the difference between us." She sounded sad.

Marty wiped tears from her cheeks and eyes. Frustrated and weakened by her past, she didn't want to end their conversation. She wanted to feel the comfort of Liz's arms around her and hear her assurance that they'd work it out together, but she'd already been given that chance.

"Okay. I'll call Rachel."

"Thank you. Those words mean a lot to me."

To overcome her defeat, she attempted to keep Liz on the line longer. "I'm anxious to see the new script."

"You'll approve of the work. Good-bye, Marty."

"Do you have to make that sound so damn final?"

"I'll see you Tuesday."

"Tuesday." Marty choked on the word and closed the phone. She rested her arms on the railing and stared at New Jersey. Footsteps came from her left.

"You okay?" Felice asked. Marty shook her head. "I guess today isn't a day I'd want to be you. Do you want to talk about it?"

"No." She wiped more tears away.

She didn't say much on their walk back to her apartment. Liz was too prevalent in her thoughts to give any real attention to Felice's attempt to converse. She couldn't shake Rachel from her mind, either.

Marty had dealt with monsters in her theatrical life. Monsters who'd threatened her legally, monsters who'd promised to throw her to the dogs, and none of them could lay a scratch on her or her reputation. She wasn't afraid to stand up for herself. Marty worked in logic. That was easy. Working in matters of the heart, that was obviously altogether different. She had to locate some form of logic for the degree of fear that held her prisoner.

"Do you have a boyfriend?" Marty asked.

"Yes. David. Nice guy."

"How long have you been together?"

"About two years."

"Are you happy?"

"Yes. He travels a lot, so he can be gone for weeks at a time, but I know he'll be back. When he returns, he's all mine."

"Do you ever feel—never mind."

Felice looked over at Marty. "Do I feel what?"

"If you went home tonight and—" She stopped.

"No, go ahead. Do you think Liz is cheating on you?"

"Not really."

"So finish. I go home tonight and find what?"

"And you find your boyfriend in bed with your best friend. What would you do?"

Felice stopped dead. "Liz did that to you? Oh my God."

"No. It happened in another lifetime."

"Oh. Good. What would I do? After I trashed his face, I'd send both of them out the window. That would be good. Our apartment's on the third floor." Felice smiled. "Well, not the last part, but I'd trash his face. Maybe just slap the crap out of him. I'm not really violent, but I might be violent in that situation. Maybe I could go nuts. Damn. I don't know now. I might talk to him about why he cheated. Then I'd trash his face. I just pity the bastard if it happens. Wow." Felice threw a right hook into the air. "Bam!"

Marty laughed until leftover tears streamed down her cheeks. Felice talked gibberish just as freely. Nina was in for a treat.

Felice's eyes widened. "You did find her in bed with someone else."

"No. That happened in another relationship."

Their walk continued in silence until Felice stopped in front of Marty's apartment. "This is where I leave you."

"Do you want to come in for a while?"

"And ruin my reputation?" Felice smiled. "Maybe another time." She held up the business contacts paper. "Thank you." She turned away and stopped a cab.

Marty entered her apartment and headed directly to the bar. She poured a glass of wine. At her desk, she opened the massive Manhattan phonebook and searched the name Carr. There was no listing for Rachel Carr. She closed the book and fished around in a drawer until she found an old address book. When she opened it to the letter C, Rachel Carr was the first entry, and her name throbbed like the neon in Times Square. She sat back in the chair and swooshed the wine around in her glass. Her stomach trembled with negative anticipation of Rachel's voice. She dialed Nina's number instead.

"Hey, sugar. I thought I'd hear from you sooner."

"I've been busy."

"Are you okay? You sound down."

"Just thinking about a call I have to make soon."

"You need some support? Is that why you called?"

"Yeah."

"Okay. Go get 'em," she said and laughed.

"I knew I could count on you. Did Anna make any headway on Felice's costumes?"

"She finished both. Felice is thin as a rail. Nice girl, too."

"Turncoat."

"Who do you need to call that you're frazzled?"

"Rachel."

"What took you so long?"

"Obviously, I'm the only clueless one regarding her. What do you mean?"

"You never closed that door. You threw them out of your apartment but kept the vision of them inside you. You've been happy with Liz, but now you're gloomy. I talked to her a few minutes ago and she sounded gloomy. I'm guessing Rachel is the key to putting some spark back into both of you."

"Maybe you're right." She finished her wine.

"Just make that call and then come cry on my shoulder if you need me."

"Okay." She hung up the desk phone and looked back at the neon-black name. She closed the book. "Screw you, Rachel. I'll get through this."

Marty worked fitfully to occupy her weekend with exercise—dance for her body and reading for her mind. Three pages into a murder mystery, she realized she'd read the last page twice, and still hadn't a clue what she'd read. Distracted and dwelling on Liz and Rachel, Marty was unable to concentrate. She returned the book to the shelf and went into her dance studio. With her stereo blasting, she'd perform some warm-up exercises.

Jelly. Not just her hands, but also her limbs were jelly. Everything quivered in negative ways. Her dance timing was off, and her body refused to move where and how she'd wanted. Instead of working the boards, a simple turn and break flung her into an uncontrolled twist that threw her backward and ass first onto the floor. She landed with a thump and loud "Ooph." With a second attempt, she tripped herself at the ankle and never pulled through to the break. Marty quickly crumbled into a sweaty heap. Staring sideways at worn lacquered floorboards and a dust bunny, she blew a quick breath and the dust slid across the floor. She sat up and looked at her disheveled appearance in the mirrored wall. She brushed her hair back with her hands.

"Focus, Martina. What is it you need?" She glanced at the dust bunny. "Aside from a housekeeper?" She looked over at the freestanding ballet bar, and then to the bar mounted on the mirror.

Ballet bars weren't her immediate need. She scanned the room in the mirror and stopped at her desk. The house phone, in plain view, held her attention. "I can't make that call," she told the mirror. "I thought Rachel was an old wound, and I don't want to hear her voice." She stood, headed toward the front door, kicked the dust bunny under the chair, and left her apartment.

Through the din of traffic, Marty crossed the scrambled street patterns of the West Village. She wished the phone in her pocket would signal a call from Liz. She checked the battery level twice. Three times, she stopped short of pushing speed dial number one. A short call would be fine, if only to say hello, but that call never came. Liz was busy with the play. Wasn't she?

She continued her route, beyond the construction site of the new World Trade Center, until she reached Battery Park. There, she purchased a bottle of water and found a spot under a shady elm. Sweat slid down her back and between her breasts. After a long swallow of water, she turned her attention to the distant and green Statue of Liberty in the harbor.

"Tempest tossed. That's me."

Her phone rang. Nina. It rang again. Clive. With each call, she jumped. She obsessed. "This is nuts. How do I stop the crazies?"

An hour later, she reversed her course and headed home.

"I'm not needy." She slipped into bed. "I can live without Liz, but I'd prefer she shared my life."

Marty had lived better weekends.

Chapter Fourteen

Clive called late Monday afternoon. Liz had e-mailed a completed script to him.

"It's a fun read. She's rewritten almost everything. Will you come into the theater tomorrow?"

Marty looked forward to reading the new script. For her, there was magic in Liz's writing, with her sickeningly intelligent and evocative word placement. She expected the new script would deliver the same quality of work as Liz's novels.

"I'll be there at eight. Is Liz home?"

"She'll return tonight. Also, I've hired two of the readers as understudies for you and Felice."

She perked up even more, anticipating the sight of Liz. "Good. It sounds like we almost have a show. Did you locate any money?"

"A boatload. I called in some favors and they agreed to back us. We're looking good for a while. I'm sorry for the fiasco last week."

"Ah, Clive, that was last week. We'll start fresh in the morning."

"Okay. See you tomorrow."

She closed her phone and jumped from the ring that instantly followed. She turned the illuminated face of the phone slowly toward her, hoping the name would be Liz. Blue letters spelled the name and Marty's heart skipped a beat, or maybe half a dozen, while she waited for the third ring.

"Hello."

"Hi, Marty."

Liz sounded happy and her voice was enough to collapse Marty into her chair. With each word, Liz sat on Marty's lap and cradled her heart in her hands.

"Hey, Liz," she simply said, but wanted to say how much she missed her. Instead, she remained businesslike. "I hear we have a new show already."

"I finished the script late yesterday, sprawled on a secluded beach I'd found. My tan looks great, too."

She thought back to those tan lines and how they curved and dipped around her breasts. She wanted to know in person how the whiter flesh of Liz's breasts clashed with her newer tan.

"I'll bet you look lovely."

"Thank you. I worked like the devil to finish the play. Did you read it? I e-mailed a copy to you."

"I told Clive I'd wait until tomorrow. I'm looking forward to a first read-through with Felice."

"You like her, huh? That's a relief for the rest of us."

Marty smiled. "She's okay. Are you home from sand and sunshine?"

"Yes. We signed the papers early this morning. I just walked through the door a few minutes ago."

A block away still felt like the distance between Manhattan and Nassau. If nothing else, she'd called quickly.

"I won't keep you, then. I'm sure you have a lot of things to do before tomorrow."

"Not really. Unpack. Bathe. Not an evening packed with fun. I've missed you. It's good hearing your voice."

"I've missed you, too. I'd hoped you would have called to say hello."

"I needed to focus on the show. By the way, I got in touch with Betty Tomlinson. We should have some songs by the end of the week. You said Monday, but we have to give her a break on time."

"You did well, Madame Producer. Betty knows what I like. I'm sure they'll be good songs. Do we have an orchestra?"

"We're going a different route. *A cappella*. At least we'll try it that way first."

"Just voice? That's intriguing. We're breaking the rules of Broadway left and right, aren't we?"

Liz laughed softly. "Breaking rules has always been our way, ki—uh, Marty."

You almost called me kitten. "Yes, it's our way, Liz."

"I guess I'll unpack and make some dinner. I'll see you tomorrow morning."

"Good night." She hung up the phone with a smile on her heart. "I'll do this. I won't let this be the end."

Marty dug out her address book again. Time would stand completely still if she didn't get past the call to Rachel. She punched in Rachel's phone number and waited. Four rings. Five rings. Voice mail. "Shit." She waited through Rachel's announcement.

"You've reached Rachel Carr. I'm on vacation and I'll return your call soon. Please refer any business to my office number."

Anxiety set in, just hearing Rachel's voice after two years. "Rachel, it's Marty. Would you give me a call soon? I need to speak with you. Thanks." She closed her phone. No indication of when Rachel would return left her in a funk.

"Damn it. She could be away for weeks."

On Tuesday morning, Marty found Felice—in the role of quintessential tourist—standing outside the Stanwyck. Felice looked up at the marquee and smiled broadly. Her neck bent at such a severe angle that she might be in for some serious injury, or at least a few nights of hot compresses and mild pain relievers. The illuminated sign, splashed of white lettering and a bright blue background, read *Marty Jamison-Felice Tate*. Below, in larger letters and the perfect exclamation point, the title read *I've Got You!*

"What do you think?"

Felice kept looking up. "I'm playing on Broadway and I might miss it because I'll still be standing here looking at this gorgeous marquee. Isn't it beautiful? I can't believe that's my name beside yours. Let's get some pictures. Can we do that?"

Marty enjoyed sharing a step forward on Felice's timeline. "At some point. Come on." She put her arm around Felice's shoulder. "Let's get to work."

They entered the house and sat in the third row. The curtain was down, but spotlights lit the massive red drape and gold arch. The ambience fit her mood—colorful and bright—now that Liz sat near. She and Clive sat in the row ahead and had their heads together. Both looked behind them when Felice said a quiet "good morning."

"We've got stars," Clive said. "Let's make 'em shimmer."

Dressed in white, Liz looked fabulous and healthy with her Bahamian, light chocolate tan. She smiled sweetly at Marty who returned a bigger smile and wished a hug were involved.

"Good morning," she said, and then looked over at Felice. "Nina has bagels and coffee in Marty's dressing room. We need about twenty minutes before we can use you two." She turned back to Clive.

❖

"Good morning," Nina said when they entered the dressing room. "You'd think you two were something special."

Marty looked at Felice. "Ignore her," she said and poured a cup of coffee. She sat at the vanity. "What's the big secret?"

"I don't think it's a secret. Your set is nearly completed. Clive paid the set designer, Bert, and their crew to work all weekend."

"I guess he did find some money."

"I can't wait to see the set," Felice said. "The script, too."

Nina handed a single white teddy to Felice. "Here's your wardrobe. I hope the lights will keep you warm." Then Nina handed Marty one pair of silk pajamas. "They've changed your wardrobe, sugar."

"Black pajamas. I guess I'm the old broad now. At least I won't have to worry about YouTube." She tossed the sleepwear onto the daybed.

"Do I have a dressing room?" Felice asked.

Nina motioned to the right with her thumb. "One door down. It's small, but I've spruced it up for you."

"Thanks. I'll see you later, Marty." Felice grabbed a bagel and closed the door behind her.

"Did you call Rachel?"

She looked into the mirror at Nina standing behind her. "Voice mail."

"Bummer." Nina played with Marty's hair. "Do you want any special look to your hair for the show?"

"No. Nina, I'm about to ask you a question with the maturity of a fifth grader."

"What is it?"

"Has Liz ever said anything to you about me?"

"Plenty." She dropped Marty's hair. "But I'll be damned if you'll get it out of me."

"I figured as much. We're kind of separated."

"I know." From behind, Nina wrapped her arms around Marty's shoulders. "She's nuts about you, sugar. That's all I'm saying."

She turned in her seat. "I hope I hear from Rachel soon."

"It'll happen. Come on." Nina pulled her to her feet. "Let's join the others."

Nina had made a point to steer her away from entering through the stage. "Clive wants to knock your socks off when he brings the curtain up," Nina said.

Felice met them and followed them through the hall. They entered the house from the main auditorium doors and joined the others in the first few rows of seating. Clive and Liz were looking at the script. Nina took a seat in the fifth row. Allison and the additional understudies sat together in row four.

"Let's work," Marty said and sat with Felice in row three.

Clive turned to face them. "We'd like to do the read-through a bit differently. Instead of a table reading, we want you to do it on stage. Sit and walk around at your leisure. Get comfortable in your bedrooms. You know, make them yours."

"Really?" Marty asked and looked at Liz who nodded. Marty wanted to smother her with kisses, so she turned to Felice. "Is that okay with you?" Felice agreed. "We're good to go."

"Good." Clive looked toward the stage. "Bert," he yelled, "would you bring up the curtain, please?"

The spotlights went off and her eyes turned to the stage when she heard the curtain rise. The set itself was dark and the only item readily seen was a white pillow, placed down center, just before the curtain line.

Liz turned around to face them. "Felice, you're set for stage left. Marty is stage right."

"Stage right? Do I make any exits? I don't do stage right exits."

"No exits. You're in a bedroom all night. There's nowhere to go." He turned to the rear of the theater. "Light the stage lights, please," he said louder.

The split stage resembled Liz's earlier diagram. Marty's bedroom was on the audience left. The furniture positions mirrored Felice's, but decor and props were different. Marty's room was set with lavish but muted colors, and contemporary furniture. Even the artwork begged for a pick-me-up. Everything was elegant and comfortable but boring.

Felice's bedroom was bright with colorful lights fashioned in a manner that placed Marty's mind into the middle of Times Square at night. There was a circus feel to her half. That room exuded positive energy.

Clive made a note to his papers and then spoke. "Marty, we've established your character in her present time and we've jacked up her age to mid-fifties. She's regretful, angry, and ready to take a powder. Your subconscious character is set thirty years earlier, her mid-twenties. She's young, vibrant, and ready to take on the world with her optimism."

"Cool," Felice said. "I get it. All those years ago, I wanted the lights and excitement of Broadway. I was full of hell and anxious to make a mark." She looked over at Marty. "Then I grew up and now I'm boring." Her voice trailed and then she laughed. "Is that what I have to look forward to? Beige?"

Marty laughed. "Yeah, pretty much." She paused when Liz snickered. She looked over at her and smiled. "I like the set. It works for the characters."

"Come on, you two," Liz said.

They followed her up the steps and onto the stage. Marty sat on her chair near the armoire and Felice sat on her bed. Soundmen wired the actors and Liz gave pencils and copies of the script to Marty and Felice. Marty examined the pencil tip.

"Sharpened to the likes hitherto unknown to mankind."

Liz nodded. Their eyes lingered. "Hitherto. Break a leg, kitten."

"Thanks."

Thanks? For what? For just having made her day? For having sparked a glimmer of hope that maybe, just maybe, Liz would soon warm up to her? Maybe thanks for setting her heart all giggly and gooey? She watched Liz descend the stairs. Yes, she was thankful for all of those reasons.

"Felice, show this woman what good acting is all about," Liz said and took her seat in row two.

"Whenever you're ready," Clive said. "Just say the lines however you feel them."

Marty opened the script, and after taking a moment to consider her approach, she read her first line. *"A woman can't get any sleep when she's contemplating suicide."*

Felice groaned. *"Again with that? If I don't get some decent sleep soon—"*

"What do you care? You have your whole life ahead of you."

Sleepily, Felice cocked her head toward Marty and said, *"I'll wake up looking like you."*

Marty waited for their light audience to stop laughing. She looked over at Felice and shot her a sarcastic grin. *"I have news for you, sweetheart."*

Another bit of laughter and the actors warmed quickly to each other. They took off like rockets. Both dug instantly into the comedic and dramatic scheme, and their deliveries were perfect. With ease, they moved about their sets, often speaking directly to each other. When they reached the end of the first act, both sat at their vanities.

"Damn empty chambers," Marty said.

She set down her handgun and poured a glass of prop whiskey. Felice poured a glass of wine. Both took a drink and then stared into their mirrored images.

"When did you start drinking whiskey? Drink enough of that and you won't need another bullet." Felice dipped her fingers into her wine.

"I don't need another bullet."

Felice spritzed Marty with the wine. *"I've got you,"* she said, and act one ended.

Marty blinked, her eyes narrowed, and an eyebrow twitched. She heard "Uh-oh" from Clive, and then a spate of clapping from the others.

Petty theft, an action that she attributed to Felice's acting inexperience. Marty saw a quick lesson in Theater Protocol 101: Working with Marty Jamison, in Felice's immediate future. She got up from her chair and walked to Felice's side. She removed her mic, turned her back to the others and spoke softly.

"The good news is you were terrific, Felice." Felice beamed a wide smile back to her. "The bad news is, and I'll say this only once politely, you stole my line."

Felice's beaming smile vanished and she spilled into a fountain of apology. "I'm sorry, Marty. It just came out. It fit. I couldn't stop it. Your character killed the drive in mine, and I needed to tell her. I don't know what I was thinking. Of course it was your line."

Once again, Marty enjoyed Felice's frightened look. "Relax, this time. The line worked better your way. For your future reference, I don't mind losing lines if it's necessary, but don't spring changes on me that way. We'll discuss them with Liz and Clive."

"Okay. Got it." Felice stood. "The way you looked at me, I thought I was about to die."

"Not this time. Aside from that." She threw her arms around Felice and squeezed. "I just had a hell of a lot of fun."

"Is everything okay up here?" Clive asked when he approached the stage.

"We're good," Marty said and Felice nodded. "I think we're ready for act two."

"Yes," Clive finally shouted. "We have a show."

Their morning progressed through the final acts. There were three sections marked as song inserts, and Marty ached to know what Betty had in store.

When the imaginary curtain came down on act three, Marty couldn't show her happiness enough. She hugged everyone, including Bert, and felt as though the curtain had settled after a successful opening night.

"All right," Clive said at the end of the day. "I feel good about this. You work well together. I say we wrap this up for today and come back in the morning."

❖

"I have a great vibe about the show," Marty said as Nina was about to leave. She checked her phone for a message from Rachel. "She won't call me. She's vacationing. Everyone's getting sun but me."

"Extended sun isn't good for you anyway." Nina leaned over and kissed Marty's cheek. "Your show is a winner, and I'm proud of you for bringing in Felice. I have a chicken to roast. See you tomorrow, sugar."

While Marty gathered her belongings, footsteps echoed in the hallway and grew louder. Their patter stopped at her door and she turned around. Even with their strained relations, Liz turned her into a bundle of bliss.

"Hi."

Marty smiled. "Hi back at you. How was your day?"

Liz entered the room and approached her. "Oh, I had a read-through with some zany actors. I think today was the most fun I've ever had in a work environment."

"Theater is addicting." She dug in her bag for her sunglasses. "Your script is good. I'm on my way home. Will you have a drink with me?"

"I can't. Trish sent some book covers and galley proofs for me to look over. Lots of reading for the next few nights."

Okay, babe. I'll make dinner while you work and then we'll settle in for the night, talk about the show, share some kisses, and try to make a baby. "Consider the offer a rain check, then." She put on her sunglasses. "Your tan looks terrific."

"Thanks," she said with a smile. "You two knocked our socks off, by the way."

"Wasn't she great?"

"It's too bad Clive cut the pillow scene. That was my favorite." Her eyes moved slowly over Marty. The warm glow that enveloped her sent her right back to the night they had sat in the muck of Times Square.

"And so goes the theater." Marty took her glasses off and gave Liz a curious look. "Are you flirting with me?"

"Did you think I wouldn't? I'm upset with you, but you aren't any less attractive to me."

That irked Marty. "You won't see me, but I'm okay to flirt with and ogle? That makes me feel like a slab of meat."

Liz stepped closer. She grasped Marty's arm and Marty hoped she would never let go. She looked genuinely sorry, but Marty had more than playing hurt on her mind.

"I'm sorry," Liz stammered. "What I meant…was…oh hell."

Without a long look into her eyes, without waiting for any hint of reaction from Liz, Marty pulled her into her arms and kissed her with the passion of bursting suns. Excitement ran deep into the pit of her stomach. Liz's thrill streamed through Marty's ears in melodic whimpers. They held tightly and stopped their kiss only when they gasped for air. Their mouths remained close, moist, and warm.

"I flirt back, Liz. I'm just more direct."

Liz pulled away. "I get the message." Flustered, she turned to leave the room and then turned back. "I'm waiting for you." Marty stood at the threshold and watched her walk down the hallway.

When she was out of sight, Marty took the script from the vanity and stretched onto the daybed. Briefly, she studied her lines until her thoughts seized Liz's image. She smiled, dropped the play to the floor, and hugged a pillow. Seeing Liz again, Marty realized she hadn't been careful, even though she'd promised the daisies.

"Instead of Liz unpacking last night, she deserved bone-busting embraces, lip bruising kisses, and whispers of sweet everythings," she said and grabbed her play. "That sounded like something she'd write."

Marty managed to break her thoughts away from Liz and studied for an hour. When the rumble in her stomach signaled hunger, she left the Stanwyck and walked down Broadway. A sudden, mouthwatering aroma of charred steak beckoned her into a steak and clam bar.

The waiter quickly greeted her. "We always have a table for you, Ms. Jamison," he said and she followed him.

Not ten feet into the restaurant, she looked to her left and saw Paul Chandler sitting alone. He glanced up, saw her, and motioned for her to join him, but she smiled politely and followed the waiter to a table. Seated with her back to Paul, she soon felt a hand rest on her shoulder.

"Hello, Marty," he said.

"Hello, Paul."

"Would you like to join us? Liz just excused herself, but I'm sure she'd be surprised to see you at the table."

Marty's ears prickled at his mention of her. "Liz is with you?" Was Paul talking about the same person that had a ton of work but not a few minutes to have a drink? Without an ounce of doubt, yes, she would be surprised. "Thank you, Paul," she said and pushed her chair from the table. "I'd love to join you."

Paul seated her next to Liz's chair and then poured a glass of wine for her. "How've you been? Liz tells me the show has taken a new turn."

She reached for her glass. "Yes," she said, "turns ooze from the woodwork."

"Well, I hope you're more comfortable in your role."

She tipped her glass against her lips and, over the rim, she watched Liz approach the table. If she had blinked, she'd have missed the moment of hesitation in her step. Liz smiled. Marty lowered her glass and smiled mockingly larger.

"Hi," Liz said. "I'd have thought you were home by this time."

"Had you given me thought," Marty muttered. "No, I've been working. When steak beckoned me, Paul was thoughtful enough to invite me to your table." She looked at Paul. "Isn't that right?" He nodded while he repositioned his tie. She looked back at Liz. "Have you completed your work already?"

"I haven't been home yet," she said without a hint of discomfort.

"Liz has been great through all of these things I keep throwing at her. Excuse me for a few minutes."

Paul left his seat and Marty watched him walk away. She sat back in her chair and Liz took her hand. Marty slowly turned her head to see her. Deflated at seeing her with Paul, she said nothing. Liz displayed a look of innocence and smiled.

"I'm happy to see you sitting here."

"You don't want to see me outside of the theater, but you're holding my hand and you're happy I'm at your table." She wondered how Liz's smile appeared genuine. "You lied to me. Is this your concept of waiting for me?"

Liz shook her head. "I didn't lie to you. Paul called and asked me to meet him here. He needed some papers signed and I circled back for this dinner."

"One drink. That's all I asked."

"I had to come. My signature netted me twenty-five thousand dollars a few minutes ago."

"Yes, that's reason to come," Marty said. "A drink with me would have been worth much less."

"Don't put words in my mouth. I expected to go home and work, but signing those papers was important." She closed her eyes, sighed, and opened her eyes again. "I'm digging an early grave."

Marty pushed her chair back. "When you get your important things straightened out with Paul, maybe we can try this again." She shook her head. "I feel like crying and screaming, but none of those will come out. I had the impression that you were warming up to me quickly."

"I've never cooled down. Do you know how I felt when you kissed me today? I had to force myself to stop. I missed you all weekend. Stay, please. Afterward, we'll go to your place and talk."

Marty got up from her chair. Liz still held her hand. "It breaks my heart, but I'll follow your lead. Outside of work, we shouldn't see each other." Marty pulled her hand away and walked from the table.

"Kitten, wait."

She turned a quick about face. "I'm just Marty. Marty Jamison."

"And you own this town, but you don't own me."

Marty turned away and left the restaurant.

CHAPTER FIFTEEN

Weeks had gone by since Marty's initial read-through of the script. Bringing Felice on board had moved their schedule effectively forward. Betty Tomlinson's songs were the only things that kept Marty in control of her emotions. Relating to Liz strictly on a business level agonized her. Evenings were lonely, long, and an immeasurable void remained inside. She filled her free time with Nina and sometimes others. Even Felice showed up at Marty's apartment to pass an evening with theater talk or watch a classic film. Nina and Felice, they weren't Liz.

Clive had scheduled a full preview performance with a limited audience. He invited one hundred members of various schools of acting, including the drama division of Juilliard, and one hundred civilians. Another breach of protocol, the press wasn't invited.

"I want gut reaction, not a clinical study from martini sipping newspaper columnists who don't know comedy from commodes," Clive had told Liz and his cast. "They almost killed *Avenue Q*. Who won Best Musical in 2004?" They didn't need to answer him.

Marty sat alone on the stoop of her apartment. The curtain would go up at three o'clock for the preview. She looked at her watch. It was two. She wrote a note and a possible line change onto her script and then took a Newport from a fresh pack and lit it. She inhaled deeply. Something felt wrong surrounding today's performance. She was on edge and she couldn't zero in on the cause of her anxiety. A taxi pulled up and Nina motioned her over. Marty mashed out her cigarette.

"Let's go, sugar. Bert's gonna be pissed off if you miss his final call."

"It's not a real show, Nina."

"Tell that to Bert." Nina opened the door and slid over.

❖

"What's wrong with you?" Nina asked while she handed Marty her pajama top. "You've been jumpy ever since you got into the cab."

"My stomach's doing flip-flops, and I feel as though I should run out of here and never come back." She put the top on.

"Why are you in such a dither?" Nina asked.

"I don't know." She turned loose with anxious babble-speak. "The show's good, isn't it? The songs are okay? Where's Felice? How's she feeling?" She lit a cigarette. "Did the understudies get here? I wonder how the audience feels. If they're not in a pleasant mood, we're screwed." Marty took another hit. "What time is it? Did Bert say they're ready for us? I didn't hear anything."

Nina took the cigarette from her and dropped it into a mug of old coffee. "You can't smoke in here. Settle down, Marty. This is a preview."

"Where's Liz?"

"She's out front. Clive is welcoming the guests and you have at least fifteen minutes."

A knock came to the door. "It's Bert. Can I come in, Jamison?"

"Yes." Her cell phone rang and she checked caller ID. "Oh shit. It's Rachel."

Bert entered the room. "I'm not holding you to a time frame. Clive is gonna give the audience…" He looked closer at her. "Do you feel okay? You look a little pale."

Marty shoved the phone into Nina's hand and ran into the bathroom. Her stomach instantly emptied what small amount it had taken in earlier. "Damn it," she said and washed her hands and face.

She took a swig of mouthwash, spit into the sink, and returned to the room.

Bert had left, and Nina still held the phone. "I took the call," Nina said. "She's just returned from a religious retreat and you can call her tonight."

Marty laughed sarcastically. "Rachel found God? At least knowing we'll speak tonight gives me time for getting my head together for her." She looked into the mirror. "Will you fix my makeup, please?"

She turned in her chair to face Nina. She didn't have enough time to think about Rachel before Liz walked through the door with Paul and Felice. Marty was thankful her stomach had already exploded. She stared at Liz's hand on his arm.

"Paul wanted the royal tour and then wanted to wish you success." She handed a bottle of champagne to Marty. "This is for a successful preview."

"Champagne gives me a headache," she lied and Liz's shoulders dropped.

"We've had champagne three times together."

Marty's mouth moved, Liz's mouth moved, but Marty was nowhere within the conversation. She kept glancing at Liz's hand holding Paul's arm. The gesture seemed vulgar and inappropriate in her presence. She wanted to toss Liz and Paul out of the room, but at the same time, wanted to fall into her arms for reassurance that the preview would blow the audience's socks off.

Marty finally snapped to attention. "What did you say?" Liz guided her to the daybed. "What are you doing?"

"You're pale. Even with makeup you look like you're about to pass out. Are you okay?"

Nina craned her neck and glanced over Marty's face. "You're right."

"I lost my lunch a few minutes ago. I need something to eat before I go on stage."

Liz felt Marty's pulse. "Your heart is racing. Do you want Paul to have a look at you before you go onstage?"

Marty gave Liz her best "have you lost your mind" expression. "No," she said, brooding.

"Here." Nina handed her a dry bagel and a cup of tea. "Get these into your stomach."

Liz sent Paul back to his seat. Marty chewed on the bagel and her mind struggled with having Liz at her side and thoughts of Rachel. "Please leave, Liz."

"I'm concerned about you."

"We haven't had a civil conversation outside of this show in weeks. Don't placate me."

"Marty—"

"Come on, Liz. Maybe she'll see you later." Nina escorted Liz from the room and closed the door. Marty finished her bagel while Nina diverted her attention. She knew the key words of support. "Your command of an audience…You'll have them on their knees. Use your gimmick. Find a subtle way to bring them to your feet and those two hundred people will buy out future box office today. If act one fails miserably, I'll pull the fire alarm without charge."

A boisterous laugh flew out of Marty. "Yup, you still have confidence in me." She stood, energized with professionalism, and now looked forward to stepping on stage. "Let's go."

Nina walked with her to the wing and then retreated to sit with the audience. Clive stood onstage, in front of the curtain, completing his welcome and history of the show. Felice waited at the wing, anxious to strut for a different public. Marty was pleasantly shocked seeing Felice with dark hair for the first time.

"I don't care if they're a preview audience," Felice said. "This is my day."

Marty smiled at her. "You aren't scared? Nervous?"

"Hell no. That's my name on the marquee, beside the famous Jamison, and that gives me the okay to say I'll knock 'em dead."

Bert approached. "Hey, Felice. Jamison, I'm glad you could make it on time. Get to your marks. Clive's almost finished." Felice headed toward her bed, and when Marty took a step toward the stage, Bert stopped her. "Are you sure you're okay to go on? I can hold them for a few extra minutes. Free admission and wine makes the audience less restless."

"I'm good to go."

"You'll be swell," he said and gave her a wink.

Marty took her position in bed and the curtain rose to begin act one. They weren't just swell. They were great. Reaction spilled on target for each laugh expected, and sarcasm extracted loud groans from the guests. Throughout their performance, Marty was proud of the Jamison-Tate duo. The only question in her mind arose when their songs didn't receive the spirited round of applause that she had anticipated. Some seemed into the music, but most were bored and some looked at their watches.

In the middle of the first act, Marty opened the bottle of Jack Daniel's. She poured a shot and capped the container. She studied the label on the side of the bottle.

"I am a star. It says so right on the bottle. 'Star of excellence.'"

Felice sat, buffing her toenails. *"Did you bother to read the opposite side?"* She looked up at Marty. *"The part that says 'The oldest registered.'"*

Two hundred voices filled the house with laughter. When Marty knocked back the drink, she thanked God the audience approval covered her gasp for breath. Bert had slipped his handy dandy personal bottle of whiskey onto the set. While the burn eased in her throat, she looked with alarm at Felice's wine bottle and then looked at Bert on the wing. He smiled.

Twenty-five minutes later, Felice spritzed her and spoke the final line of the first act.

"I've got you!" She took a long swallow of wine and the curtain came down.

"You nailed it, Felice."

Felice coughed. Her face glowed red and her eyes were the size of spotlights. She choked. "I think that was white lightning. My throat's on fire."

"Clear the stage," Bert said.

❖

Marty and Felice entered her dressing room in such a fine mood that Liz's presence didn't bother her.

Felice flopped onto the chair and Liz talked excitedly. "Clive and I listened to the audience chatter. They approve, and it appears that everything's coming up roses for Jamison and Tate." She brought a rose from behind her back and handed it to Marty. Marty shook her head and walked away.

Marty vigorously brushed her fingers through her hair. "I feel wonderful." She took a cool cloth from Nina and sat on the daybed. "Thanks," she said, and proceeded to cool her face. "I think the second act will go as well, if not better. I almost wish the press were here."

Obviously disappointed that Marty hadn't accepted the rose, Liz placed it on the vanity. "I need to get out front and listen to the buzz." Liz touched Marty's shoulder. "Excellent work, Marty. I'll see you after the final curtain."

"And maybe you won't," Marty said when Liz closed the door.

Nina gave her a bathrobe. "Put that on. It's too cold in here for just pajamas."

"Thanks." Marty slipped into the robe and stretched out on the daybed. "We had fun, didn't we, Felice?"

"Yes, but is Bert trying to kill me?"

Marty laughed. "We'll get him back. I'm happy and I'm singing after all. Theater doesn't get any better than this."

"Right," Nina said, "and you're probably still feeling a tingle where Liz touched your shoulder. Are you two working on your relationship or is it completely over?"

"We're stagnant," Marty said and wouldn't admit that she did feel that tingle. "We work together. Aside from that, I haven't a clue what she's doing."

"She's trying to find her way back to you," Felice said. "Can't you see that? I'm going to my dressing room."

Nina handed Marty a glass of orange juice. "Here, keep your sugar levels up."

She sat up and took a drink of the beverage. Without Liz, nights were often tearful, and it took all her strength not to call her. She wondered if Liz went through the same long hours. A few months or a year from now, maybe they would see another curtain rise for them, but she couldn't imagine a revival in their near future.

"Try to put her out of your mind. The show will keep you busy," Nina said.

Marty perked up instantly. "Act two will be even better than our first. Felice has some great lines." Her cell phone rang. "Can you take that call for me?" She looked over her shoulder when Nina nudged her. Rachel Carr, she read in bold blue letters. Marty's joy deflated.

"Voice mail," she said.

"Do you want me to check the message?"

"Yes. No." Marty thought. "I'll do it later." She took a deep breath. "Nina, I need a few minutes alone."

"I'll make sure Bert calls for you. Are you okay?"

"Yeah. The day's too good to let Rachel bring me down again."

"Don't forget to touch up your face," Nina said and left her alone.

Marty reluctantly retrieved Rachel's message. *"Hello, Marty. It's Rachel again. I won't be home until after eight tonight. Give me a call then. Bye."*

Memories of Rachel in bed with another woman blinked through her mind, but died an early death. She no longer felt the anger that had sent her cheating mate into the street with nothing but a blanket wrapped around her. She knew only the silence of streaking neurons and the splay of overworked dendrites that formed unanswered questions. *Why* did Rachel sleep around? Had Marty completely lost Liz—the possible love of her life? She could only wonder.

"Jamison?" Bert knocked twice. "You have five minutes to get to your position on my stage."

"Thanks, Bert." She wiped her tears with the cloth and then touched up her makeup. "I will not allow thoughts of Rachel Carr and Liz Chandler to screw up our show."

The second act ran smoothly and the audience sounded with regular laughter. In act three, their final song united the characters as a stronger, single woman who wasn't afraid to face the next day. Marty and Felice sat back to back on the mega pillow. Marty held the revolver in her hand.

When they completed their song, they waited for applause to subside. They repositioned themselves, arm against arm, and faced the audience. Marty looked at the gun, and then at Felice. Felice smiled and shook her head. Marty returned a smile and threw the weapon over her shoulder. They joined hands and spoke two lines to each other.

Felice spoke first. *"Tonight isn't curtains for me."*

And then Marty. *"I'm not that lost of a soul."*

In unison, they looked toward the audience and spoke the final line together.

"Tomorrow, it's curtain up."

Marty felt a tight squeeze from Felice's hand when the audience stood with ovation and the curtain fell on the final act.

"Can I let out a yell?" Felice asked.

"Yes," Marty said and they gave a holler. "The show worked." Without letting go of Felice's hand, she pulled her to the apron. "Come on. Let's take a bow."

The house lights were up and Marty saw all two hundred smiling faces. "Go ahead, Felice," she said and waited while Felice took her first nearly official Broadway bow. Eventually, and to uproarious applause, they took a final bow together and returned to the wing.

"They're still clapping," Felice said.

"Want to go back out? Get a little more lovin' from your audience? Go ahead, hon. They're calling your name."

Felice bubbled. "I can't believe this. Those two hundred are louder than a full audience for my past shows."

From the stage, Clive motioned. "Come on out." He smiled. "They want both of you. Marty, would you say a few words to them?"

They stepped out together. Before the audience quieted, Marty reached under the curtain and pulled out Nina's pillow. She placed it in front of them. When the house grew silent, she spoke.

"Thank you for attending our preview. This production has been through hell, before we managed to bring it together. It wasn't too long ago that I sat on that pillow"—she pointed toward the cushion—"three sheets to the wind and madder than hell." The audience laughed. She pointed at Felice. "Wasn't she great?" When their applause and yells of "yes" subsided, Marty took a step back. "Felice?"

Felice looked into the small audience. Though she was flawless with her performance, now she shook. Marty nudged her and she produced a crooked smile. "Good-bye," she finally said, but a quick exuberance took over and Felice rushed more words. "Tell everyone you know to come and see us."

Following their ego boost, Nina met them on the wing and gave them their robes. "The photographers are waiting outside for the photo shoot."

"Excellent," Felice said as they made their way through the hall.

"I told you there'd be time," Marty said.

Outside, a hydraulic lift and platform awaited them. Shimmering black velvet covered the floor. Several photographers waited, some from the newspapers that Clive refused to invite to their initial preview.

"I promise a full show to the press in a few days," Clive said as Marty and Felice stepped onto the platform. "Let's just get some fabulous shots of our actors."

An operator raised the platform to meet the marquee. When Marty and Felice threw their robes to Nina, the onlookers, press, and photographers echoed wolf whistles and catcalls.

"Eat your hearts out, boys and girls," Marty said and flashed a wide smile.

With the show title behind them, they primped and posed, laughed, and wiggled for the photographers. They held their tumbler and wine glass together in toast and then stood back-to-back. At Felice's suggestion, they stood face-to-face and exaggerated the pose of angry boxers ready for a showdown.

"This is fun," Felice said.

A sharp glint of light, unlike that of a camera flash, struck the corner of Marty's eye. She turned toward the crowd and looked into the group of press and onlookers. The light flashed again and nearly blinded her. A watch, strapped to a buxom brunette's wrist, sparkled a third time. She felt her blood drain. She leaned against the marquee when she focused on the woman's face. Rachel.

"Shit. This can't happen now." Stomach acid simmered degrees from a hard boil.

"Something wrong?" Felice asked.

"I'm afraid of heights." She motioned to Clive. "Let's wrap this up." She looked for Liz and found her talking to a staff writer of *Playbill*. Liz's back was turned away.

Marty looked back at Rachel. Rachel smiled but received no acknowledgement. There was no lingering attraction for Rachel, but Marty's gut screamed that it hadn't forgotten the anger at all. While the platform lowered to the ground, her stomach cranked up another notch. Rachel zoomed closer with each increment of the descending crane. Clive thanked the photographers and then helped Marty and Felice step down.

"Great pictures," Clive said to them.

Marty grabbed her robe and rushed to cover herself. While she walked over to Rachel, bitterness rose from her toenails to the top of her sternum, but stopped there. Had her emotions gone further, she would have verbally assaulted Rachel, and the press would have had a field day. She knew her place as she stood eye to eye with her.

"Hello," Rachel said. "I heard you were down here. I can't believe you're working with Tate. You can't possibly be that desperate for press."

"Felice knows her stuff, and you'll regret never having signed her." She pulled her robe tightly around her. "How was your religious retreat? Did you work your way into any new habits?"

"Are you kidding? All of those nuns and me? I was in hog heaven."

"How fitting that you equate yourself to a pig. I'll call you tonight."

"I can't imagine why. We haven't spoken in two years."

Marty looked over at Liz and the gap between them. She looked back at Rachel. "I'm working, and this isn't the appropriate place for our conversation. Tell me now if you won't be home tonight."

Rachel pulled off her sunglasses and tapped them against her lips. She looked toward Liz and returned her eyes to Marty. "I'll be there. You look wonderful. You must be in love."

The comment wasn't worth a thank you. "You look tired." Marty turned away and walked through the entrance to the theater.

"Marty," Clive called to her, "Liz and I need a meeting with the cast and understudies. We'll meet on stage in five minutes."

She wandered down the hall, onto the stage, and then stretched out on the big pillow and waited for the other production members to arrive. Talking with Rachel wasn't overly gruesome, and she relaxed until Clive arrived.

"Okay," Clive said through the shuffle of footsteps. "I have some good news and some bad news. First of all, our cast did a bang-up job today, but the first thing we need to do is make a few changes to dialogue."

Marty sat up and ignored Clive's speech. She looked over at Liz and smiled internally. Seeing her, sensing the delicate blend of her perfume, remembering her soft breaths while she slept, and her tears of joy and unhappiness, she wanted all of those things back. Liz had been the object of her promise of care, but Marty miserably failed the test. Each time Liz had to leave, Marty weakened.

When Liz surrounded her, as she did that moment, she felt peaceful. Her eyes followed the course of curves that became Liz's ear. She was worth an aggravating conversation with Rachel, if that talk might help their relationship. Not walking over to her and kissing Liz took all of Marty's strength.

When she noticed that Liz's eyes were on her, the emotional gravity pulled her closer. Did Liz miss her at all? Her eyes said yes. Marty broke away from her thoughts when Clive asked her a question. "What was that, Clive?"

"We're waiting for your reaction," he said, as Felice exited the stage.

"Oh. Sure, whatever you think is best." It seemed a harmless response and she could ask Felice about his comment later, but the air had gone dead around her. "Did I miss something important?"

"A biggie, Marty. I'm cutting the songs from the show."

When his announcement sunk in, her eyes widened. "Why? They're the best work Betty's done." She got up from the pillow.

He sighed. "You weren't listening. The audience consensus is that the songs are good, but they take away from the impact of the characters sparring. They wanted the music to end and hear more dialogue. Betty's songs have some great dialogue that Liz will work into the show."

Marty paced a slow distance from the pillow and back again. Her bad vibes returned and she saw herself in that bedroom with Rachel. Rachel's influence irritated her memory, and Marty's self-doubt had again surfaced with Clive's statement.

"You've got to be kidding me," Marty said. "Singing is what I do best."

"That's crap. You're a terrific actor and a better dramatic actor than you give yourself credit for. The songs are fine, but you and Felice can carry this show without a lot of pageantry. We'll come off stronger as a dramatic comedy."

She stopped pacing. She turned so abruptly that her hair swished around her shoulders. "Pageantry is my style, Clive. I give it to them big, loud, and sometimes belting a song that makes them weep for days."

"Not this time. Sorry." He sat back against his chair. "Sometimes you have to take a stage right exit."

"And you're making this decision on the comments of a small audience?"

"It's not like they were a roomful of dumb blondes." He looked over at Felice. "I mean no disrespect."

A roomful of blondes. Didn't anyone tell Clive it took only one blonde, attached to Rachel's face, to fuck up my life? She looked at Liz. "And what does Madame Producer say?"

"I'm inclined to agree with Clive."

Marty fumed. "You're inclined to agree? Is that your way of saying you haven't a clue what a seasoned producer might think?"

Liz backed away from her. "I beg your pardon?"

Clive stood. "Settle down, Marty."

She tried his patience. "I will not settle down. I could have walked out of this production weeks ago, but Betty's music kept me here."

Clive stood, shaking his head. "No more. Pampering you stops now." He motioned toward the aisle. "Walk. You'd be stupid to leave, but don't let us stop you. This is theater. Things change quickly and you know that. The songs are cut, and if you can't accept that, the door's yours." He headed toward the wing. "Everyone else, let's regroup tomorrow at nine."

She glared at Liz. "Where's Felice? She should be here for this discussion."

"Felice knows, and it's not open for discussion. Don't take Clive's decision personally. It's a business decision."

Rachel had told her not to take it personally, but she did, and she took Clive's music decision the same way. "My audience wants to hear a soundtrack."

Liz shrugged. "Then they'll have to see *Wicked* or *West Side Story* or some other show. You and Felice kicked ass on stage. Don't you see that? They're just songs."

Marty folded her arms. No, she couldn't focus on the need of the show or on Clive's directive. She focused on her final minutes with Rachel.

"It's nothing personal," Rachel said without emotion. "It's just sex."

Marty pointed to the bedroom door. "Get out of here." Rachel reached for her clothes. "Get out now."

"Let me get dressed."

Marty stormed toward Rachel and shouted again. "Now!" She grabbed a music box from the dresser and threw it at her. Marty just missed clocking her. Rachel dove across the bed to avoid a bottle of perfume to her head. She grabbed a blanket and wrapped it around her. "Are you still here?" Marty side-armed another bottle of perfume. It exploded against the doorway. Without a scratch, Rachel fled the apartment and Marty never saw her again.

Marty sat on the pillow and stared at the base of the proscenium arch. Everything had fallen apart: her relationship with Liz, the songs, and her self-respect. Everything she needed was suddenly unavailable.

"I feel as though someone has torn every bone out of my body."

"Marty," Liz said and moved quickly to her. "Come on. It's just a few songs."

"No, it's much more than a few songs. This is about my need to back away and figure out what the hell has happened to me."

Felice entered the stage. "Liz, your taxi's here."

"Your taxi?"

Liz hesitated. "I'm flying to Aspen tonight. Another real estate sale."

"What about the show? You have a responsibility here."

"You're right. I'll cancel and reschedule after the show is established. I'll be here for you, now."

"Just go." She looked away from Liz. "Do whatever you have to do."

Liz leaned over and softly kissed her cheek. "We'll talk soon." She made a quick exit.

"Soon," Marty muttered. "Soon after Aspen? Tonight? Maybe we shouldn't talk at all." Marty looked over at Felice. Felice's eyes bore into her. "What?"

"Jamison hits jackass mode again. Liz brought champagne for you and you told her it gives you a headache. I saw the hurt in her eyes. I mean really, Marty. I've seen you drink champagne in your dressing room with her."

"So?"

"You were intentionally discourteous. Then she tried with a rose and you snubbed her again. Don't you understand she wants the two of you to make things right?" Felice pointed to Marty's side of the set. "That'll be you, if you don't straighten up your act. Alone, bitter, and beige."

Marty turned her head toward the set behind her, but stopped half way. She looked back at Felice. "You have a lot of nerve."

"I've taunted you, but I've also had respect for you and the esteem your name holds. That respect disappeared today. Is playing jackass your new act? You're rude. Fix it."

"Don't even think you can talk to me in that tone."

"Someone has to tell you. Clive will, if you dare go into his office." Felice laughed a little. "So you're stuck with Tater tot. Knock it off." She turned and walked down the stage steps. "Good night. If I don't see you here tomorrow, you're a fool."

Alone on stage, Marty paced. "Intentionally discourteous. You're rude. Pampering you stops now. The songs are cut." She shouted to an audience of none. "They're just songs, Marty." She crossed the stage and leaned against the arch. "Just songs," she repeated softly and scanned the darkness of the hollow auditorium that became her. "You're rude. Fix it!" She waited for her echo to disappear and then shouted a final time. "Anyone else care to take a swing at me?" Quick clapping sounded from the back of the mezzanine and strengthened as a shadowed figure approached the stage from her left.

"*Brava!*" Rachel shouted. "Remind me to leave a few bucks at the box office for that performance. Having a bad day, Martina?"

"Fuck you, Rachel."

"Now that's a warm welcome."

"How did you get beyond security?"

"I walked through the door, like everyone else. Security knows me." She stopped walking when she reached the center edge of the apron.

"Lucky me. Go home. I'll call you later."

Rachel smiled and reached for a footlight. "Allow me to recap. Your director offered to replace you." She gave a quick turn to the light and it flicked off. "Your girlfriend is off to Colorado with Paul." She darkened a second light. "Your costar thinks you're a jackass, and I can attest to that observation." She twisted off the third light.

"I'm not going to listen to this. You have—"

"You better listen because you need to hear this." She looked back at the footlights. "What else? Ah! I missed this one: The songbird was reduced to a dramatic comedian." She twisted off a fourth light. "Now for the final light. What's happened to our lovely queen?" She turned the fifth light until it flickered continually. "Have you lost your luminous star quality?" Rachel tapped the sensitive light and it darkened. "Poof." She grinned.

Marty looked up from the darkened row of lights. "Everything onstage is larger than life. Things aren't that bad."

"Is that so? I'm thinking differently. Otherwise you wouldn't call me." She walked up the steps and stood beside Marty. "I'm curious. What do you want from me?"

Uncomfortable under Rachel's gaze, Marty moved to the armoire. She tightened her bathrobe.

"Oh, don't worry, Miss Jamison. I have no interest in your precious body."

"If anyone is aware of your disinterest, it's me." With her back to Rachel, she found the nerve to ask the ultimate question. "Why did you do that to me?"

"Why did I do what?"

Marty swung around and wanted to smack the smile from Rachel's face. "Don't play stupid. Why did you take that woman into our bed?"

"That was two years ago. My little tryst still haunts you?" She walked to the vanity and stopped.

"Just answer the question."

Rachel slowly ran her finger over the top of the dressing table. "Because she was there and I wanted her."

"We were in a relationship. Did I mean nothing to you?"

She laughed. "I loved you. I wanted to give every damn drop of my intellect and emotion to you, but I wasted my time. My love was unrequited."

Marty's eyes widened with anger. "What? I loved you. I took you everywhere with me. All the awards dinners, my guest appearances, I even took you to the White House."

"Our photos were all over the newspapers, all over the world, for the endless procession of your events."

"Oh, please. Don't tell me you didn't enjoy rubbing elbows with—"

"I did enjoy those things at first, but it took me a long time to understand that you were all about Marty Jamison and the show, and then the next show. I was never a priority with you."

Marty glared at her. "That's not true. I had you with me because—"

Rachel stepped closer. "Like it or not, I was an obedient puppy that you didn't want. You took me out for walks in public, but when you took me home, life still wasn't about us. You were too tired to talk with me, but you had the energy to plan your outfit for dinner the next night."

"You never complained," Marty shot back. "You didn't complain when Paris welcomed us."

"Parisians welcomed Marty Jamison. You dumped me onto the perimeter while you mesmerized everyone with a stroll through the Champs-Elysées or stuffed your face with vichyssoise."

"I never touched vichyssoise."

"Or me."

"How can you say that? I introduced you as my girlfriend." She followed Rachel to Felice's side of the stage. "The President of Goddamn France knew you were my lover. Of course I touched you."

"Sometimes you'd remember and squeeze me in between engagements. Let's talk about one of those times. Do you remember the third night in Paris?"

"Do you honestly expect me to remember a particular night three years ago?"

"Try, Marty. Humor me this one time."

If thinking about that night would get Rachel out of the Stanwyck a minute sooner, Marty would relent. She sat at the edge of Felice's bed. Try as she might, she couldn't remember that night. She looked up at Rachel with the hope that her face would dislodge a reminder of that evening.

"You see?" Rachel said. "I'll remind you. For the first time in months, you said all the right things and touched me in all the right places. You were *très affectueux,* and I was so…damn…forgiving."

"Then we did make love."

Rachel shook her head. "Not quite. You killed the mood when you laughed."

"I laughed?"

"You were kissing me and suddenly stopped to laugh. Do you remember your reason for laughing?"

Marty looked out to the house and thought hard. "Something about a reporter?"

"You cheerfully said to me 'Did you hear that photographer tell me he'd shoot his wife for me?' We were making love, Marty, and you were thinking about a fucking photographer. Do you know how much you hurt me?"

"Oh damn. I remember now." She lowered her gaze to the floor. Had she been that cold? She pushed herself from the bed and walked to Rachel's side. "We should have talked about it."

Rachel walked away and sat at Felice's vanity. Her anger turned softer. "Talk. Yeah, we should have." She looked up at Marty with a smile that wasn't one of happiness, but one of hurt. "When we were about to talk, your manager called and he topped your priority list for an hour."

"You fell asleep. I turned out the light and—"

"I wasn't sleeping. I was crying. In three years with you, I never made it to your priority list."

"Why didn't you insist we talk about your feelings? I never meant to hurt you." She pulled her chair next to Rachel.

"You always put me off for a meeting or a photo shoot, whatever became the flavor of the day for your career. You blew this city away when you took over the lead in *Bourbon Street*. The world suddenly wanted Marty Jamison at their dinner tables, but you never had the time to fold a napkin for ours."

She couldn't dispute Rachel's charges. Caught in the glitz of limelight, she'd given fame full control. "You had affairs after France. I was always suspicious but never knew for sure."

Rachel nodded. "I decided I'd take advantage of all of those wives and friends you introduced to me. I set aside my emotional needs, but I craved physical attention. Those women were my playmates."

"I can't blame you. I neglected you." She ran her hand over Rachel's shoulder. "You're right. Everything was about me."

"A small part of me still believed you would come around. I convinced myself that the next day would be my day. Always the next day, but that day never came."

It pained Marty when tears streamed down Rachel's cheeks. "Oh, Rachel. Why did you put up with me?"

She wiped her eyes with her hand. "To answer your initial question further, I wanted you to catch me with that woman so you would throw me out of your life. I knew you wouldn't come looking for me."

"Why didn't you just leave?"

"I couldn't leave on my own. I was *afraid* you wouldn't look for me."

"Oh, God." Liz's words came back to her. *I'm afraid you'd never find me again.* "I'm so sorry for what I've done to you. I've wanted to slap you silly, but you're the one who should take that swing at me."

"No. I'm sorry for the way I ended us. I can't imagine how you felt, but I wasn't proud. I was in pieces." She took a breath. "Maybe we can find it in ourselves to forgive each other? We don't ever have to see each other again."

Marty put her arms around her. "I wish you had handled me differently, but now I understand your action. I'm sorry, Rachel. You deserved better than what I gave you."

Rachel pulled back and looked directly into her eyes. "Yes, I did deserve better, but so did you. I'm sorry, too. What a pathetic pair we were." Rachel gave her an awkward hug. "I wasn't on a religious retreat, you know."

"No nuns, huh?" She asked with a smile. "That's a relief."

"I was in Hyannis, with my girlfriend."

"You're happy with her?"

"Yeah. She's not in the business and we've been together for almost a year." She stood and took Marty's hand. "Come on. We need to fix your lights."

They walked to the darkened footlights. Marty knelt, assuming they would twist the lights on, but Rachel stopped her when she reached for the first bulb.

"No. That's not how you'll get the lights back on." Rachel sat on the floor and pulled Marty down beside her. She pointed to the first light. "Tell me why Clive offered you the door."

"I…I've been bossy. I've insisted things go my way." She felt like a heel.

"Uh-huh. It's still all about Marty Jamison. You need to learn that that's not true. Joyce told you everything was about the show. Did you ever stop to think that your private life was the biggest part of the show?"

"I took Joyce too literally. She always had time for her husband and daughters and grandchildren."

Rachel nodded. "I'll give you this light. I think you have sense enough not to walk, but to let Clive run the show."

"Gee, thanks." She watched as Rachel turned the light on.

"Moving on to the second light…oh, wait. That light was Liz. Let's come back to her." Rachel pointed to the third light. "Ah, yes. Felice Tate called you a jackass and said you'd wind up like your character: alone, bitter, and beige." Rachel turned the light on. "I'm giving you this one because I think it's great she told you like it was, and I also think this light has something to do with Liz's light."

"To which we'll return."

Rachel smiled. "Exactly."

"Do we have to do all of these? I feel badly enough."

"We're almost done. The next light is the songbird that's lost her voice." Rachel shook her head. "Again, and with more precision, the show is not all about you." She turned the singer's light on without waiting for a response. "The fifth light, our queen. We'll do her light last." Rachel pointed back to Liz's light. "Tell me about her. What does she mean to you, and who is Paul?"

Marty tearfully told her story from the beginning. When she finished, Rachel was quiet. "Felice is right. I'm a jackass."

"Yes, you are, but part of your problem stems from me and the big lie. If I had been more honest with you, you might not feel afraid of Liz. I'm an equal jackass."

Marty removed Liz's light and held it in both hands. "She's never given me reason to feel insecure, other than the night of her dinner with Paul. When I think back, she was probably telling me the truth."

"How do you feel about her?"

Marty flinched when butterflies invaded her tummy and her flesh danced happily. "I love her."

Rachel took the light from Marty and turned it into the socket. "That light stays dark for now. Liz told you she's waiting for you. What will you do about that?"

"I don't deserve her."

"She thinks you do. Don't let our bungling interfere with your relationship. Your life with Liz is the show that matters."

"I'll try talking to her when she returns from Aspen. Maybe I haven't destroyed everything."

"Maybe you haven't." Rachel looked at the darkened Queen Marty light. "What becomes of that one?"

Marty turned the light until it shined. "I have some work to do, but I'll get it back before I do any permanent damage." She looked back at Rachel. "I lied to you. You don't look tired. You look great."

"Thanks." Rachel stood. "You'll be fine. Things don't seem beyond repair, and I have to leave now." When Marty stood to walk her to the entrance, Rachel stopped her. "I know the way out." She proceeded down the steps and up the aisle. "You stay here and think about Liz's light. Good-bye, Marty."

"Good-bye, Rachel." She watched her leave and knew they'd never see each other again, unless accidentally, and that settled well with her. Their show had closed.

Marty faced the dark house that swallowed her. "Jonah and the whale." She walked back to the armoire. She picked up the prop gun from the floor, faced the empty auditorium, and pointed the gun to her head. "Bang." She threw herself backward and onto the bed. "I don't need another bullet." She stared at the catwalk. "I need lessons in respect and then groveling." Light footsteps followed her words. Expecting Bert to tell her to clear his stage, she sat up. "Liz," she said after a lost heartbeat. Liz stood near the darkened footlight.

"That whale saved Jonah," she said and then pointed to the dark footlight. "Looks like you need a replacement."

"No. I need to find out if it's beyond repair. I thought you were on your way to Aspen."

"I told you I'd be here for you. I meant it. Come talk with me." They settled in front of the darkened light. "Clive and I had a brief meeting. Then I stopped by your dressing room and Nina said I might find you here." She looked around the stage. "We've come full circle."

Heavy hearted, she took Liz's hands into hers. Marty's eyes blurred from tears, but she looked into Liz's eyes. "I've missed you and I've mistreated you. Will you forgive me?"

"Time and I are old pals. I'm still here." She brushed away Marty's tears.

"If you knew how wonderful that sounds." Marty pulled Liz into her arms. She felt peaceful but still regretful for any hurt she'd caused.

"I'm the one who cries at night when you aren't there. We've talked about falling in love haven't we? We can't do that unless both of us are present."

"I cry, too," Marty said and tightened her embrace. "I talked to Rachel just now." She felt Liz stiffen.

Liz pulled away and cleared her throat. "I…about Rachel. Since we're here, I have another confession." Her expression was full of concern and fear, just as it had been their first night on stage together.

"I'm easy to talk to."

"I invaded your privacy."

"How?"

"I came backstage to find you. When I heard you and Rachel talking, I stood in the wing and listened."

"You heard everything?"

"At least from vichyssoise onward."

"Great." Marty shook her head and stared at the dark light. "For you, that clarifies my ignorance of people."

"I apologize for listening, but I'm not sorry. I needed to hear what she had to say as much as you needed to listen."

Marty suddenly looked up at her. "Then you heard me say—" Liz's smile and nod stopped her.

"I love you," Liz said.

Marty knew what to do. She knew to tell Liz she loved her. She knew to hold her so closely that it would take that bitch of a glacier to separate them. She also knew she'd wanted so badly to hear those words that she'd never prepared herself for the moment Liz might actually say them, and there they were, larger than the theater around them and small enough to burrow deep into Marty's heart. Liz reached over and turned her light until it brightened. She looked back at Marty.

"Is there something you want to say to me, Ms. Jamison?"

"Yes." Marty took Liz into her arms. When their lips met, Marty's body turned giddy in full thank you. Every inch of her returned to life. She kissed Liz gently first, and then as though they'd never been apart. "I love you. You've had faith in me when you should have walked away."

"I want to be with you. I know you aren't a monster, but felt you needed a little education. I'm glad Rachel appeared here today." She rested her head on Marty's shoulder. "We'll work beyond what's happened."

"The irony is that I remember thinking you'd have a warehouse of baggage."

"If you learn to trust your intuition again, we'll be fine."

"Trust myself?"

"From the moment I kissed you in your dressing room, you were determined to find out what I was all about. I tried forgetting our encounter, but I couldn't. The day I pried the apple from your mouth—well, I needn't go further."

"When you told me you were straight, I wanted to bust a gut laughing. What changed your mind? Why did you come over that day?"

"Honestly?" Liz laughed. "Hormones and twenty years of lusting for you walked me to your door. You were smart, keeping me on my toes at my apartment. When we talked on this stage that night, I loved hearing your tale of what this theater means to you. I adored your passion for the Stanwyck. Then I wanted to know you and not just your body."

Marty listened, but her head swam from the scent of Liz's delicate perfume. She was quietly intoxicated. "Paul's kiss wreaked havoc on my brain. I need to de-program." She touched Liz's cheek. "Do you still want me?"

Liz smiled broadly. "I want my kitten home with me tonight, and we'll talk until daylight if we have to."

"I'm sorry about the champagne and rose."

"You damn well better be." Liz pulled Marty up from the floor. "Let's go and get them."

Considering all things, Marty's day on 44th Street turned out the best ever.

Chapter Sixteen

M arty extended several apologies within the cast and production team, and added a promise that the Diva Jamison was no longer a part of the show.

Five days after their initial preview, *I've Got You!* played favorably to Clive's martini-drinking theater critics. Clive invited all of them to Sardi's afterward, where he personally mixed their cocktails. Preliminary reviews were favorable.

Liz applied some brush strokes to selected dialogue and, several previews later, their show opened to the public to an almost full house. Marty and Felice had such fun sharing the stage that Marty never missed the songs Clive had cut. Reviews were flattering, touting the duo of Jamison and Tate as surprisingly palatable.

One month after their opening, Marty and Liz shared a hot bath. Liz read her favorite review.

"'No respectable audience or management team ever dreamed the duo of Jamison and Tate lurked on the horizon. Chances are Jamison and Tate never dreamed of the moment. Given the tenure of her Broadway mystique, Jamison audaciously shucks her dramatic skin and slips easily into a relaxed style of dramatic comedy. Tate, known for her flare of publicly ribbing the Grande Dame of Broadway, was ever on the heels of Jamison's self-deprecation and gun slinging. With perfect timing, sharp retort, and comedic skill, Tate foils Jamison's nightlong flirtation with suicide.'"

"Imagine that," Liz said. "I'm in a bathtub with the Grande Dame of theater."

"And don't you forget it," Marty whispered into Liz's ear. She pushed her hair away from her neck and nibbled Liz's soft shoulder.

Liz set the review on the floor and splashed warm water and bubbles over her breasts. She turned her head toward Marty. "You're happy, kitten. Your talk with Rachel has done wonders for us."

"I'm deliriously happy." Her biting segued into kisses.

Liz moaned and then leaned against Marty again. "You spent two hundred dollars on an antique brass box today. What will you do with it?"

"I thought I'd polish it and place it right there." She blindly pointed to the vanity and never missed a beat with her nibbling lips. "It's perfect for Q-tips."

"A girl can never have too many Q-tips. You know, of course, I might ask you to marry me one day."

"Maybe I'll ask you first." Marty reached between Liz's arms and cupped her breasts. She moved on to shoulder kisses, in between her words. "Maybe I was thinking ahead with the brass box." She turned in Marty's arms. She glowed and her words came softly.

"One day we might get hitched. I know how you are with timelines." She warded off a poke in her ribs. "Marty?"

"Yes?"

"I need a lot of years to show you how much I care for you."

Marty wondered again if Liz saw rockets fire and heard champagne corks pop. Her heart fluttered and burst into shimmering pieces again. Marty drew Liz closer. "Let's make love until the sun comes up."

"I'm sorry, kitten. I'd love loving the night away with you, but I can't chance missing the video conference with my associates. I like producing. I like the greater scale than just writing."

"You're a natural for the job. You still don't know what show they want to do?"

"I'm clueless, but I'll find out in a few minutes. They've promised something big." She snuggled against Marty's shoulders. Liz looked up at Marty. "Kiss me."

With all the love in her heart, Marty kissed her.

❖

Liz powered up her computer. "Come and watch, kitten. Maybe you'll find the meeting interesting."

Marty pulled up a chair and watched Liz insert a DVD. For a conference? She was even more puzzled when Liz and Felice appeared on the monitor and stood on the stage of The Stanwyck.

"What is this?"

"Shh. Just watch."

Felice paced in front of the brightly lit stage curtain and she babbled. *"I don't think she'll do it. Not with me. Maybe with knocked-up Allison. God, I think I hate Marty for not wanting me there. Why does she have to be so damn fussy? I'm a good actress. I think you should make her play the ass end of Caroline the cow."*

Marty laughed.

"She'll play Rose," Liz said. *"It's her life dream. Marty would dump me in a minute for the chance."* She walked to the end of stage left and manually raised the curtain. Larger than half the size of the stage, a sign lowered. Its lights flickered and then fully brightened.

Marty read aloud. "Marty Jamison and Felice Tate." The names disappeared and, in lights larger than she'd ever seen on a marquee, the show title flashed. *"Gypsy."* Marty looked over at Liz. "If this is a joke, it's not funny. What does this mean?"

"You'll have a contract in your hand tonight, if you'll do the show. When *I've Got You* finishes its run, we'll begin production for *Gypsy.*"

Marty stared at the illuminated title. *Gypsy.* That wasn't work. *Gypsy* was her *piece de resistance* of musical theater, and she'd almost take the role without pay. Move over, Midler. Step aside, Tyne. Clear the stage Ethel, Bernadette, Patti, and those who appeared between them. Marty Jamison was born to play Mama Rose.

The camera operator zoomed in on Felice. She put her hands on her hips and looked directly into the lens. *"Well, hot shot? Do you think you're still woman enough to work with this Broadway actress?"* The lens panned back to the show title. Liz let the title flash on her monitor.

Marty glared at Liz. "Absolutely not. This is not proper protocol for signing Marty Jamison to a work contract." After a moment of letting Liz feel the disappointment, she embraced her. "Gotcha back. Yes! Of course I'll do the show. I'm not crazy."

They celebrated with a pint of Ben and Jerry's Cherry Garcia ice cream.

"Am I playing Rose?" Marty teased and dipped her spoon into the ice cream carton.

"Would you prefer playing the ass end of Caroline, as Felice suggested?"

"My purr is much more interesting than my moo. And I'll have a talk with Bert about Felice." Marty kissed her full on the mouth and then took the mouthful of Garcia that Liz offered her. "Can I safely assume you don't actually have a video conference?"

"You may safely assume I have no meeting."

"And that means we can make love until the sun comes up?" Marty leaned toward Liz and licked at a drop of ice cream that had melted at the corner of her lips.

"That's what it means, kitten. I have to keep the Grande Dame of Broadway happy, after all, and that same Grande Dame had better pull out all the stops tonight if she wants that contract."

"I'll break a leg." She dropped her spoon into the now empty carton and turned Liz toward her. "I'm happy. Thank you for *Gypsy*, and I would never choose any show over you."

"Good, and I expect you to thank me all night long," Liz said and threw her arms around Marty. "I do love you."

Marty's heart burst again and beat in time to the flashing show title on the monitor. "I love you, too." She held Liz tighter.

Life was damn sweet.

About the Author

Bobbi Marolt was born in Pennsylvania and upon graduation from high school enlisted in the United States Army, where she specialized in telecommunications. After an honorable discharge and two and a half years in Texas, she ambled into Connecticut "to go to school." That stunt landed her between New York State and Connecticut for the next several years, jammed into quality assurance positions in various types of manufacturing. After a brief move to Las Vegas, she again resides in New England. Somewhere in the midst of these journeys, she published the romance *Coming Attractions*, from Rising Tides Press. Her interests include films and classical music.

Books Available from Bold Strokes Books

Blood Hunt by L.L. Raand. In the second Midnight Hunters Novel, Detective Jody Gates, heir to a powerful Vampire clan, forges an uneasy alliance with Sylvan, the wolf Were Alpha, to battle a shadow army of humans and rogue Weres, while fighting her growing hunger for a human reporter, Becca Land. (978-1-60282-505-5)

Loving Liz by Bobbi Marolt. When theater actor Marty Jamison turns diva and Liz Chandler walks out on her, Marty must confront a cheating lover from the past to understand why life is crumbling around her. (978-1-60282-210-8)

Kiss the Rain by Larkin Rose. How will successful fashion designer Eve Harris react when she discovers the new woman in her life, Jodi, and her secret fantasy phone date, Lexi, are one and the same? (978-1-60282-211-5)

Sarah, Son of God by Justine Saracen. In a story within a story within a story, a transgendered beauty takes us through Stonewall-rioting New York, Venice under the Inquisition, and Nero's Rome. (978-1-60282-212-2)

Sleeping Angel by Greg Herren. Eric Matthews survives a terrible car accident only to find out everyone in town thinks he's a murderer—and he has to clear his name even though he has no memories of what happened. (978-1-60282-214-6)

Dying to Live by Kim Baldwin & Xenia Alexiou. British socialite Zoe Anderson-Howe's pampered life is abruptly shattered when she's taken hostage by FARC guerrillas while on a business trip to Bogota and Elite Operative Fletch must rescue her to complete her own harrowing mission. (978-1-60282-200-9)

Indigo Moon by Gill McKnight. Hope Glassy and Godfrey Meyers are on a mercy mission to save their friend Isabelle after she is attacked by a rogue werewolf, but does Isabelle want to be saved from the sexy wolf who claimed her as a mate? (978-1-60282-201-6)

Parties in Congress by Colette Moody. Bijal Rao, Indian-American moderate Independent, gets the break of her career when she's hired to work on the congressional campaign of Janet Denton—until she meets the remarkably attractive and charismatic opponent, Colleen O'Bannon. (978-1-60282-202-3)

Black Fire: Gay African-American Erotica edited by Shane Allison. Best-selling African-American gay erotic authors create the stories of sex and desire modern readers crave. (978-1-60282-206-1)

The Collectors by Leslie Gowan. Laura owns what might be the world's most extensive collection of BDSM lesbian erotica, but that's as close as she's gotten to the world of her fantasies. Until, that is, her friend Adele introduces her to Adele's mistress Jeanne—art collector, heiress, and experienced dominant. With Jeanne's first command, Laura's life changes forever. (978-1-60282-208-5)

Breathless, edited by Radclyffe and Stacia Seaman. Bold Strokes Books romance authors give readers a glimpse into the lives of favorite couples celebrating special moments "after the honeymoon ends." Enjoy a new look at lesbians in love or revisit favorite characters from some of BSB's best-selling romances. (978-1-60282-207-8)

Breaker's Passion by Julie Cannon. Leaving a trail of broken hearts scattered across the Hawaiian Islands, surf instructor Colby Taylor is running full speed away from her selfish actions years earlier until she collides with Elizabeth Collins, a stuffy, judgmental college professor who changes everything. (978-1-60282-196-5)

Justifiable Risk by V.K. Powell. Work is the only thing that interests homicide detective Greer Ellis until internationally renowned journalist Eva Saldana comes to town looking for answers in her brother's death—then attraction threatens to override duty. (978-1-60282-197-2)

Nothing But the Truth by Carsen Taite. Sparks fly when two top-notch attorneys battle each other in the high-risk arena of the courtroom, but when a strange turn of events turns one of them from advocate to witness, prosecutor Ryan Foster and defense attorney Brett Logan join forces in their search for the truth. (978-1-60282-198-9)

Maye's Request by Clifford Henderson. When Brianna Bell promises her ailing mother she'll heal the rift between her "other two" parents, she discovers how little she knows about those closest to her and the impact family has on the fabric of our lives. (978-1-60282-199-6)

Chasing Love by Ronica Black. Adrian Edwards is looking for love—at girl bars, shady chat rooms, and women's sporting events—but love remains elusive until she looks closer to home. (978-1-60282-192-7)

Rum Spring by Yolanda Wallace. Rebecca Lapp is a devout follower of her Amish faith and a firm believer in the Ordnung, the set of rules that govern her life in the tiny Pennsylvania town she calls home. When she falls in love with a young "English" woman, however, the rules go out the window. (978-1-60282-193-4)

Indelible by Jove Belle. A single mother committed to shielding her son from the parade of transient relationships she endured as a child tries to resist the allure of a tattoo artist who already has a sometimes girlfriend. (978-1-60282-194-1)

The Straight Shooter by Paul Faraday. With the help of his good pals Beso Tangelo and Jorge Ramirez, Nate Dainty tackles the Case of the Missing Porn Star, none other than his latest heartthrob—Myles Long! (978-1-60282-195-8)

Head Trip by D.L. Line. Shelby Hutchinson, a young computer professional, can't wait to take a virtual trip. She soon learns that chasing spies through Cold War Europe might be a great adventure, but nothing is ever as easy as it seems—especially love. (978-1-60282-187-3)

Desire by Starlight by Radclyffe. The only thing that might possibly save romance author Jenna Hardy from dying of boredom during a summer of forced R&R is a dalliance with Gardner Davis, the local vet—even if Gard is as unimpressed with Jenna's charms as she appears to be with Jenna's fame. (978-1-60282-188-0)

River Walker by Cate Culpepper. Grady Wrenn, a cultural anthropologist, and Elena Montalvo, a spiritual healer, must find a way to end the River Walker's murderous vendetta—and overcome a maze of cultural barriers to find each other. (978-1-60282-189-7)

Blood Sacraments, edited by Todd Gregory. In these tales of the gay vampire, some of today's top erotic writers explore the duality of blood lust coupled with passion and sensuality. (978-1-60282-190-3)

Mesmerized by David-Matthew Barnes. Through her close friendship with Brodie and Lance, Serena Albright learns about the many forms of love and finds comfort for the grief and guilt she feels over the brutal death of her older brother, the victim of a hate crime. (978-1-60282-191-0)

Whatever Gods May Be by Sophia Kell Hagin. Army sniper Jamie Gwynmorgan expects to fight hard for her country and her future. What she never expects is to find love. (978-1-60282-183-5)

nevermore by Nell Stark and Trinity Tam. In this sequel to *everafter*, Vampire Valentine Darrow and Were Alexa Newland confront a mysterious disease that ravages the shifter population of New York City. (978-1-60282-184-2)

Playing the Player by Lea Santos. Grace Obregon is beautiful, vulnerable, and exactly the kind of woman Madeira Pacias usually avoids, but when Madeira rescues Grace from a traffic accident, escape is impossible. (978-1-60282-185-9)